A BREAK IN LOVE

RRASHIMA SWAARUP VERMA

VISHWAKARMA PUBLICATIONS
VP™

A BREAK IN LOVE

1st Edition Published in India by Vishwakarma Publications in December 2021

ISBN - 978-93-90869-73-2

Disclaimer
This is a work of fiction. Names, characters, places and incidents are either the product of the author's imagination or are used fictitiously and any resemblance to any actual person, living or dead, events or locales is entirely coincidental.

Published by:
Vishwakarma Publications
34A/1, Suyog Center, 7th Floor, Gultekadi Marketyard Road,
Giridhar Bhavan Chowk, Pune: 411037, Maharashtra, India.

Mob.: 9168682200
Email: info@vpindia.co.in
Website: www.vishwakarmapublications.com

Cover : **The Book Bakers**

Typeset and Layout : **Vishwakarma Publications**

Printed at : **Spectrum Offset, Pune**

To all my fabulous readers.
Thank you for your love and encouragement –
that, truly, is the most precious gift for an author!

Introduction

"No one who achieves success does so without the help of others" - Alfred North Whitehead

Writing 'A Break in Love' has been one of the most rewarding experiences of my life. I have truly savoured every moment of it. This journey has indeed been a fulfilling one, enriched immeasurably by some incredible people who have showered me with support and encouragement and have worked tirelessly with me for the successful completion of this book.

My deepest gratitude to my literary agent, Mr. Suhail Mathur, and his team at The Book Bakers, for their unparalleled wisdom, support and guidance. I am truly touched by their unwavering faith and encouragement and the meticulous attention to every little detail that they have given to my book. They have advised and guided me every step of the way and turned my dream into a marvellous reality. Suhail, I am deeply grateful to you for bringing my book to such a wonderful outcome. A special thank you to The Book Bakers team for also designing a book cover that beautifully symbolizes the essence of the book.

My heartfelt gratitude and appreciation to my publisher, Vishwakarma Publications, for giving me the opportunity to share this story with the world. I would like to sincerely thank their CEO, Mr. Vishal Soni, and his entire team for believing in me, having faith in my work and welcoming me with so much warmth into the Vishwakarma Publications Family. I would also like to express my gratitude to Nupur, Stanley and Chaitali from the Vishwakarma Team. It has been a wonderful experience to work with all of them and I am deeply grateful for the diligent attention and care that they have given to my book.

I would also like to take this opportunity to thank all the channel partners who have worked with dedication and commitment to make this book available to my readers.

This note of gratitude would not be complete without a huge thank you to my loving family. I feel truly blessed. My parents for instilling an ardent love for books in me. My father, Swapn, is my sounding board as well as my most uncompromising critic even at risk of offending me sometimes. My mother, Shirley, who loves me unconditionally and constantly smoothens my life in so many ways, allowing me to devote my time and attention to do what I love doing most, writing. My husband, Puneet, who shares and supports my dreams and showers me with more love than I could have ever wished for. And, of course, my darling son, Eshan, who is truly the sunshine in my life. Watching him bloom is a constant source of joy and delight.

Contents

Welcome home Karan

'Hello? Anybody home? Lisa? Lisa?' Karan Chopra entered the house and flung his jacket and laptop on the couch as he strode in. At six feet, two inches, with an athletic frame and purposeful walk, the first impression about him was that he exuded authority. At this moment, however, he just looked plain exasperated. He'd been ringing the bell for more than five minutes! The least he expected was for someone to open the door for him when he came home after an exhausting trip. He'd finally used his key to let himself in but he hated doing that. He looked around for Lisa but she was nowhere to be seen. Out as usual!

Shaking his head in exasperation, Karan marched into the kitchen and opened the fridge. He needed a glass of cold water desperately. This had to be the hottest summer in the past ten years. Delhi at the end of July was certainly not pleasant. What the hell! No cold water! There wasn't a single bottle in the fridge.

'Rama, Rama,' he called for their twenty-something, live-in maid who was invariably never at home. But where was Lisa? She knew he was returning from Mumbai that day and the least she could have done was to ensure that the house was in order. The living room was a mess, the kitchen was filthy with unwashed utensils lying in the sink, and the fridge was becoming a garbage dump loaded with rotting food! What in the world was wrong with her?

He poured himself a glass of water, dumped four cubes of ice into it (mercifully Rama had remembered to keep a tray in the freezer) and drank it thirstily as he thought about his trip. It had been exhausting but very promising. He'd managed to meet the president of that automotive company they'd been trying to meet for ages and the meeting had gone off pretty well. The guy had been impressed with the presentation that Karan had made and had even asked him to email it to him so that he could send it to his entire South Asian team. His other meetings had also gone off well and Karan was pleased with the results of the trip. And of course, he always enjoyed going to Mumbai. Despite the humid weather and crazy traffic that most Delhiites constantly complained about, Karan had always liked Mumbai. Sure, it was fast paced and chaotic, and the city in general always seemed like it was bursting at the seams, but Gurgaon was no better these days. Besides, the people in Mumbai were professional and right on the ball about work. In fact, this time he'd even managed to catch up with an old friend over dinner. All in all, he'd enjoyed the trip. So much so, that he actually hadn't been looking forward to coming home. He was amazed that he felt that way, but it was true. Coming home just wasn't the pleasure it had once been. He sighed as he loosened his tie and flicked on the percolator to make a cup of coffee.

Karan worked for a leading international business-research and consulting company which had five offices in India. This was his seventh year with the company. After completing his MBA from Columbia Business School in New York, he'd returned to India to join his father's well-established auto component business. It was, after all, what was expected of him and even though he went in with an open mind and gave it an honest try, it didn't take him long to discover that it just wasn't his true calling. So despite his father's coaxing and his mother's ardent protests, Karan finally apologized to his parents and decided to embark on something he would enjoy.

The consulting job came his way almost immediately after that and Karan had loved it from the start. The excitement and stimulation that came from working for some of the biggest corporations across a varied spectrum of industries, the thrill of meeting with leading business magnates around the world and the knowledge and experience that he gained in the process – within six months Karan knew that this was what he had been looking for. He loved every bit of it – the travelling, the deadlines, even the crazy pressure. And now his hard work and commitment were finally paying off. He had become his boss's blue-eyed boy and had recently been promoted to Senior Project Director with a significant salary raise and greater responsibility. But this also meant that Karan had to deliver in spite of tremendous pressure and stiff competition. However, he thrived on the challenge. It was exciting, stimulating, inspiring and addictive. If he proved his worth for a couple more years, he would soon be one of the youngest vice-presidents in the history of the Indian consulting industry.

The coffee was perking and he poured it into a cup and strolled out onto the balcony. His mind turned to Lisa, his wife of five years. Five years! Somehow it didn't seem that long to Karan as he mused over it. He couldn't help marvelling at how the time had flown. He slowly sipped his coffee as he watched the world go by. In spite of the sweltering heat outside, Karan needed the air. He'd been cooped up in a narrow aircraft seat for too long and then the traffic had been terrible on the way home. But he wasn't thinking about all that now. There were far more important things to think about, and as he stood there on the balcony, sipping his coffee, his mind turned back to how wonderfully perfect everything had been in the beginning.

He had met Lisa at a mutual friend's New Year party six years ago. Serendipitous though that first meeting had been, later it had seemed to the both of them that it was just meant to be. It was still all so vividly clear in Karan's mind even today. He remembered how lost he'd been feeling that evening since he didn't know anyone at the party except his hosts, who after the initial exchange of pleasantries, had been too occupied with greeting the throngs of guests who were steadily pouring in. He'd just downed his second drink and had been thinking about slipping out when Lisa had walked in. He had to admit that plenty of heads had turned when she'd entered the room, his included. After all, she was easily one of the most attractive women at the party.

The attraction between them was instant and mutual. He still remembered how lovely she'd looked that evening in that short, black dress with her sexy, high heels and her hair all fashionably mussed up. She'd smiled coquettishly at him across the room as he tried not to stare at her. Never had he seen a more sensual woman before. He'd wanted to kiss her there and then but restrained himself and behaved like a perfect gentleman, looking after her all evening and making sure she was comfortable. He soon discovered to his delight that she was not only gorgeous but also extremely intelligent and well informed. Indeed, he was admittedly impressed when she told him that she'd just gotten her master's degree in Journalism from the University of Wisconsin, Madison, which he knew was one of the finest journalism colleges in the world.

Lisa too had been instantly drawn to him – the way he tilted his head to one side when he was listening to something, how handsome he looked when he smiled, how passionately he talked about his work – in fact, he seemed like a genuine, wholesome person – a rarity not to be found anymore – and she liked that there was no artifice about him.

They'd spent the entire evening together and it had been a little after midnight when they'd finally stepped out on to the terrace to share a cigarette. The truth was that Karan was secretly very glad that he hadn't left early after all. It had been a magical evening, and he'd called her the very next day and asked her out. After that, they spent almost all their free time together and unsurprisingly, their mutual attraction soon turned into love. It did not take them long to figure out that they were meant to be together. Despite the fact that they were very different people with entirely diverse personalities, they were sure that they wanted to spend the rest of their lives with each other.

Lisa was an outgoing, gregarious and vivacious person with a real zest for life. She loved her job, her friends, and the life she led. A naturally creative person, she was a prolific writer, always brimming with new ideas and thoughts. She hated sitting around at home, and was always on the go. There was always something she had to do or somewhere she just had to be! Karan, on the other hand, was more relaxed and calm and definitely a lot less adventurous about most things. There was still something of a child in Lisa, while Karan sometimes seemed more mature than men who were much older. But somehow all that just didn't seem important the night they made love for the first time, and Karan went down on one knee and proposed to Lisa. In fact, the contrast in their personalities was the last thing on her mind as she stared at him incredulously, let out a whoop of joy, and flung her arms around him. The moment she'd been waiting for had finally come, and Lisa thought her heart would burst with joy as Karan slipped a simple platinum band with a sparkling solitaire on the third finger of her left hand.

However, when the two families met, it was clear that the parents weren't as crazy about each other as their children obviously were. Karan belonged to a traditional and conservative business family and his mother, who was fiercely possessive about her only son, adamantly refused to believe that he'd done something as stupidly outrageous as to fall in love! That too, without her approval!

'You are completely under her spell!' she said furiously one day when he emphatically stated that he would only marry Lisa or not marry at all. 'Can't you see she's trapped you?' It was a ridiculous question so Karan did not bother answering it. What he did do, however, was state even more clearly that Lisa was the love of his life and he couldn't live without her. This obviously didn't go down well at all with his mother and she cried incessantly for days afterwards. 'I knew it was a mistake to send you abroad! I knew….'

'I met her here, Mom. What does going abroad have to do with it?' he asked as she continued to cry. The quintessential Bollywood movie scene would have made Karan roar with laughter had it not concerned his own future.

To make matters worse, Lisa's parents didn't approve of the match either. They were both professionals, with her father being in education, and her mother a leading lawyer, and they couldn't see their only daughter adjusting in a family like Karan's.

'This is marriage you're talking about,' Lisa's mother had said to her reprovingly. 'You can't be flippant!' She was convinced that Lisa was making a huge mistake, and she and her husband had obvious reservations about the match the first time they met Karan's parents. His mother's excessively proprietorial attitude towards Karan didn't help either and they were both deeply concerned about the situation.

'She is not even a Punjabi! How will she adjust in our family?'

'Her father's a Punjabi, so she's familiar with our culture,' Karan had tried to coax his mother. The truth was that he couldn't care less whether she was a Punjabi or not, but if it made a difference to his mother's attitude, he was willing to try whatever it took. He'd looked at her hopefully but she shook her head vehemently in response.

'Her mother's an Anglo-Indian and she won't fit into our family. You're behaving as though this Lisa is the last woman left on the planet!'

'I really love her, Mom.' He'd looked at her beseechingly but she had stood her ground.

'I don't want you to marry her.'

This was stated emphatically and very firmly but Karan and Lisa were also both very firm about being together. They'd both sworn that they were crazily in love, couldn't live without each other, and had never been surer of anything else in their lives. It took several months and plenty of perseverance on their part for their parents to come around, but eventually the two families grudgingly gave in to what was so clearly, true love. Unbelievable though it seemed to them at the time, the young couple were finally engaged and waiting to start a happily-ever-after life.

They'd bought the apartment a few months before the wedding. Lisa, who had been born and raised in Delhi, had been skeptical about the move to Gurgaon but Karan's office was in one of the spanking new corporate buildings on Sohna Road, and he was clear that trudging back and forth every morning and evening and spending half his life in the car was not his idea of fun. He also stressed that the Millennium City was a major corporate and business hub, and in comparison, Delhi seemed awfully tired. Even Lisa had to agree that it made sense and then, as Providence would have it, she got a job with one of the country's leading fashion and lifestyle magazines as a senior journalist. Apart from paying well, it would give her the opportunity to tread new ground, and the publication's corporate office was in Gurgaon.

After talking to several real estate agents and looking at innumerable apartments in the countless complexes in and around Gurgaon, Karan and Lisa settled on a cozy, two-bedroom apartment on Golf Course Road with a panoramic view of the Aravallis. They had both fallen in love with it instantly. The living room opened out into a spacious balcony where they could sip their morning tea in companionable silence as they read the newspaper, or enjoy a drink together in the evenings when the weather was agreeable. The kitchen was already fitted with most modern-day gadgets; the bathrooms were small but elegant, and even though the apartment wasn't huge, it was actually just what they needed. They hadn't planned to have children soon anyway. They were both young, were enjoying their freewheeling existence, and had all the time in the world.

Buying the apartment was a wise decision from an investment point of view as well – so the estate agent had informed them. There was a high-end shopping mall coming up on one side and a four-star hotel on the other. The complex was well equipped with a three-tier security system, and even though Karan had tried to appear unimpressed and blasé in front of the agent, he knew that it was that very house in which they both wanted to start their married life. He was actually relieved that they could even afford it for they were both young and owning a house like this in one of India's fastest growing cities was something to be proud of.

But they were both doing well and Karan, particularly had always been prudent and cautious with money. So, they discreetly conferred with each other and took the decision to buy it almost as soon as the estate agent was out of earshot.

In the beginning, Lisa was as excited as a little girl. She'd never owned a house before and this was an entirely new and exhilarating experience for her. In fact, she just couldn't stop raving about how pretty the complex was, how nice the neighbours were, and how she couldn't wait to start doing the place up. She would sit with the interior designer for hours, poring over wall colours, designs of woodwork, and bathroom tiles. Karan would smile indulgently at her every weekend when she dragged him to the home furnishing stores to buy furniture or curtains, or something or the other for their new house, but even he had to admit that all her effort paid off in the end. The house was as pretty as a picture when it was ready. They moved in immediately after they returned from their honeymoon, and gave a splendid house-warming party for their family and close friends.

Their first year together was almost as delightful as they'd hoped it would be. They would both rush home from work, eager to be with each other. The days had acquired a dreamlike quality, and it was almost as though they existed in a world of their own. Holidays were always spent together as a couple, and friends and family were soon complaining that they never got to see them anymore. But the two of them had never been happier. They were in love after all, and it was a love story out of a fairy tale. Karan could recall it all so vividly, with every moment spent together clearly etched in his memory. Those lazy monsoon mornings spent contentedly wrapped in each other's arms as they watched the rain fall from their bedroom window… those long walks together during the early autumn months when the leaves were changing colour and everything was bursting with beauty… the freezing winter evenings when she would smile at him over a cup of hot chocolate and he would feel as though his heart would melt. Love's young dream, their friends called it and that's what it was.

And then the fairy tale started to show cracks. Nothing sudden or even dramatic. Little by little, inch by inch, hardly noticeable in the beginning but unravelling gradually, and slowly but surely. The real world came sharply into focus, making its demands with uncompromising firmness. The conference she had to attend despite the fact that he was sick with a raging fever; the evening that he forgot that Friday nights were date nights and went out with a bunch of buddies instead; another evening when she'd promised to make his favourite pasta for dinner but didn't because she was too exhausted; the first time when he refused that third glass of wine because he was too distracted with work to make love to her. Suddenly, prioritizing each other wasn't a priority anymore. Simple, spontaneous demonstrations of love became rarer and rarer. They were always too tired or too busy or too pre-occupied with other things but somehow, despite the frequent disappointments, he always believed that there was deep love between them that held everything together, and would help them wade through difficult times. However, disillusionment mounted as the disappointments turned into disagreements, the disagreements into constant arguments, and the arguments to a bitterness that seemed to have taken over their relationship. Now, five years later, it was almost as though they were different people.

Karan looked pensive as he thought about his life and slowly walked into the bedroom. He gently placed his empty coffee mug on the side table and ran a hand through his hair. How had things come to this point? It had all been so perfect in the beginning. The first major fight had come as a rude shock to the both of them. Now, sadly, he actually couldn't remember the last time they'd agreed on something or spent even a few hours together without getting into an argument or heated debate. Sometimes, it took them mere seconds to get exasperated with each other, and these days, the most trivial things turned into full-blown issues. When people, including both their families and even some friends, had warned them that they were as different as chalk and cheese, they'd simply laughed it off and talked instead about the theory of, 'Opposites Attract'. But now it was difficult to not wonder if the differences between them were finally catching up with them. Or was it simply the stresses of surviving in their crazy worlds. They were both ambitious after all, and their jobs were demanding. They had loans to pay off, and of course, the added responsibility, particularly for Lisa who was an only child, of caring for parents who weren't getting any younger. Could monotony and boredom have set in because they'd been married for five years, or heaven forbid, had they actually fallen out of love with each other? Karan didn't know the answers but as he mused about their relationship, he couldn't deny the fact that it bothered him. Yes, of course, it bothered him. But what could he do? Did she expect him to turn a blind eye to the fact that he'd come home from an exhausting trip to an empty house and a messy one at that, or perhaps she expected him not to notice that she hadn't bothered to call him more than once in the last three days, and every time he'd called, she'd been so preoccupied with other things that her tone had seemed almost perfunctory to him. It was not an encouraging thought and Karan shook his head wearily as he walked toward their en-suite bathroom, almost tripping over the towel she'd left on the floor and obviously forgotten to pick up when she'd gone out that morning. He sighed and picked it up from the floor. Tossing it into the laundry basket, he switched on the geyser and closed the bathroom door behind him.

□

1 hour later

Lisa was humming to herself as she entered the house and shut the door noisily behind her. She was feeling very upbeat. The last three days had been great and she had to admit that she'd enjoyed having the whole house to herself. Work was busy as always but she'd managed to catch up with Sameera and Ayesha for drinks and dinner last night at their favourite pub. The trio was complete again ever since Sameera had moved to Gurgaon, and it was wonderful to have both her close friends around. It had been a great evening and they'd all been more than a little tipsy when they'd left the pub. Since Karan was travelling anyway, the girls had stayed over and it had been just like old times. They'd spent hours on Facebook and tracked down old friends, raided Karan's bar and conjured up the most fabulous Margaritas, watched movies, gossiped about their old boyfriends and listened to blaring music. Everything had been absolutely perfect and they hadn't had that much fun in ages. Lisa smiled to herself as she thought about it and then took off her sunglasses and slipped them into their cover.

She was just about to switch on the percolator to make a cup of coffee, when she suddenly noticed Karan's laptop and jacket lying innocuously on the couch. She stared at them for a few seconds and then closed her eyes briefly, as though bracing herself. Jesus! She'd forgotten that he was returning that day. He'd sent her his flight details but it had been such a stressful day at work that it had promptly slipped her mind. When she opened her eyes, with a rather firm expression, she resolutely tucked a stray strand of hair behind her ear. Well, if he wanted to nag her about not being home to welcome him, she wasn't in a mood to listen to him. She did feel a tad guilty about it but she'd had a frenetic day! She just hoped he wasn't in a disagreeable mood. The smile had by now disappeared from her face, and she took a deep breath before swinging open the bedroom door.

'Why is it so dark in here?' she asked as she entered the bedroom and blinked in surprise. It was very unlike him to be in bed at seven-thirty in the evening, and she stared at him as he stirred and then opened his eyes. He'd obviously been taking a nap but now he threw off the double duvet as she flicked on the lights and dumped her bag on the recliner chair in the corner. She noticed that he'd changed into a clean pair of shorts and a T shirt but the bed was still unmade from the morning.

'I was sleeping. I have a headache,' he finally said in answer to her question, pulling himself into a sitting position. So, what else is new, she wanted to ask him. They were becoming more and more frequent weren't they, these headaches he was always complaining about? Was it her? She noticed then that other than the unmade bed, the bedroom was looking tidier than it had been when she'd left that morning.

'So, when did you get in?' she asked, shutting the door with the back of her foot.

He glanced at the wall clock, squinting as his eyes tried to adjust to the light. 'About an hour ago. Where were you?' He tried to make it sound as casual as he could but Lisa didn't miss the edge in his voice when he asked her the question. Why was he always asking her so many questions, demanding answers and explanations?

'I was at work. Where else would I be?'

'It's almost eight.' He knew she worked late sometimes, and usually he was perfectly fine with it, but he was disappointed that she hadn't made an effort to get home a bit earlier that night. Hadn't she missed him at all?

'I was famished and grabbed a sandwich with Preeti before heading back. No big deal.' She shrugged her shoulders as she sat down on the edge of the bed, and he watched her kick off her shoes. New! Again!

'Are those new?' he asked, narrowing his eyes. 'I thought you said you wouldn't...'

'Oh, come off it, Karan,' interrupted Lisa in an exasperated tone. She couldn't believe that he was picking on her within two minutes of meeting her! 'You've just gotten back. Is that all you can ask me? Don't you have anything nice to say to me?' She stood up with both her hands on her hips and stared at him angrily, perfectly poised for a fight.

He looked at her wearily for a moment as though too tired to argue with her. Finally, he sighed and got up to give her the ceremonial hug and kiss, but she pushed him away almost immediately and shook her head.

'Don't bother! I don't want you to think you have to. Do it when you really want to.' She turned on her heel and before he could say anything else, she marched into the bathroom and banged the door behind her. Two minutes later, he heard her turn on the shower.

'So, how was your trip? Did you manage to meet that hotshot you've been chasing?'

Karan looked up from his book to see that Lisa was done with her shower and distinctly seemed to be in a better mood. The shower must have done it. It always did. She was wearing her white terry cloth robe and her hair was still damp. She looked young and fresh and vibrant. Desperately trying to conceal the longing he now felt, he wondered what it was about her that, despite all the disagreements and bickering, reduced him to jelly and made him want to take her into his arms then and there? But then that was hardly surprising since she really was a very attractive woman. All of five feet, five inches, Karan at his six feet, two inches, usually had to bend a little to kiss her but he didn't mind that. He'd always found her exquisite. She had flawless skin that turned the colour of honey the moment she saw the sun, big animated eyes that accurately reflected whatever mood she was in, and a consistently slender figure thanks to the Pilates classes she was so diligent about.

'Yeah, I did,' he answered as he desperately tried to focus on what she was saying instead of how she looked. 'The meeting went off well and at least now we're on their list of preferred consulting companies.'

'That's great!' Lisa smiled at him and he couldn't help but notice that it was the first time she'd smiled at him since he'd returned. 'Hey, I almost forgot! There was an unbelievable sale at that new mall and I got you something.' She placed the bottle of body lotion she was holding on the dresser and walked over to the closet. She pulled out a bag and handed it to him with a slightly hesitant look.

'I hope you like it. I know it's not what you usually wear but I thought, you know, just for a change…' She stopped when she saw his incredulous expression as he pulled out the black shirt with the bold multi-colored print emblazoned all over.

'Lisa! You can't be serious!' He stared at her, unable to conceal his amazement, and turned the shirt around in his hand as he shook his head disbelievingly. 'You know I can't possibly wear this! And where do you think I'd wear it? In the boardroom in the office? Or perhaps under a pinstriped suit when I meet my new clients next week! Honestly, I never saw anything quite so inappropriate!'

Typical! Everything she did was always inappropriate wasn't it, she thought as she held her hand out for the shirt.

'Well, don't wear it if you don't like it. I just thought it would be a nice change from those boring, insipid suits you wear all the time. This, by the way,' she gestured to the shirt with her hand, 'happens to be all the rage right now.'

'Frankly, it looks like something heavily inspired by street fashion,' said Karan shaking his head, all attempts to be nice to each other now clearly tossed aside and forgotten. 'Anyhow, I can't wear it. It's completely outlandish and just not my type. You know I'm in a serious profession and I can't make a fool of myself. I'm sorry.'

He handed the shirt back to her and she put it back into the bag. She never should have bought it for him anyway. She should have just bought him yet another white shirt. That's why she no longer shopped for him since he never liked anything she bought.

'And by the way, where is Rama?' His voice snapped her out of her thoughts and she looked up in surprise.

'Rama? She's taken a few hours off. She'll be back any minute. Why?'

'Well, the house is a mess or didn't you notice?' He knew where this would lead but he couldn't help it. He thought it was very inconsiderate of her to give the maid a day off when she knew he was returning from a hectic trip. He looked at her reprovingly as she stared at him, wondering why she suddenly felt like a truant child who was being scolded by her parents. 'I think you're too lenient with her,' he continued. 'How many days has she taken off this month?'

'She's not a slave, Karan,' said Lisa, feeling very irritated now. 'She's entitled to time off now and then. And anyway, do you have any idea how difficult it is to get a good maid these days? I don't want her to run off because of your nagging.'

She couldn't believe that he hadn't even kissed her after three days of being away and was bickering away about the maid instead.

'Come on, Lisa!' said Karan, wondering why she always contradicted everything he said. 'I don't nag and you know it.'

'Don't you?' she asked, raising her eyebrows disbelievingly. 'I know you've had a chip on your shoulder ever since she broke your favorite decanter. Anyway, if you don't like it the way it is, then why don't you find us a better maid? All you do is complain! You don't do a thing around the house. It's all my duty isn't it? Typical!'

'Oh, I do my fair share,' shot back Karan. 'But you know how demanding my work is these days and how hard I've been working on that new project.' If she only knew how badly he wanted to make love to her right then. It had been quite a while hadn't it? And she looked so sexy in that bathrobe with her hair all mussed up. Oh God! He shook his head, admonishing himself for thinking about something like that in the middle of a heated debate about who did more around the house, but he couldn't help it. Well, if nothing else, at least it proved that he was still hopelessly attracted to her, even after five years of marriage! He wondered if she felt the same way.

'Well, I work jolly hard too,' snapped Lisa with a scowl that was enough to jolt him back to the argument. 'My career's important too!'

'Yes, but my work is a lot more stressful than yours. You can't compare!' He said this emphatically, as though stating an irrefutable fact.

'How dare you say that!' she retorted irately. 'You have no idea how hard I work! Do you think it's easy to work for someone like Milind Mehta? Haven't you read about how merciless and brutal he can be? And besides…'

'You're kidding, right? When did writing about how to get a peachy tan or which kick-ass hair styles work best in the summer become stressful work?' He didn't notice Lisa's furious face, or the fact that she looked as though she'd like to throw something at him. 'I admit you're good at what you do, but writing for a fashion magazine isn't like consulting.

Everyone knows that consulting is one of the hardest jobs around. We have to literally sell our souls.'

'Well, at least more people read my articles than your dull reports.'

'Dull reports! Oh, I'm sure that article you wrote on designer maternity jeans was very insightful.'

'You have some nerve! I've had enough of your belittling comments about my work. I work for a leading fashion magazine and I get paid very well.' She was livid!

'Well, if that's the case, how come I never get to see the money? Oh, I know! You obviously need it to buy a new pair of designer shoes or bag every month, don't you? The Spendthrift that you are, you would have squandered everything away if I wasn't so careful. It's because of my prudence that we were even able to pay off the loan on the house in time.'

It went on and on and on till finally Karan, too exhausted to argue anymore, threw his hands up in resignation and stormed off to the bathroom. Later, as he showered, he couldn't help feeling distressed that they'd had an argument as soon as he'd returned. What had happened to them? It was as though every issue, every word, even every thought triggered an angry debate. Well, those people who had warned them about the differences between them had been wrong about one thing at least, he thought bitterly. They had one glaring similarity – both of them could not control their awful tempers. Despite the fact that they hadn't seen each other in three days, they hadn't exchanged a single pleasant or loving word. Ironically, he couldn't help but remember the first time he'd come home from a trip and how Lisa had welcomed him. They'd been married a little over three months then. She'd opened the door and kissed him passionately when he'd arrived, obviously delighted to see him. The house had been spotless; she'd remembered to chill a bottle of his favourite wine and he'd even remarked jokingly about what a perfect wife she was. And afterwards they'd made love, twice in a row, first in the bathtub and then in bed. All that was clearly out of the question now, he thought gloomily, as he towelled himself dry and stepped out of the shower.

Over the next hour, Lisa got Rama, who had dutifully returned at the promised hour, to clean the house, clear out the fridge and cook a decent dinner, but she was quiet and withdrawn with Karan all evening. He did actually feel a little guilty about the harsh things he had said to her. He hadn't even meant any of it – it had just been thoughtless things said in a spurt of anger but his small attempts at making up either went unnoticed or were deliberately ignored. She made it clear to him that she was upset, responded to his questions in monosyllables, and went about her tasks with the sort of indifference that he found quite distressing. After the heated argument, the silence between them felt oppressive to him. But there was nothing to be done about it, so in the end, they ate dinner in silence. And later, when they did reluctantly get into bed together, she pointedly turned the other way and slept with her back to him. He didn't know that it took her a long time to actually fall asleep, just lying there, trying not to cry. The truth was that she too was extremely distressed at the current state of their once perfect relationship. Imagine going at each other's throats like this after three days of being away. You'd think that any normal, loving couple would have been in each other's arms by now, whispering sweet nothings about how much they'd missed each other and how three days had seemed like several weeks. But their egos seemed to have got the better of them, and it was all she could do not to burst into tears about it. Karan, of course, didn't know how upset she was as he stared at her ostensibly sleeping form for a few minutes, wondering if he should do something to make up with her. He finally decided that she'd probably fallen asleep and would only get irritated if he woke her up.

'Well, Karan, welcome home,' he murmured to himself as he turned over to the other side as well. It had been a long day and he needed to be in the office early tomorrow. He sighed, closed his eyes and then, as though finally succumbing to exhaustion, drifted off to sleep.

□

No Quinoa in the house!

When Karan awoke the next morning, the sun was streaming in through the windows. It was already almost seven o'clock and he usually liked getting up earlier. He'd always been an early riser. But this morning, he'd allowed himself the extra sleep. It had been a demanding trip and he'd been exhausted last night. The rest seemed to have done him good since he felt much fresher this morning. Almost ready to conquer the world!

He sat up in bed with a huge yawn and stretched, squinting at the bright sunlight that was pouring into their bedroom. They'd forgotten to draw the curtains last night and he jumped out of bed to do it now. Lisa was sleeping peacefully, her face resting on the palm of her right hand. Karan quietly drew the curtains and then bent down to pick up the blanket that she'd tossed aside sometime in the night. As he gently covered her with it, he couldn't help noticing how beautiful she looked in her sleep. A lock of her dark brown hair fell carelessly over her smooth, unlined forehead and her face was serene and calm as though she was in the middle of a beautiful dream. In spite of the tension of the previous night, Karan smiled to himself as he stood there, quietly watching her.

After he had washed his face and brushed his teeth, Karan poured himself his first cup of coffee and took it out to the balcony. Downstairs, the condominium had already come alive: there were several early risers heading for morning walks – some alone, some in pairs, some with dogs, others in groups. A cluster of drivers and car cleaners were chattering among themselves as they went about their morning task of washing and cleaning the assorted mix of cars lined up in the parking area. Karan inhaled big gulps of the fresh morning air that was crisp and springy at this hour before the usual construction dust started flying around. Looking out over the towering buildings and skyscrapers that had enveloped the city of Gurgaon over the years, he was still sometimes amazed at how much the city had changed. He'd heard tales about how quiet and peaceful the city had once been from friends who'd grown up here and wished he could have seen the vast expanses of lush land and experienced the simple, modest living that had existed here at that time. Karan almost laughed out loud as he imagined Lisa's reaction to living in the Gurgaon of yesteryears.

'Jesus! I'd be bored to death!' she'd have said instantly. She certainly needed her malls and cafes and pubs! Karan smiled to himself as he sipped his coffee, grateful for these rare, quiet moments before another crazy day began.

'Good morning! Did you sleep well?' He smiled at her as she emerged from the bedroom, rubbing her eyes. It was almost a quarter to eight by then and Karan had already had two cups of black coffee and finished reading the newspaper.

'Yes, thank you.' Her tone was formal and a bit guarded as she joined him at the dining table. 'What about you?'

'Fine, fine,' he said pleasantly, rising from his chair to kiss her. He was trying to make up for last night, and even though it was a light kiss, at least she didn't pull away from him. He knew that she usually took longer than him to bring things back on an even keel and would take a little time to forget and forgive his harsh words from the previous night. He continued to smile at her however, as he handed her the newspaper. She noticed that he had already shaved and was looking clean and fresh and very handsome. But then he was a very handsome man. Despite the travelling, he was also extremely fit since he meticulously visited the gym five times a week whenever he wasn't travelling and followed a disciplined diet. Even now, Lisa could see the ripple of his muscles and the taut torso under the thin fabric of his T-shirt, and she couldn't help that all too familiar feeling of utter longing that she'd felt last night as she'd lain next to him, pretending to be asleep.

'Would you like a cup of coffee?' His tone was warm and his manner amiable. Lisa was glad that he seemed to be in a better mood. She nodded in answer to his question and glanced at the percolator. 'Is there any in there?'

'Yes, I made an extra cup,' he answered as he rose to fill a mug for her as she raised her eyebrows in surprise. Well, he certainly seemed to have taken his gracious pills this morning. She couldn't help smiling to herself as he poured out the steaming hot, strong, aromatic brew that they both loved and added a dash of milk to it before offering it to her. She didn't drink it black like he did.

'Thank you,' she muttered as she took a sip and unfolded the newspaper. 'Any earth-shattering events this morning?' 'Thankfully no,' answered Karan with a laugh. 'But there is a picture of you on Page 3. I think that after-party you attended at Olive. You look very nice in it.'

'Thanks!' She smiled at him this time as she turned the Gurgaon Times to the right page, her smile broadening when she saw the picture. Karan was right, it was the Olive bash and she did look great in it. And she'd been photographed standing between one of the hottest models of the season and one of the most respected fashion designers who was visiting from Italy. Her boss would be very pleased.

'Oh, by the way, I wanted to ask you –' Karan's voice interrupted her thoughts and she looked up from her paper – 'did you pay the maintenance bill?'

Lisa sighed and rolled her eyes. There he went again! You'd think he'd let her have a peaceful cup of coffee before he started his daily dose of nagging. She tried not to let her annoyance show and shook her head in answer to his question. 'I forgot. I'll do it today.'

'Well, make sure you do,' he couldn't help adding, 'it's embarrassing when they levy those late charges almost every month. Oh, and could you ask Rama to make sure breakfast is ready in twenty minutes? I need to be in the office on time. Vivek is supposed to leave for a presentation before lunch, and I need to meet him before he leaves to fill him in on the trip.'

'Well then, don't let me keep you,' retorted Lisa brusquely. 'All you can talk about anyway is things like maintenance bills. And don't worry, breakfast will be ready on time,' she added dryly.

Shaking her head in exasperation, she picked up the Gurgaon Times again. Karan watched her as she took a sip of coffee and turned to the movie page to see what movies were currently playing. It was clear that she just wasn't interested in talking to him any longer and Karan didn't try to offer any further explanations. He didn't want to start another argument after last night.

They were back at the dining table precisely twenty minutes later. True to her word, Lisa had ensured that breakfast was ready on time and she glanced questioningly at her husband as he poured himself a glass of orange juice from the pitcher on the table.

'Do you have a meeting today?' It was a question she asked him every time he appeared for breakfast, looking all crisp and business-like in one of his pin-striped suits with the two Mont Blanc pens he was so proud of, placed neatly in his jacket pocket.

'Yes, I do,' he said as she leaned forward to straighten his tie and he smiled at her. She never forgot to do it and it was one of those little gestures that seemed to have evaded all the arguments and disagreements of the past few months.

'A client from Bangalore is in Delhi and I have to meet him for lunch at the Radisson,' he continued as Lisa called out to Rama to bring in their breakfast. 'His company is in the business of medical devices and they recently made an acquisition in South America. There was an article about it in the Economic Times and – oh, that reminds me! Can I take the Eco Times with me? You don't read it anyway.'

'What is that supposed to mean?' demanded Lisa, looking indignant. 'You think all I'm interested in is Page 3 news, don't you? Do you think I'm a bimbo? Well, I'll have you know that I can hold my own in any conversation, Karan. Talk to me about the budget. Talk to me about government policies. Talk to me about the economic challenges in the US. Go on,' she challenged as he stared at her, wondering why she got so angry these days? Why did she take everything he said so seriously? Did it mean that they couldn't even have a normal conversation anymore without biting off each other's heads?

'I didn't say you can't,' he clarified finally but she continued to look sulky. 'Trust me, it wasn't meant like that. I was just –'

Rama appeared with their breakfast before he could finish his sentence and he stopped abruptly as she glanced at them nervously. It was as though even she could sense the constant friction between them. Karan almost wanted to tell her to mind her own business as she placed a hot case and a bottle of mango pickle on the dining table quickly, glancing at them anxiously again before disappearing back into the kitchen.

Clearly irritated now, Karan shook his head exasperatedly and whipped open the hot case. His eyes widened in astonishment when he saw four heavily fried, aaloo parathas staring up at him. Each paratha looked as though it contained a thousand calories, while even the tissue paper on which they'd been placed was drenched in the yellow oil. For Karan who was a very health-conscious person and zealously counted every calorie he consumed, it was one of the most unappetizing sights he had ever seen.

'Lisa! I can't eat this!' he pounced. 'You know I can't bear oily food! Besides, I've just returned from a trip and all I've been eating for the past three days is junk. Ask her to get me my quinoa and grapefruit.'

'Um…I think we're out of quinoa.' She looked sheepishly at him, 'I haven't had the time to go to the supermarket.'

'Well you obviously had the time to go out for a drink with your friends the other day when I called from Mumbai,' retorted her husband then. 'The fact is that you don't have your priorities in place. You know I need quinoa for breakfast every morning. Doesn't that make any difference to you? Don't you care at all?'

Lisa looked at him in surprise. Of course, she cared! But why was everything always her responsibility? Lisa didn't believe in gender-defined roles, and personally thought that Karan didn't do enough around the house these days. She couldn't help remembering the first time that Karan and her had gone shopping for their new house. They'd just moved in and everything had been a whirlwind of activity. They'd made a list of things they needed and then promptly lost it before they even reached the store. Afterwards, they'd both been like excited children running around the store. Lisa had wanted to pick up everything in sight and it had taken Karan a while to convince her that they really didn't need a microwave, a grill and an OTG or three dinner sets. They'd come back laden with stuff and so happy that they'd promised each other that they'd always do the household shopping together. And they had for a while. Actually, Lisa couldn't recall when the pleasure of shopping for their home together had became a household chore, or when she had started fitting them in between work and other commitments and doing them on her own because Karan was just too busy to go with her. Trying not to dwell on the past, she focused on the present instead.

'I'm sorry, Karan. I'll get the quinoa today. I'll ask Rama to make you an omelette now.' She knew how finicky Karan was about his diet preferences so she had decided to be gracious about it and apologise.

'Do you really think I have the time to stand around waiting for breakfast to be ready? As it is, I'm late!' He pushed his plate away and got up.

'But you can't go without breakfast,' objected Lisa. 'What about a sandwich? There's that lean chicken ham you like and –'

'No thanks,' answered Karan shortly, 'I can't wait. I'll eat something at the office.'

He picked up his car keys, swung his laptop bag around his shoulder and marched out of the house before his wife could say another word. She was too taken aback to say much anyway. For no logical reason in particular, she suddenly felt tears pricking the ends of her eyes but she blinked them back angrily. What was there to cry about? It certainly wasn't all her fault after all! Bloody quinoa! But her appetite had vanished too, and as she hated eating alone anyway, she pushed her plate away and got up. She called out to Rama to clear the table and then slowly walked back into the bedroom to get ready for work.

□

Boiling point in the Boss's office

It was pandemonium in the office when she entered. 'Milind's lost some papers,' whispered Nishi, Milind's new assistant who'd joined them the previous month and was petrified of Milind's unpredictable temper. 'He's furious!'

'Well, he is the Editor-in-Chief of Diva India,' said Lisa, placing her bag on her desk. 'This isn't an easy job. Of course, he's stressed!' She was wondering whether to risk calling him on the intercom when he buzzed her himself.

'Get in here,' he commanded and Lisa charged to his room, nearly knocking two people over. His door wasn't shut, so she didn't bother knocking and went straight in.

He was sitting at his desk reading an article, his carriage as erect as ever and his brow furrowed in concentration. Almost forty-two years old, Milind Mehta was an extremely intelligent and perceptive man. Having spent almost twenty years in fashion publishing, he was one of the most respected and admired individuals in the industry. In fact, more than once, Lisa had heard people say that there was something remarkable about Milind, that he had the Midas touch. Over the years, she'd seen him accomplish what no one else could and solve problems which were dead-ends for others. He had created trends and talking points which were unique. No wonder he commanded the wholehearted admiration and respect of his peers in the industry as well as his employees.

Though not conventionally handsome, he had a lean, athletic body and was extremely stylish and chic, which was imperative in his business anyway. He loved experimenting with clothes and accessories, dabbling in frequent changes in styles and hated being restrictive about what he wore. The only consistent thing in his ensemble was his Platinum Patek Philippe watch with the black leather strap. The watch had been a gift from his ex-wife on their tenth anniversary and he was crazy about it, albeit they'd been divorced for nearly five years. The good thing was that the divorce had been amicable and they'd stayed friends. There had been some rumours afterwards that the main cause of the divorce had been a rather sweet and young, male fashion photographer who'd been visiting from Japan, but there had never been any proof. Milind was either very discreet or it was just the tabloids coughing up another one of their sensational stories. Incidentally, he hadn't remarried, but had had a couple of girlfriends since then. Some people even claimed that he was bi-sexual. His sexual preferences were, however, the furthest thing from Lisa's mind now as she stood there in front of him, wondering why he looked more stressed out than usual today.

'Please sit, Lisa,' he said finally, barely looking up from the article. 'I won't be a minute.' He waved vaguely to one of the chairs in front of his desk, but both of them were piled high with papers, shoe boxes and other stuff. His office was a mess as usual. There was another pile of papers stacked on his desk and Lisa could hardly see the couch which was almost totally loaded with fabric samples, jewellery and clothes. If one were to ignore the mess, however, it was a beautiful office. The walls were a bright, bold red, dotted here and there with paintings by famous artists and photographs of Milind with important people. There were interesting souvenirs and bric-a-brac that he'd picked up from his travels around the world, along with a huge, life-sized mannequin of a French fashion model that caught everyone's attention at once. For anyone coming into his office for the first time, it was like entering a new world, but for Lisa, who went in at least twenty times every day, it was business as usual as she shifted the shoe boxes that had been piled high on the chair opposite Milind's desk, to the floor, and quietly sat down.

She watched her boss as he finished reading the article, his dark, intelligent eyes darting from line to line. Lisa couldn't help but admire him as he crossed out almost complete paragraphs and made quick changes. But this was nothing new. Milind Mehta was almost never satisfied with anything and was a perfectionist to the core. He ran a tight ship and stood no nonsense from anyone. Working for him meant being on the fast track, and Lisa had been in awe of him ever since she'd joined the magazine. Even though he was a very moody man with a famously short temper, Lisa had, over time, come to like and understand her boss. Despite having accomplished so much, there was nothing supercilious about him and he was a genuinely compassionate person. The thing she liked most about him was his smile – there was something wonderful about it – it reached his eyes and lit up his whole face. Today, however, he wasn't smiling as he finally put the article down and peered at Lisa.

'So where were you all morning? I've been yelling for you for ages!'

Lisa stared at him in surprise and then smiled. She was used to his habit of forgetting.

'Well, I had to meet our ad agency reps this morning. I told you about it yesterday, remember?'

'Yesterday!' exclaimed Milind, widening his eyes. 'Who cares about yesterday, Lisa? Yesterday is gone, over, done with! We have no time to think about yesterday!'

'Um…I understand,' muttered Lisa, looking a little embarrassed. 'I'm sorry. Was there….um…. something urgent you needed to talk to me about?'

Milind clicked his tongue. 'Urgent! Everything these days is urgent, Lisa! We're completing ten years in India this year. I want every single issue leading up to our anniversary to be special! I want every article, every interview, every word that we write, to say something about us, about who we are, what we think! Your columns are getting a great response but you need to keep up the drive. Get as many interesting interviews as you can, cover as many important events. So, tell me! How did it go?'

'How did what go?' Lisa looked completely blank for a minute and Milind sighed in exasperation as she surreptitiously sneaked a peak at his pin board for inspiration. As usual, it was crammed full with indiscernible bits of paper and Lisa couldn't make head or tail of it.

'Lisa! I'm speaking about that photographer! Did you talk to him? Sam's pictures in last month's issue were too parochial.'

'Oh that! Of course, I did,' said Lisa enthusiastically. 'It's all set. And that meeting with Collins Advertising went very well. We're working on some great tie-ins for the fall. And…' She was interrupted by the sudden ringing of her cell phone which made them both jump, and she immediately started rummaging around in her bag to turn it off. She knew Milind hated cell phones. He said they interfered with his creativity.

'Jesus, Lisa! Can you turn that damn thing off before I lose my mind?' he yelled as Lisa's hands shook even more frantically. She found it at last and switched it off immediately.

'Don't bring that thing into my office again,' grumbled her boss and then suddenly frowned again. 'Oh, I almost forgot! Where's that article on the Harry-Potter-inspired, Halloween make-up?'

'Milind, I already gave it to you yesterday,' said Lisa in surprise. He was being more absent-minded than usual. 'Remember? It was just before the staff meeting, you were on the phone and you didn't want to be disturbed, so you asked me to leave it on that desk and…'

'Jesus Christ, Lisa!' Milind flung his pen down on the table, looking exasperated. 'You don't expect me to remember stupid things like that, do you? Find the article!' he roared and Lisa shot out of her chair and out of the room.

Eventually the article turned up in the dustbin. Milind admitted that he remembered tossing it in there. He said he'd been deep in thought and on the verge of getting 'the' brainwave. He further grumbled that Lisa should never have left it with him in the first place for he wasn't supposed to get involved in checking routine articles. Lisa murmured an apology and scurried out of his room as her colleague, Preeti, smiled at her sympathetically.

'Be careful. He's in a really rotten mood today,' Lisa whispered to her as she went back to her desk and switched on her computer. How could Karan think her job was easy?

In the afternoon, she decided to head out for lunch with Preeti. There were several restaurants and cafes around their office in bustling Cyber City. The choices were plentiful, and it was good to escape the office occasionally when the atmosphere got too stressful. Besides, she enjoyed Preeti's company. They'd both joined the magazine around the same time and had gotten along like a house on fire from the very beginning. They were both ambitious, hard-working girls, and had been put on the senior level editorial team together. Their writing styles were very different but they were both prolific writers and enormously talented in their own way. Though they hadn't known each other for a long time, there had been an instant, obvious camaraderie between them from the very beginning and now it seemed as though they'd been friends for ages.

'Remember, all we have is forty minutes,' pointed out Preeti as they settled down at a corner table and unwrapped their sandwiches. They were at their favourite café, which besides coffee and sandwiches, also did early lunch specials on weekdays. As usual though, the café was full. 'We're lucky I was quick enough to spot this table. Look at this place! It's swarming with people.'

'Maybe we should have let that exhausted looking lady with the screaming toddler take the table,' remarked Lisa then, feeling a tad guilty. 'The poor thing looked totally stressed out.'

Preeti shrugged. 'Well, if we're not back in time, our heads will be on the chopping block. Anyway, you were telling me about the quinoa issue. So, what happened? Did he actually leave without breakfast?'

'Oh, he just stormed out of the house! It's as if he has a chip on his shoulder when it comes to me,' said Lisa, shaking her head. It felt good to talk to someone. It hadn't been an easy morning and she was glad they'd come out for lunch. 'You should have heard the whole house reverberate when he banged the door. Just because I forgot about the damned quinoa! I mean, it's just quinoa for God's sake!' She rolled her eyes and opened a sachet of demerara sugar, pouring its contents into her cappuccino and stirring it around vigorously. A few drops of the steaming coffee splashed onto her arm and she tried not to squeal as she wiped them away with her napkin.

'You mean this entire thing happened because there was no quinoa in the house?' Preeti looked at Lisa in surprise. She knew Karan well enough, and he'd always come across as a sensible and reasonable person. 'Well, if that's the one thing he's so particular about, why don't you try and make an extra effort to ensure that you always have quinoa in the house? You know, we all have our quirks and Karan's actually quite mature and – '

'Not all that mature!' objected Lisa, shaking her head. 'Have you forgotten what happened on Valentine's Day? We were supposed to go out to dinner. He not only forgot about it but went to the pub with those guys from his office instead! He came home at one o'clock in the morning and was too sloshed to even apologize for standing me up like that. On V Day too!'

'He did apologize the next day,' pointed out her friend, 'and got you that huge bouquet of flowers.'

'Big deal!' Lisa looked unimpressed as she rolled her eyes. 'Most of them were wilted anyway. And anyhow, it's not just the quinoa.' She took a sip of her coffee and shook her head. 'Even yesterday, he couldn't stop nagging me about the most trivial things. He'd just returned from a trip but he didn't even give me a hug. Instead, all he talked about was how frivolous and careless I am, how the house is always messy, how I don't manage the maid properly…' She dipped her panini into the ketchup and bit into it angrily. 'He even made all kinds of rude remarks about my career! Can you believe his nerve? Just because I'm not one of those boring, stiff-necked, corporate types who think they know everything and sit in dull meetings all day! But Karan has never been able to understand the demands of my job. After all, he's grown up in a typical business family and gone straight into a conventional, archetypal corporate job. But I just can't believe how insensitive he is these days.'

Lisa sniffed back the tears that were threatening to start falling any second. She was actually amazed at how easily she could cry these days. She didn't want to look like a weepy wimp in front of her friend, but she just couldn't help it. 'The problem is that he just doesn't seem like the man I married any more. Life with him these days is so boring! There's no romance, no passion, no fun! The Karan I was in love with and married was crazy about me. I remember it like it was yesterday.'

'You remember everything like it was yesterday,' teased her friend.

'Yeah, but all he talks about these days is how much money we need to save, how much goes out in installments every month, how important it is that the bills get paid on time – you know – dreary household stuff like that. I'm totally fed up!'

Preeti didn't know what to make of this unusually maudlin mood that her friend seemed to be in today. She made a commiserating sound and leaned across to squeeze Lisa's hand. 'Well, all that is important too,' she pointed out gently, 'it just shows that he's a practical and level-headed man who's aware of his responsibilities.'

'Why are you on his side? You're supposed to be my friend!'

Lisa shook her head and glanced out of the window. It had just started drizzling and people were scurrying about all over the place, looking for cover. She stared at them in irritation. It was just a little drizzle, not a deluge for God's sake! Nothing to get so harried about.

'Okay, enough about me and my stupid old problems. Let's talk about something else.' She turned back to Preeti and managed a watery sort of smile, as a waiter brought them the apple pie they'd ordered earlier à la mode. The two girls dug their forks into it. 'How's Aman?'

Aman was Preeti's fiancé and a successful cardiologist with one of Gurgaon's biggest private hospitals. The couple had met in a gym four years ago, and everyone knew they would get married eventually. They were perfect for each other. Lisa liked Aman: he was charming, affable and got along with everyone.

'Aman's fine,' answered Preeti with a smile. 'He's in China. Some medical conference. Then he's flying to Singapore for a week.' She glanced at her watch and signalled to the waiter for their bill. Their extended lunch break had crossed its outside limit of fifty minutes, and Milind would start yelling for them any minute.

'So, when are you guys planning to get married?' asked Lisa as they finished the apple pie, paid the bill and got up.

'Soon. In fact, we're talking about a winter wedding this year. Frankly, our families are relieved that we're finally doing it. They all think it's been way too long.' She rolled her eyes and laughed.

'Well, four years is about as long a courtship as you'll be allowed.' Lisa smiled at her friend and tucked her arm into hers as they walked out of the café together. It was amazing how much a good cup of coffee and a heart-to-heart with a close friend could help. She already felt better. 'Karan and I only went out for a year before we got married.'

'Oh, that's because you guys couldn't wait a second longer,' laughed Preeti blithely. 'Both of you were too much in love with each other.'

Lisa didn't comment but she knew Preeti was right. Karan and her had been much too in love with each other. It was hard to believe that they were the same people, so much had changed. She shook her head, willing herself not to think about all that. She needed to focus on other things. She still had the rest of the day to get through, and Milind would be waiting for her.

Karan's day had been equally demanding and stressful. There was always so much pending work after a trip – a string of emails to get through, proposals to check, teleconferences that couldn't be postponed – in fact, he hadn't had one free moment by the time he wound up the lunch meeting with his new client at the Radisson. To make things worse, the traffic on the highway was terrible even in the middle of the afternoon, and Karan was already running late for his three-thirty telecom when he finally walked into the office and switched on his laptop. He hadn't even had time to read the brief that Maya, the Business Development Executive, had mailed him earlier. He hated being unprepared for anything. He glanced at his watch and then groaned. It was almost time for the call. He was just about to pick up the phone, when Maya called him on the intercom.

'Three-thirty is cancelled. The client will call you back tomorrow.' Karan heaved a sigh of relief and flopped down into his chair. Thank God for small mercies! This at least gave him a few minutes to breathe. He was just thinking about ordering a cup of tea from the cafeteria, when his colleague Mayank, popped his head in at the door.

Mayank had joined the company a couple of years ago, and Karan and him had worked on several projects together since then. They were both around the same age, and had taken an instant liking to each other since they'd shared their first cigarette one evening after a particularly stressful day at work. Mayank was a nice, easy-going guy with a great sense of humour that could tickle even the most austere of people. He was reasonably attractive and had the look of an outdoorsman since he played tennis regularly and swam a lot. Unlike Karan though, Mayank wasn't married, and was well known for his weakness for good-looking women. He'd been through several relationships, but after one particularly bitter break-up and three casual flings which had clearly been on the rebound, he was still very much single. He seemed to have a problem finding the right girl, but he was basically a sweet guy with an amiable disposition and Karan was fond of him.

'Got time for a smoke?' he asked and Karan nodded and grinned, 'Your timing is perfect! I'll be right out.'

'Too much stress in there,' commented Mayank as he jerked his thumb behind him in the general direction of the office and sighed. He took a cigarette from a packet of Classic Milds, lit it, and took a long puff.

Exhaling slowly, he almost instantly looked visibly relaxed. 'God, I was dying for a smoke! I just hate this "No Smoking" rule in the office.'

'Yeah well, look at it this way,' said Karan. 'At least we have an excuse to step out now and then.' He smiled and accepted a cigarette from Mayank who was now puffing away furiously on his. They smoked in silence for a few seconds before Mayank spoke again.

'By the way, I've been meaning to ask you. Who's the new hottie reporting to Sumit these days?'

'I don't know who you're talking about. I come here to work, remember?' Karan laughed and leaned back against the wall.

'Oh, come on, Karan!' Mayank looked exasperated at Karan's obvious disinterest in something so important. 'I'm talking about that new girl with the perfect figure and pouty lips. I think she was wearing red yesterday, looking quite irresistible if I may add and...'

'Esha Malhotra!' Karan's eyes lit up in realization and Mayank raised his eyebrows meaningfully.

'Oh, so you did notice after all, huh?'

'Can't help seeing her around,' muttered Karan nonchalantly. 'So, what about her?'

'Oh, don't pretend as though you don't care dude! She's got the most coquettish smile I've ever seen!'

'I couldn't agree more!' Sameer from the Finance Department joined them and laughed. Tall and rangy with a thin pale face, Sameer wore round, rimless glasses, that made him look every bit the brainy chartered accountant that he was. Now he smiled pleasantly at his colleagues and to their utter astonishment, declined the cigarette that Mayank was offering him. Sameer was more of an addict that anyone else in the office. It was common knowledge that he took twenty breaks a day just to grab a smoke whenever he could.

'I'm trying to give it up,' he declared, taking a sip from his coffee cup instead. 'My new girlfriend's an environmentalist,' he explained. 'She's warned me that she'll never go out with someone who pollutes the environment for his own selfish reasons. Her sister, by the way, is a social reformist. Yesterday, she asked me if I ever feel at least a wee bit guilty about all the material comfort that we've all so unashamedly gotten used to and take for granted most of the time.'

'What an awful family!' Mayank looked stunned, and then as though to prove a point, he lit another cigarette and blew a cloud of grey smoke right into Sameer's pale face. 'Anyway, you shouldn't let her dictate terms to you.'

'And what if this Esha Malhotra loathes smokers?' asked Karan with a grin.

'Oh well, that's different. With a face like that, she can dictate terms as much as she likes.'

Karan looked heavenwards as he stubbed out his cigarette and Mayank looked at him defensively.

'Well, don't you think she's gorgeous?' he demanded but Sameer was quick to shake his head.

'Oh, it's no use talking to Karan about this. He'd never look at another woman, he's a steadfastly loyal husband.'

Karan didn't comment, but he knew that what his friend had said was perfectly true. It was hardly surprising that given his looks and charm, lots of girls had been drawn to him and there had been plenty of opportunities for casual affairs and flings, but he just wasn't interested in any of that. He was a naturally faithful husband.

'Well, that's something even I can't argue with,' conceded Mayank then. 'He's definitely a loyal husband and of course, Lisa's a lovely girl – intelligent, warm, beautiful – it would be hard not to be crazy about her. You guys really are perfect together.'

'No wonder Lisa likes you,' laughed Karan. 'In fact, you're one of the privileged few among my friends she's fond of.'

'Come on, time to get back,' said Sameer suddenly as he saw Sonal, the new HR Head, passing through the reception. 'That new HR Head is a nightmare! There's been a draconian atmosphere ever since she joined. She times everyone's lunch breaks and keeps a close tab on everyone's in and out times.' He nodded at Mayank who took a final puff of his cigarette, gazed longingly at what remained of it, then finally sighed and stubbed it out.

'Back to the grind,' he remarked as they headed back to the office and went their separate ways.

His friends didn't notice how wistful Karan looked as he walked back to his cabin. He was thinking about Lisa and the morning's argument. Why wasn't anything perfect between them these days if everyone else thought they were so perfect for each other? It was something he just couldn't figure out. And hadn't she also accused him just that morning of being boring and dull? That, despite the fact that all she ever talked about was how much she did around the house and the dratted maid, and when she had nothing else to crib about, she would pick on his mother. For all her claims of him not caring and not being interested in her, he couldn't remember the last time she had said or done something to make him feel loved or cared for.

□

Marriage doesn't guarantee sex!

Lisa leaned back into the soft contours of the leather couch that was the most recent addition to Kriti's already over-furnished living room. It had been several days since she'd seen her neighbour. Today, she'd managed to get home earlier than usual, and so had taken the chance and dropped in. Actually, it was amazing how they lived next door to each other and still didn't bump into each other for days, sometimes even weeks. To her credit, Kriti had invited them over for dinner to her house several times but Lisa and Karan had never been able to accept, mostly because of their extremely busy schedules.

Kriti Sehgal had been their neighbour for the past three years, ever since she'd moved into the apartment next door. Even though she was just a year older than Lisa, she'd been married young and had had two children in quick succession. Ever since then, she had devoted herself almost completely to taking care of her house, husband and children. She was a qualified physics teacher but had permanently given up work after the birth of her first son. To top it all, Kriti also had her sixty-five-year-old mother-in-law living with her and prided herself on the fact that she also played the role of a dutiful daughter-in-law to perfection. The only other things she was interested in besides fulfilling her wifely and motherly duties as Lisa called them, were her yoga classes which she was extremely particular about, and the occasional times that she volunteered to teach arts and crafts at her younger son's kindergarten school. Kriti was, in fact, someone Lisa's mother-in-law would call, 'extremely virtuous'. It was therefore no wonder that Lisa and Kriti didn't have much in common with each other, but even though they weren't great pals, they had a cordial relationship and got along reasonably well.

Now as she sat back and watched her neighbour pour out cups of milky, instant coffee for both of them, Lisa wanted to remind Kriti that she did not drink instant coffee. Instead, she accepted the cup without a word as well as one of the rich chocolate walnut cookies that Kriti offered her.

'Made them myself,' said her neighbour conversationally as Lisa bit into the cookie. 'Hey, you look a little preoccupied!' She looked at Lisa with concern, as though noticing her friend's restless demeanour for the first time. 'Everything okay?'

Lisa looked thoughtful as she took a sip of coffee. It had been a week since Karan had returned from Mumbai and things were still a bit chilly between them. She had to admit that the growing distance between them had started bothering her. They seemed to be squabbling over the smallest matters these days. They'd barely made up after that argument they'd had about the quinoa, when again, there had been that disagreement about that silly sister of his.

'I don't know. I guess I'm just tired of all the responsibilities,' she said at last in answer to Kriti's question. 'Sometimes it's all so... well, almost claustrophobic! Work, home, being a wife...' She stopped abruptly when she noticed that Kriti was staring at her with raised eyebrows and shaking her head disbelievingly at the same time.

'Responsibilities? Responsibilities! What do you know about responsibilities? Ask me!' She nodded her head emphatically and Lisa rolled her eyes, knowing very well what was going to follow. 'You have a fabulous job, a nice, broad-minded husband, lots of friends, the freedom to do exactly what you want, no children! Believe me, you don't know what responsibilities are till you have children. That's when your world changes! No time for anything! No time for frivolous things like pedicures and hair do's and lunch with girlfriends!'

Lisa almost instantly regretted talking to Kriti about her issues. She should have known Kriti wouldn't understand. They were too different; their lives were too different. And then, of course, the one-year age difference between them gave Kriti the feeling that she could teach Lisa a thing or two about life in general.

As though, almost on cue, her younger son suddenly started bawling and she sighed exaggeratedly as she turned around to give Lisa a 'You see what I mean look,' before she rose from the sofa to pick him up.

'Yeah, but I'm so bored and fed up with everything, and work's been such a bitch!' Even as she said the words, Lisa acknowledged that she sounded self-indulgent even to herself, but she couldn't help it. She wanted to add: 'And Karan hasn't even kissed me properly in weeks!' but she didn't want to scandalize her prudish neighbour. Besides, they weren't that close.

'Oh, Lisa!' Kriti looked at her wearily as she broke a cookie into small pieces and tried to coax her son to eat it. 'Why are you so negative today? You have a good life and a nice husband. Your in-laws don't live with you.' She glanced meaningfully in the direction of her mother-in-law's room as she spoke: 'What more can you want? What issues could you possibly have? Don't mind my saying so, but I think you're being a bit self-indulgent.'

Lisa made a mental note right then never to discuss her life with Kriti again. It was useless. In all honesty, she actually couldn't help feeling a little sorry for Kriti. The girl never got a minute to herself! Her house, her life – in fact – was one crazy whirlwind of two bawling children, inflexible school timetables, and a dominating, chauvinistic husband. Lisa couldn't remember the last time Kriti had visited the salon on a whim or gone for an impromptu lunch with a friend. It was actually difficult to believe that she was just a year older than Lisa. Maybe that's why she was so particular about her yoga classes. If anyone needed the deep breathing and stress management, it was Kriti.

Nodding politely at her neighbour, she picked up her cup of instant coffee. Trying not to notice the thin film of congealed milk that had formed on top of it, she gulped it down. She was suddenly in a hurry to get home. A warm bath would help to ease the stress of the day. And maybe a glass of Sula Satori to go with it. Talk about decadent indulgence! She almost laughed out loud. So, what is so wicked about being self-indulgent sometimes?

'I guess you're right, Kriti. Maybe I am being a bit self-indulgent. Anyway, I'd better get home.' Lisa picked up her bag and got up. 'I have to tell Rama what to cook for dinner and…'

'You see!' Kriti looked triumphant as she walked Lisa to the door, 'At least you don't have to cook yourself. Kartik would never eat food cooked by a maid. I have to cook all three meals myself or he refuses to eat.'

'Yeah well, your Kartik is the biggest jerk I've ever seen in my life,' Lisa thought to herself as she smiled sympathetically, thanked Kriti for the coffee, and walked back to her apartment.

She had just stepped out of the bath when Karan got home from the gym. He was eating a banana and barely even glanced at her when she walked into the living room. Lisa pursed her lips. So, he still didn't want to make up after that argument about his sister huh? Seething, Lisa wondered how Karan couldn't see that his sister was a spoilt brat and only ever thought of them when she needed something. She didn't even bother to remember their birthdays or anniversary half the time! Well, if that was going to be his attitude then so be it. Two could play that game! She strode into the kitchen, pretending not to notice the rippling muscles in his arms and chest as he stripped off his T shirt and headed off to the bathroom for a shower. He always did look so good after his work out. It was actually a pity that they weren't on talking terms.

As Karan massaged his anti-hair-fall shampoo into his hair and scalp, he couldn't help thinking about how gorgeous Lisa had looked when she'd walked into the living room. With her hair all wet and slicked back from her face, and those tiny water droplets still running down her arms and legs, it had been obvious that she'd just stepped out of the bath. He'd instantly felt like taking her into his arms and kissing her with the kind of passion he hadn't felt in months, and it had taken all his self-control to stop himself and walk away. Why, oh, why had they had that silly fight about his sister? It all seemed so meaningless, didn't it? It had been five days, and even though they hadn't had another quarrel, it was as though a cold truce existed between them. He could have tried to make up with her but he'd been the one to do it the last time. Damn ego! But then you'd think she could make the first move sometimes too. But women were women after all! When did they ever admit they were wrong? For all their talk of gender equality and women's empowerment, they were the ones who didn't believe in having equal relationships most of the time. Now they'd probably spend the rest of the evening nurturing their individual egos in stony silence. Personally, Karan could think of more appropriate ways to conclude the evening, but he knew it was no use. And if this was the way his life was turning out, then it really was no wonder that his hair was falling! He shook his head wearily and turned on the shower.

'He looks so hot when he's just worked out,' whispered Lisa to Ayesha on the phone. She hadn't been able to stop thinking about him since he'd walked in. 'Why did we have that silly fight? It's just not fair!'

'Yes, but after the fight comes the make-up sex!' exclaimed Ayesha, 'Trust me, it's the best way to end an unresolved argument.'

'Seriously, it's not that easy,' sighed her friend.

'But Lisa, he's your husband!' laughed Ayesha. 'I mean, you can have him whenever you want, right?'

'Oh, really?' said Lisa sardonically. 'You think marriage guarantees sex? Believe me, that's the last thing it does!' Why did single women have these stupid notions? Were they really that unrealistic?

'Well, if it doesn't, it should,' said Ayesha indignantly. 'I mean that's the least it should do. What's the point of being married to someone as hot as Karan if it doesn't even guarantee that much?' Lisa gave a bitter laugh and shook her head. If only things were that simple!

'By the way, when was the last time you guys... you know...?' asked Ayesha curiously. After all, if a couple like Karan and Lisa were having problems in their sex life, then it was certainly good to know what to expect for herself.

'I don't keep count,' answered Lisa dryly. 'Besides, I don't think I remember. And I certainly won't tell you even if I did.' She hated admitting it even to herself that there was definitely a lack of intimacy between them these days. There was just no denying it any more. It was astounding really, given how passionate they'd been about each other. Somehow, she'd never imagined that they'd have a problem in that area.

'Don't worry darling! Your secret's safe with me.' Ayesha laughed raucously at her own joke. 'No one will hear a dicky bird from me, you can be sure of that. Anyway, if you don't even remember, then it probably means that it's been way too long.'

She sounded almost matter-of-fact about it and Lisa wanted to throw something at her through the phone. 'Well, we'll see if you can do better than that,' she thought to herself.

'Hey, do you know studies say that in India, Mumbai couples have sex most frequently. I wonder where they find the time! Hell, they spend half their lives on the road! Crazy isn't it?'

'Why do they do these ridiculous surveys?' asked Lisa, very irritated now. 'I mean, come on! Is that like an average figure or something?'

'Dunno,' said Ayesha. 'It's just interesting to know. You would know, considering that you write about it all the time.'

'Not all the time,' protested Lisa. 'We write about plenty of other things too.'

'Anyway, what are you going to do now? I take it you're not going to get lucky tonight, right?'

I wish I would, thought Lisa ruefully. 'No,' she answered shortly, 'I'm going to check on dinner and then I'm settling down with Sex and the City – Season 5, and a huge bowl of chocolate ice cream.'

'Well, chocolate is the next best thing anyway,' agreed Ayesha. 'And Sex and the City is timelessly inspiring.'

Absolutely, thought Lisa, as they hung up. After all, men, whether they were in New York or good old Delhi, were always difficult.

The rest of the week whizzed by. They were both immensely busy at work and hardly got any time together. Lisa had to travel to Bangalore for two days to attend the launch of a new cosmetics brand, and she had some friends coming in from Mumbai by the time she returned. They were people from the fashion industry who she occasionally worked with and she wanted to invite them over to the house for dinner. Karan however, made his disapproval clear. He was wary of people from the fashion industry and thought them too eccentric. The last time she had invited people over, things hadn't gone well. There had been that male model who'd arrived wearing those hot pink Capri pants with gold lamé sandals. And that gay photographer who'd unashamedly hit on the model throughout the evening and even patted his behind after dessert. Even her boss – he was a bit strange, wasn't he? He had that peculiar way of flying off the handle at the drop of a hat and waving his hands wildly about all the time, which Karan found quite discomfiting. Lisa however wasn't very sympathetic. After all, didn't she put up with his boring, stuck up, dreary colleagues all the time? Why did he always have to be such a killjoy?

In the end she took her friends out to dinner instead of inviting them home. She thought the atmosphere at home would be too stressful, and so they went to an Italian restaurant in Mehrauli known for its 'arty' theme and absolutely delicious cocktails. The restaurant was very popular with the fashion fraternity; the food was good, the music better, and they all had a great time together. It turned out to be better than doing it at home since Lisa was able to join in the fun instead of having to run to the kitchen every ten minutes.

By the time the weekend rolled in, the weather was more pleasant since the temperature had fallen a little. By Saturday morning, Lisa seemed to be ready to forget and forgive, and Karan was trying to make an extra effort to be nice to her as well. And even though they both had to work on Saturday, surprisingly, Karan came home early and Lisa wasn't too late either. He had already made a fresh pot of coffee by the time she got home and they both smiled tentatively at each other as they sat down at the table together.

'What are you planning to do tonight?' she asked him as she sipped her coffee. She was hoping he'd suggest that they go out for dinner. Despite all the disagreements that seemed so commonplace between them these days, sometimes she really missed the simple pleasure of going out to dinner with her husband and sharing an easy conversation with him over a glass of wine. It had certainly been a while.

'No plans really. It's been a hard week and I was hoping to stay home and relax.'

That was that then, thought Lisa as she nodded, trying to conceal her disappointment. Did he even remember how long it had been since they'd gone out to dinner, just the two of them?

'But,' said Karan suddenly, 'I was thinking – we could get a pizza, open a bottle of wine and watch a nice movie together. What do you say?'

Oh thrilling! Did he expect her to jump for joy? Pizza and a movie at home on a Saturday night! Were they eighty? But not wanting to hurt him, she smiled at him over her coffee mug and nodded.

'Sure! Which movie?'

'How about something really mushy?'

Lisa raised an eyebrow then, surprised that he'd suggested a mushy film. Karan was usually more the action flick type of guy.

'Really? I wouldn't have thought you'd be keen on one of those.'

'Well, last time you watched that Sean Connery film with me, didn't you?' he said generously, 'How about Pretty Woman? I've always had a thing for Julia Roberts so I won't hate it either.'

The evening turned out better than she'd expected. True it wasn't exactly the most exciting they'd ever had, but she had to admit that there was a certain intimate quality about spending time at home sometimes. After they'd finished the pizza, they opened a bottle of wine and settled down to watch Pretty Woman. By the time she was on her second glass of wine, she was laughing uninhibitedly at his little jokes and he felt at ease enough to slip his arm around her shoulder and pull her closer. When he leaned over and kissed her a moment later, she stiffened for just a couple of seconds before slipping her arms around his neck and returning his kiss with equal fervour. Karan didn't know whether it was because he was wearing her favourite cologne, or that the movie was at a particularly romantic climax when Richard Gere was climbing up an apartment building to declare his undying love for Julia Roberts, but who cared? Things were definitely looking better.

After the movie, they listened to jazz and finished the bottle of wine. They were both very relaxed by the time they went to bed, and the worrisome sense that things weren't right had temporarily abated. In fact, Lisa was even talking with the exaggerated slur of someone who's had a bit too much to drink. But then to be fair, she had had a bit more than him. He smiled at her as she kicked off her slippers and stretched out on the bed. He then went to brush his teeth. Tonight, might be the perfect opportunity to try and bridge some of the gaps that had sprung up between them recently. He had to admit to himself of course, that it was to a great extent his own fault. After all, his frenetic work schedule of late hadn't left much time for romance in their life. Half the time, despite being hopelessly attracted to her, he was too tired. Perhaps he should have been more pro-active. And then the frequent arguments and disagreements hadn't helped. Anyway, if the way she had kissed him back tonight was anything to go by, things should start looking up for them soon. And he was happy to set his ego aside and make the first move now. It was high time that they started behaving like a proper couple and worked on sorting out their differences. He finished brushing his teeth, pushed open the bathroom door and almost instantly blinked in surprise.

His wife was fast asleep in the double bed. She hadn't even bothered to remove her make-up which was very unlike her; she'd just thrown her jeans and top on the chair and slipped on a night shirt. Admittedly, Karan was intensely disappointed when he saw her. Sighing, he realized that he probably wouldn't be able to sleep anyway, and there was no point in lying awake for hours thinking about what wasn't to be. He picked up his packet of Classic Milds, turned off the lights, and tiptoed out of the room. He might as well get some work done on the proposal he needed to submit on Monday. It was a far cry from how he had imagined the evening to end, but there was nothing to be done about it. He walked into the kitchen to get some water. The first thing he saw when he opened the refrigerator, however, was the bottle of Moet and Chandon that he'd bought and chilled earlier that evening, in anticipation of a different conclusion to the evening. The bottle seemed to mock him as he stared at it in frustration. 'Shouldn't I have known all along that it was a mistake to buy it?' he muttered to himself as he pulled out a bottle of water and slammed the refrigerator door shut. 'Six bloody grand down the drain and nothing to show for it!'

□

Girls just wanna have fun

Sunday morning dawned nice and bright. It had rained the previous night and the usually dusty city looked as though it had paid a visit to the drycleaners. When Lisa stepped out of bed at eight-thirty, she was surprised to see Karan still fast asleep in the king-sized bed. He must be tired. She pulled on her dressing gown and tiptoed out of the bedroom. The living room was bathed in warm sunlight; there were birds chirping merrily in the balcony and Lisa smiled to herself as she switched on the percolator. She couldn't help remembering how they had done this house up together – every little piece of furniture, every painting, every bit of crockery. It had been five years to the day but even then, just thinking about it brought an instant smile to her face as she poured out her coffee and took it out to the balcony along with the Sunday Times.

It was a beautiful morning and she settled down in one of the wicker chairs and took her first sip of coffee. As she opened up the newspaper and started skimming through the headlines, she couldn't help thinking about the previous night. After the way they'd shared the wine and the pizza, and the easy laughing and friendly banter that had followed, and of course, not to forget the passionate kiss they'd shared, Lisa had kind of hoped that the evening would end a bit differently. They hadn't made love in – how long had it been? She shook her head wryly as she realized that Ayesha was right. She couldn't even remember and it wasn't something to be proud of. Lisa couldn't help wondering whether it was just the long hours, their travelling and the overall stress that was common to most young couples in big cities, or was there more to it? Was there a larger reason lurking there that they should be worrying about, which was responsible for the lack of intimacy between them. After all, yesterday could have been the perfect opportunity to break the ice but it hadn't happened. She'd dropped off as soon as her head had touched the pillow and she'd slept like a log through the night. How much wine had she drunk? It was strange that she didn't have a hangover. Wine usually gave her a heavy head. It must have been very good wine.

'Good morning!' Lisa smiled at Karan when he walked into the balcony half an hour later. He smiled back and placed his mug of coffee on the railing as he raised his arms and stretched.

'Morning! Since when have you been up? I didn't even hear you.'

'About an hour,' said Lisa, putting down her newspaper. 'Were you working last night?' She had no idea how pretty she looked as she smiled at him: her eyes were clear and bright and the morning sunlight was casting little gold specks all over her soft brown hair, making it look like burnished gold. She'd lost quite a bit of weight recently. The nightshirt she was wearing had always been a bit big and now looked incongruously loose on her lithe body. To Karan however, she looked incredibly sexy like that and he suddenly wanted to take her back to the bedroom and make love to her right then. He wondered what was holding him back.

'For a while,' he said in answer to her question. He took a sip of coffee and ran a hand through his hair. It was dishevelled from the previous night but Lisa thought he looked very handsome like that.

'After all that wine?' she asked him, looking amazed. 'How could you?'

'Oh, I didn't drink that much.' Karan grinned meaningfully and she blushed as she remembered how she had gulped down the last glass.

'Well, maybe I did have a little more than you,' she conceded.

They laughed together and walked back into the living room with their mugs and newspapers.

'Sorry about falling asleep like that last night.' She looked apologetically at him as they settled down in the living room. 'I guess it was the wine.'

He smiled at her and nodded. 'It's ok, you've been working hard. You must have been tired.' He tried not to let on how disappointed he'd felt but she didn't miss it. After all, she'd felt the same way.

'So, what are we doing today?' asked Lisa, putting her hand into the biscuit tin. She chose a Marie biscuit and bit into it. 'It's a gorgeous day. There's an art exhibit at that new gallery that might be worth a visit. Or we could go out for lunch. Since you don't like Chinese, I hear there's a great new steakhouse that's opened in that new mall.' She knew he loved steaks; he'd developed a liking for them during the years he'd spent in the US. Amazingly, despite an abundance of world cuisine available, getting a good steak was a challenge in Gurgaon.

'I wish I could, Lisa,' sighed Karan, looking up from his newspaper, 'but I have to work on a proposal that has to go to a client tomorrow morning. I have to send it to Vivek this evening. As a matter of fact, that's what I was working on last night.'

'It's Sunday,' answered Lisa simply. 'I don't think it's fair of Vivek to expect you to work seven days a week.'

'You work on weekends too sometimes, don't you? I don't hear myself complaining.'

'Not as often as you,' retorted Lisa, 'and hardly ever on Sundays!'

'That's not true! What about last month? You worked two Sundays out of four!'

'Oh, that was just because that designer was visiting from Paris. Anyway, I'd invited you to the party too. You could have joined me.'

'You know that's hardly my thing,' remarked Karan with a shrug, 'all that crazy stuff! Drinking yourselves silly, partying till the wee hours and God only knows what else!'

'You make it sound positively sordid,' objected Lisa. 'That's not how it is at all.'

'Anyway, if I want to be Vice President at some stage, I have to start volunteering to take on a little extra. Why don't we go out for dinner instead?'

'Your parents are coming to dinner,' Lisa reminded him pointedly, 'we invited them last week.' She was amazed he'd forgotten since he usually never forgot anything to do with his parents, particularly his mother. He must be busy.

'Oh, that's right,' said Karan with a nod. 'Well, maybe we can do something next week. You know catch a movie or...'

'Yeah, yeah, whatever...' said Lisa, cutting him off. At least she had tried. 'Well, I guess if you're going to be working, then there's no point in me hanging around by myself. I'll go out with Sameera and Ayesha. At least with them, I can go for Chinese.'

'Why is it so important to go out?' asked her husband with a frown, 'why can't you stay home for a change?'

'And do what?' She stared at him in surprise. Why was he always needling her about staying home?

'There are plenty of constructive things for you to do at home. Sorting out your closet, for instance. It's a total mess.'

Lisa looked at him incredulously. 'Jesus! I can't believe you expect me to stay home and clean the closet on a Sunday. I can think of better ways to spend my Sunday than doing some mundane household task. Hell Karan, I want to have some fun!'

She gulped down her coffee and got up. 'I'll ask Rama to squeeze out your orange juice and there's plenty of quinoa for your breakfast.'

He tried to ignore the pointed look she gave him then. So what was the big deal if she'd got the quinoa? It had been high time anyway!

'Better late than never,' he muttered but she pretended not to have heard as she walked out of the living room. Truth be told, Karan was actually glad that she had decided to go out. It would have been a challenge to concentrate on work with her around. Just as well.

As Lisa rode down in the elevator, she couldn't help being thankful that Sameera and Ayesha lived in Gurgaon. What would she have done without them around? They were her closest friends in the whole world and she loved spending time with them. The three of them had been friends since they'd all joined a gym together a few years ago but it seemed like forever to Lisa. It was amazing how well the three of them got on, considering how different they all were. Sameera was the mature one in the group; she was a year older than Lisa and Ayesha and had taken it upon herself to be the surrogate elder sister. The role actually came quite naturally to her since she was the oldest among three children. She was always ready with sensible advice in most situations and was usually the level-headed and wise one. Her family was in Lucknow and she'd been living alone in Delhi ever since she had started working. She was a political science teacher in one of the best private schools in DLF and was also pursuing her PhD. She was a pretty girl and most men usually found her attractive but she was very particular about whom she went out with. She preferred intelligent men – men she said she could have a real conversation with. She'd had one serious relationship only and it hadn't worked out. She had met someone recently though. He was a banker and they'd been dating for a while.

Ayesha, on the other hand, was the only child of rich parents and had been thoroughly spoilt by them. She'd been conceived after ten years of marriage, which explained the spoiling. She was an attractive girl, in a sexy, come-hither kind of way with a curvaceous figure, luminous eyes and pouty lips. Men usually found her attractive and she thrived on the attention she got from them. She was a happy-go-lucky girl who rarely took anything seriously except finding the right guy, at least these days since most of her friends had started getting married or engaged. She worked as a copywriter with her father in his advertising agency but instead of treating her job as a proper one and working hard to develop it into a career; she used it more as a stop gap arrangement till she found the right guy and got married. She couldn't help it. She just didn't have that kind of drive or ambition. But she had her heart in the right place and was basically a nice person.

Just thinking about her friends brought a smile to Lisa's face as she stepped out of the elevator and walked across the foyer to the parking area where Sameera was waiting in her white Swift Dzire. She didn't even notice how many heads turned as she passed by. She was totally unaware of the easy, effortless elegance she possessed that was so irresistible to most men. 'Hey you! Looking gorgeous!'

Sameera smiled at her friend as Lisa stepped into the car. The two friends exchanged a quick hug before Lisa laughed and reached for the seat belt. 'Thank God for best friends! At least you guys are generous with the compliments.'

'Well, didn't Karan tell you how lovely you look?' Sameera looked surprised as she pushed the car into gear.

'Nope!' Lisa laughed again and switched on the music system. 'But then, don't I always say that best friends are better confidence boosters than husbands?' She didn't want to let on how disappointed she was that Karan hadn't complimented her. She tried to push the gloomy thought away, but the truth was that there had been a time not very long ago when just being with Karan had made her feel like the most beautiful woman in the world. He'd had the ability to make her feel special then and it was very difficult to get used to his indifference and disinterest in her these days. The thought that perhaps he felt the same way didn't even cross her mind as they drove through the main gate.

The three friends had a very pleasant lunch together at their favourite Chinese restaurant. By the time they finished their meal, Lisa was in a decidedly better mood. Being with her friends always made her feel better.

'So, what did you guys do yesterday?' asked Sameera as they left the restaurant together. 'Was Karan working late?'

'Not really. But he is today.' Lisa's tone was matter-of-fact but Ayesha looked at her, appalled.

'Fancy working on a Sunday! What a dismal thing to do! I would just die!'

Sameera laughed at both of them. 'You hardly work anyway, Ayesha! And consulting isn't an easy job. I'm sure he's busy. Anyway, the important thing is to spend some quality time together. Why don't you go out for dinner tonight?'

'My in-laws are coming over for dinner tonight.'

'How awful!' exclaimed Ayesha, looking at Lisa in horror. 'Well, if you're going to be spending an entire evening with that monster-in-law of yours, you definitely need a bit of retail therapy my friend! So how about it? It's a gorgeous day and the whole world seems to be out and about, making the best of this rare spell of agreeable weather.'

'You're very convincing,' laughed Lisa as she ran a hand through her hair. 'Okay then, let's hit the mall! It's not as though Karan's sitting at home waiting for me. He's obviously totally engrossed in that proposal of his since he hasn't even called me once! Come on, let's have some fun.'

And fun was what they had! First, they went to see the latest Bollywood movie and afterwards they headed for the shops. The mall was as crowded as ever and the girls marveled at all the wonderful sales that had sprung up over the weekend.

'Look at that! Seventy per cent off!' exclaimed Lisa, trying to ignore the shameless stares and smirks that were being directed at them by a group of young boys who seemed to be hanging around only to ogle at women. As a matter of fact, she never ceased to be shocked at the brazenness with which men in Delhi, and even more so in Gurgaon, seemed to behave with women. What made it even worse was that most women seemed to have gotten used to this unwanted attention. Needless to say, of course, that despite all the talk of women's liberation, ignoring blatant stares was believed to be the only real practical option, and most women had actually become adept at the process. 'Perverts!' she couldn't help muttering as she shook her head furiously.

'Oh, it's the same everywhere.' Ayesha looked nonchalant as she spoke. 'My friend had a destination wedding in Rio de Janeiro and I must say that apart from the fact that I think Latin men are incredibly hot, most of them were a lot bolder in their advances than Indian men. But they are wonderful dancers!'

'Find one to marry then,' laughed Sameera.

Ayesha groaned. 'Speaking of marriage, my mom's totally on my case right now. Recently, she even told me I was wasting my life and I should either get serious about a career or get married! In fact, she even wanted me to meet a couple of guys my maasi had lined up for me last month.'

'Well, there's nothing wrong with that,' commented Lisa as they stopped at a café for coffee and cake. 'I thought you wanted to get married.'

'Yes, but I've told my mom very clearly that I'm not interested in the arranged marriage scene.' Ayesha shook her head very firmly. 'I mean, think about it. There's a dearth of eligible men these days. Then why would a man need his parents to find him a girl? Because he's probably not that eligible.'

'Well, make the best of your single life till it lasts,' said Lisa dryly, 'wait till you're married. Things won't be quite as hunky-dory then. A husband won't pamper you or put up with your frills and fancies without a word of protest. Believe me, marriage isn't all that it's hyped up to be.' She nodded decisively at her friends and picked up her cappuccino.

□

Monster-in-Law

'Puttar! You have become so dubla, so weak! Are you not eating properly?'

Lisa rolled her eyes at this expected comment which Karan's mother never failed to make whenever she met them. Without waiting for an answer, Anju Chopra came forward and embraced Karan as though she hadn't seen him in years and then proceeded to kiss him soundly on both cheeks, thus leaving red marks on both of them. Lisa, who knew how much Karan hated being treated like a child, always wondered how he put up with all this, but then it was hardly surprising since everyone knew how much Karan adored his mother. The troublesome thing was, Anju Chopra knew it too.

Anju Chopra was a short, heavyset woman in her late fifties with a fondness for vivid colours, elaborate jewellery and bright lipsticks. She spoke with a discernable Punjabi accent. She was tremendously proud of her business family background and their huge house in Sainik Farms and never failed to mention both to anyone who cared to listen. Even now, she was dressed in an embroidered, crepe salwar-kameez which clung to her bulky frame and matching jewellery, with absolutely no regard for the soaring temperatures outside. As she lovingly tweaked her son's cheek, she didn't seem to notice that her dupatta had gone askew, thus revealing a heavily rounded bosom that Lisa couldn't stop staring at. You'd think that with that figure she'd have the good sense not to wear the low-cut necklines and figure-hugging outfits that she wore all the time. Seemingly oblivious to her daughter-in-law's stares, Anju Chopra hugged Karan one last time before she finally turned her attention to Lisa and looked at her appraisingly.

'Hello, Lisa! How are you? You seem to have put on some weight.' Lisa knew she hadn't: she was naturally slender, but she ignored her mother-in-law's comment and allowed herself to be hugged as her father-in-law stood by patiently.

'See, a little here around the waist.' She poked Lisa's stomach, ostensibly meaning to be affectionate. Lisa slowly counted to ten. You'd think that she would have been used to her mother-in-law's ways by now. If it was at all possible, she actually seemed to be getting worse! 'You'll burst out of your clothes if you're not careful dear.'

'Can we talk inside, Anju?' said her father-in-law finally, looking exasperated, but Anju Chopra made a face at him.

'Ask a mother how she feels if she doesn't get to meet her children for days! You won't understand. You're not a mother.'

'But of course,' said Prakash Chopra with exaggerated patience, 'but I'd really like to go in. The mosquitoes are biting.' Without waiting for an answer, he strode into the house while Karan ushered his mother in. Lisa glanced heavenwards as she followed them, mentally preparing herself for what would undoubtedly be an arduous evening.

'Where is your maid?' Anju Chopra looked questioningly at Lisa as she brought in the drinks and snacks and placed them on the centre table. She'd remembered to add ice to her mother-in-law's orange squash but not to her father-in-law's whiskey since he had a sensitive throat.

'She's not well, Mom. She's sleeping in her room.'

'Yeah sure, she's got one hell of a cold,' remarked Karan caustically as Lisa stared at him. She was surprised at the insensitive remark. He was usually a compassionate person. Besides, she didn't like it when he contradicted her in front of his mother.

'She's got fever, Karan.' She looked at her husband coldly. 'She's worked hard all day. I'm sure we can manage without her for a couple of hours.'

'How much do you pay her, Lisa?' As usual her mother-in-law had butted into a conversation that was supposed to be a private one between husband and wife. But did she care? Oh no, not her. She helped herself to the chicken tikka, dipped a piece into the mint chutney Rama had made earlier, and popped the tikka into her mouth. She could actually eat and talk all at the same time which was bad manners, but interesting to watch. 'Nine thousand, isn't it?'

'Actually, ten. I gave her a raise last month,' answered Lisa, offering the corn and tofu salad to her father-in-law. She wished her mother-in-law would mind her own business. She didn't go to her house and demand to know everything, did she?

'Thanks, Beta,' said her father-in-law as he helped himself to the salad, 'very sweet of you to have remembered how much I like this salad.' Lisa knew he was trying to steer the conversation to safer subjects. He took a big helping and then poured a generous amount of the vinaigrette dressing on top of it. 'This dressing is delicious and...'

'Hain? Did you say ten thousand?' asked Anju Chopra, interrupting her husband as she stared at Lisa in consternation, 'who pays ten thousand? It's way too high! No wonder she's acting like prima donna!'

'Yes, but the rates are higher in Gurgaon and...'

'Don't squander your money away on ungrateful maids like her. It is Karan's hard-earned money after all.'

'Mine too,' muttered Lisa, pressing her finger to her temple. Hadn't anyone ever told the woman that cutting people off like that was not good manners? She could already feel a headache coming on. She wouldn't be surprised if she had a whopping migraine by the end of the day. Her mother-in-law often had that effect on her.

'Don't let her bully you like this, Puttar,' continued Anju who seemed quite oblivious to Lisa's lack of interest in her unsolicited advice. 'Talk to me! I'll get you a better maid any day.' Lisa almost laughed out loud. It was a ludicrous thought. Her mother-in-law hadn't been able to retain a maid herself for more than a couple of months at a time. Thankfully she didn't have to bother answering because her father-in-law came to her rescue.

'So, Karan, how's work?' Once again, Prakash Chopra tried to change the subject. 'I heard your Mumbai trip went well.'

'Yes, it did, Dad,' answered Karan as Lisa glanced at the clock. It was almost time for dinner. Rama had already set the table and put all the food into the proper dishes. All Lisa had to do was heat the food in the microwave and put it on the table. Karan helped himself to some roasted almonds and shrugged, 'Hasn't been easy though. This is not a good economy to work in. Unfortunately, our business model doesn't allow for much cost cutting and clients aren't reasonable about costs. The pressure's terrible these days.'

'Why don't you quit this stupid job and join your father in the business?' interjected his mother suddenly. 'I never did approve of your doing a job like this. Why should you slave away for an ungrateful boss at a back-breaking job that does not allow you to have a decent life, when you can work with your father in your own business? You are a very beeba bachha na, that's why people take advantage of you.' Lisa stifled a giggle and tried to keep a straight face.

'Don't be silly, Anju.' Prakash Chopra looked annoyed. 'Look how much he's achieved! All on his own too. You should be proud of him,' he added emphatically.

'Of course, I'm proud of him,' scowled Anju Chopra as she slurped her orange squash noisily. 'But why should he…'

'Because it's what he wants to do,' said Prakash Chopra, firmly cutting her off. 'You're well aware of the fact that he's not interested in the family business and that's fine with me. We've had this conversation before. He should do what makes him happy.'

'Let's talk about something else,' muttered Karan then. He was getting fed-up of the stressful atmosphere. Lisa too, decided that she'd had enough of her mother-in-law's continuous prattle, and glanced at her watch pointedly.

'I remember the doctor told Papa to eat an early dinner. I'll just heat up the food.' She rose from her chair and looked at her husband expectantly. 'Karan, can you give me a hand?' He nodded and was about to get up, when his mother put up a hand to stop him. She looked disapprovingly at Lisa.

'Karan must be tired, Lisa. Ask your maid to help you. She's not dying, is she? That's the problem with you young girls these days! When I was your age, I could whip up a four-course meal for ten people in no time. Tsk, tsk.'

What infuriated Lisa the most was that Karan actually obeyed his mother and settled down in his chair again. Her mother-in-law however, seemed oblivious to her daughter-in-law's mutinous expression and continued her chatter. 'Now, Amisha is one virtuous girl. Last time we visited; she made the most delicious seviyan ki kheer I have ever tasted. It makes me so proud to see how responsible she is turning out to be.'

Lisa couldn't believe her ears. Amisha! Responsible? It was common knowledge that Karan's sister, who couldn't manage her home and life without a line-up of staff and didn't even remember to keep an account of how much money she spent each month, was far from responsible. It was good for her that she had her parents and brother to bail her out of any messy situation, and Lisa could only hope for her sake that her husband would do the same. Personally, she didn't think it was the girl's fault. Lisa blamed her mother-in-law entirely for the way Amisha had turned out. Thank God Karan had lived away from home for a part of his life!

'Well, the last time we visited Amisha, she conveniently forgot to pick us up at the airport and was still sleeping in her bedroom when we reached her house by taxi at ten-thirty in the morning. Not very responsible behavior that!' she couldn't help retorting then.

There was an uncomfortable silence as Lisa met her mother-in-law's icy stare and Karan's father surreptitiously prodded Karan to get up.

'Go help your wife,' he murmured firmly, and Karan rose from his chair and followed his wife into the kitchen. His father looked on approvingly and Lisa couldn't resist glancing triumphantly at her mum-in-law as she walked past her. Clichéd though it was, this was definitely a test, and she had aced this round.

By eight-thirty, they were all seated at the dinner table. Anju Chopra had, as usual, plonked herself into Lisa's chair next to Karan before anyone could stop her. Most of their guests always checked the seating arrangements before they sat down; it was good manners after all, but then her mother-in-law was not 'most guests'. Lisa, who wasn't used to sitting on the other side of the table, shifted uncomfortably in the chair next to her father-in-law as everyone helped themselves to the food. It was the usual, run-of-the-mill North Indian fare since her mother-in-law didn't eat anything else, but Lisa wasn't complaining since it made her job that much easier. She certainly didn't want to be stuck in the kitchen, stirring pasta sauce on a perfectly good Sunday either.

'The chicken is delicious, Lisa. Is this a new recipe?'

Lisa looked at her in surprise since this was the first time she had ever complimented anything that Lisa had served.

'Oh, we don't know about the recipe, Mom,' laughed Karan before Lisa could answer. 'We'll have to call Tandoori Nights for that.'

He laughed again and Lisa turned around to glare at him. She couldn't believe that he could be so stupid! Was he really so dense?

'You mean it's not home-made!' exclaimed Anju Chopra, looking appalled. 'Puttar!' she turned to Lisa and shook her head disapprovingly, 'don't get food from outside so often,' she admonished. 'It's not good. Do you want Karan to fall sick?'

Do you want Karan to fall sick! Lisa shook her head in disbelief. Would it be tasteless to mention that her beloved Amisha had only served 'food from outside' during the entire course of their trip? Anju Chopra was now looking at Lisa sternly and expectantly. Lisa realized that she was actually expecting her to provide a suitable explanation as to why the chicken was not home-made.

'Most of the food is home-made,' she said at last. It was very difficult to control her temper but she didn't want to create a scene at the dinner table, particularly since she was the hostess. The most infuriating thing was that Karan was just sitting there, eating the offending chicken and behaving as though he wasn't a part of this.

'So, how's work, Lisa?' Unlike his son, Prakash Chopra didn't seem to be oblivious to what was happening and for the third time that evening, he valiantly tried to move the conversation away from the awkward discussion. Poor man! He was one of the most easy-going people around, with a genuine 'live and let live' attitude, and Lisa was quite fond of him. He probably didn't care where the chicken came from since he didn't eat chicken anyway. 'I picked up a copy of your magazine the other day and I must say it's a fine-looking publication. Karan was telling me that your circulation is really growing and your boss…'

'So I was saying, you must be more responsible,' interrupted Anju Chopra, ignoring her husband's vain attempt to change the subject. Lisa knew of course, that her mother-in-law was much too persistent to give up so easily, partly also since a conversation about Lisa's job was not one that she was particularly interested in having.

'And now that that's settled,' she continued, shooting her now silent husband, a triumphant glance, 'will someone pass me the paneer please?'

Expectedly, the evening did not end at all well for Lisa and Karan. As soon as her in-laws had left, Lisa, who had been goaded beyond endurance, descended on her unsuspecting husband. First it was about mothers, Karan's sister, even cousins they hadn't seen in years; then about Lisa's exorbitant credit card bills and Karan's general attitude towards her. Even though they were both tired, they argued relentlessly and were totally worn out by the time they finally went to bed. Lisa flatly refused to sleep with him and Karan, in turn, as though almost relieved, picked up his pillow and night things and stalked off to the guest bedroom. But even though she didn't try to stop him or make up, she couldn't help feeling distressed as she rested her aching head on the pillow and wrapped her arms around herself. After the small, tentative steps they'd taken over the last few days to make up with each other, this felt like a major let-down. She knew it was partly her fault too; she shouldn't let her mother-in-law get under her skin so easily. She also knew that despite sticking up so valiantly for his mother, Karan wasn't completely oblivious to her behaviour, but there wasn't much he could do about it. But the net result was that they'd ended up having another argument after a perfectly amicable weekend. What had happened to them? When exactly had things gone so wrong? Didn't they understand each other at all anymore? It was difficult to believe that they were the same people who'd once been much too in love with each other to even notice anything else. She was very upset about it and so was he, but neither tried to talk to the other or even take a step forward to make up. They slept in separate bedrooms. Lisa cried herself to sleep while Karan stared at the ceiling till about half past two before he fell into a fitful slumber.

Not surprisingly, when Lisa informed Karan three days later that she had to travel to Mumbai for a day, he was relieved. Even though they hadn't had another argument after his parents had visited, he knew that that was because he'd been leaving early every morning and Lisa had been working late every evening. They hadn't really had the time or opportunity to get into an argument. In fact, they'd been like ships passing each other in the night and hadn't so much as exchanged more than a few words at a time. Maybe it was just as well, considering that the last exchange between them hadn't been exactly pleasant.

Anyhow, it would be good to get a respite from all the bickering and admittedly, he found himself looking forward to it when he saw her pack her small overnight bag the next morning. He didn't want to hurt her so he tried to mask his enthusiasm and even offered to drop her to the airport. She was taking an early flight so it wouldn't upset his schedule. But she shook her head at his offer and curtly informed him that the office had sent a cab. She made it clear that she was still upset about their row and he didn't push her. Maybe it was just as well that she was going to be out; the space would do them both good. He kissed her goodbye and then heaved a sigh of relief as she got into the elevator. He'd be able to enjoy a nice, peaceful evening at last. And the best part was that they were showing the latest Avengers movie on TV that night. He was in luck!

He made it a point to wind up early at the office that day which was rare for him. It was grand to have the whole house to himself and he even invited Mayank to join him for a few beers at home after work. He'd already been to the gym that morning and was at a loose end. Mayank, of course, happily accepted and they were both out of the office and on their way home by five-thirty. Lisa would have been amazed to see them, particularly since Karan hardly ever got home before seven these days. But that was the last thing on Karan's mind as Mayank and he called up Dominoes on their way home to order a pizza. It was going to be a great evening; they would open some beer, watch the movie and just chill. They were both in high spirits and Karan was even whistling cheerfully when Rama opened the door to let them in. If she was surprised to see Karan back so early, she didn't show it. She greeted them politely and got them glasses of chilled water. And as predicted, they had a great evening. They listened to rock music on Karan's new sound bar, drank beer out of the bottle, watched the movie, and laughed and talked as loudly as they felt like. And Karan felt refreshed and easy when he left for work the next day. It was only when Lisa came back that evening and looked at him pointedly, that he felt something was wrong.

'How was your trip?' he asked her, but she continued to stare at him. He felt himself grow uneasy. 'Is something wrong?' he asked then.

'I think it is,' she said grimly as he wondered what had happened. 'I thought we had an unwritten rule in this house that any single friends are not to be entertained in the bedroom. I understand Mayank spent the evening here yesterday. I'm glad you had a great time but you could have remembered how I feel about outsiders entering my bedroom.'

As usual, she had come straight to the point. She was always candid and straightforward and this was usually one of the things he respected about her, but he was clearly very irritated now as he retorted: 'What is this Lisa? The Spanish Inquisition? Did Rama bleat to you? Did you ask her to spy on me or something? This is supposed to be my house too!'

But Lisa was not in a mood to be reasoned with. There were some things she was very particular about and this was one of them. She followed the same rules so what was his problem? Hell, even when Sameera and Ayesha spent the night at their house, Lisa was very clear about putting them up in the guest room. She just felt that the bedroom was off limits and there was a sanctity about it that needed to be respected. But Karan couldn't understand all that now as he stood there and argued with his wife, very irritated with her as well as the maid. In fact, he insisted that it was all Rama's fault and who did she think she was, spying on him like that. He even insisted that Lisa fire her at once since she was obviously getting too big for her boots. Lisa was livid and clearly shocked at his inability to see his own fault. She refused to talk to him after that, warned him not to say a word to Rama, and shut herself in the bathroom for more than an hour. Rama had also firmly closed the kitchen door, and Karan felt extremely alienated, almost like a schoolboy who had been sent to Coventry since both the women in the house were clearly refusing to speak to him.

□

Chalk and Cheese

Well! I think you should let me speak to Karan. These arguments have been going on for quite a while, haven't they? He should know better.' Lisa's mother looked at her grimly over her glasses as she spoke. She was looking particularly stern today which could either be because she'd tied her hair up in an extremely tight bun, or because she'd been invited to speak at a conference for the upliftment of women in rural areas. Either way, she looked as though she would stand no nonsense from anyone, let alone a man.

They were now well into August. It was a bright Saturday morning and as the homey aroma of hot chicken soup and herbed bread wafted in from the kitchen, Lisa's mind was suddenly flooded with childhood memories. Just then Shanti, her mother's cook, brought her a bowl of the hot, aromatic broth with a piece of freshly toasted bread. Lisa smiled. She couldn't help remembering all those times when she'd been down with the flu or a cold, or even the time when she'd been dumped by her first boyfriend at sixteen and had been feeling as though her world was coming to an end. Her mother's famed chicken soup had always worked its magic. Katherine always added a dash of a dry, red wine to the bubbling broth, claiming it was good for the system and the mood. But life had been simpler then; much simpler. Nevertheless, the soup was still as delicious and comforting as always, and Lisa thanked Shanti as she placed the bowl in front of her.

As she ate the soup and looked around the house she had grown up in, she had to admire her mother's sense of style and eye for detail. The newly decorated drawing room looked like a picture out of Good Housekeeping. The pastel colours on the walls complimented the elegant furnishings and beautiful silk drapes. The coffee table was scattered with books on art, history, and literature; the walls were adorned with paintings by famous artists and family pictures, and the house was full of small and big treasures from her parents' travels around the world. Since it was a pleasant day, her mother had opened the large French windows which looked out on a beautifully manicured garden. Everything was tasteful, understated and classy, unlike her mother-in-law's house which sometimes looked more like a museum than a house. Even the recently decorated kitchen was sleek and elegant, done with soft grays, whites and walnut, and well equipped with everything that a modern kitchen should have. Not that her mother ever cooked in there. In fact, her father had always been the better cook and when they did decide to cook a meal together over the weekend, Katherine Singh was usually the sous chef.

Lisa's mother was a successful Delhi-based lawyer and women's rights activist. Besides having a very successful legal practice specializing in divorce and property cases, she was also a noted legal scholar with many articles published in reputed law journals. Educated at Yale Law School, she had worked with an excellent law firm before starting her own practice. Over the years, she'd built up an enviable reputation for herself as one of the best women's lawyers in the country, besides being constantly involved in social causes like child marriage, dowry deaths, rehabilitation of rape victims, female foeticide and the general empowerment of women. She was a brilliant woman and had very strong views about most things which sometimes did make her a little difficult to talk to. Needless to say, she'd wanted a more academically or professionally inclined family for her only child, and had been visibly disappointed when Lisa had announced that she wanted to marry Karan. One meeting with his mother had been enough to make Katherine Singh dismiss them as just another typical Punjabi business family. Lisa couldn't help smiling as she remembered the fateful day when her mother and mother-in-law had met for the very first time. Karan's mother had nearly fainted when Katherine Singh had asked for a whiskey –'on the rocks please' – and in turn, Katherine Singh had glared ominously at everyone in general when Anju Chopra had slyly suggested that it would be a very nice gesture if Lisa's parents would present all the women in their family with gold earrings at the wedding. Needless to say, the meeting hadn't gone well.

'So, put your foot down,' continued Katherine Singh, snapping Lisa out of her thoughts. 'Make it very clear that you will not put up with this kind of behaviour. The weaker you appear in front of men, the more they'll take advantage.'

All this was said straight out in front of Lisa's father, who, other than the occasional hms and aahs, seemed completely absorbed in the book he was reading. But then Katherine Singh rarely ever minced words and her husband usually knew better than to argue with her unless she said something that he strongly disagreed with. He reserved his opinions for those rare occasions, and Lisa had always enjoyed the heated debates on important social issues and world-changing events between her parents. Now as she glanced at her father and he shook his head wearily, she knew that her mother's reaction had been very predictable. She should have known better than to discuss her marital issues with her.

'I know what you mean, Mum,' said Lisa at last. 'It's just that we don't see eye to eye a lot of the time and…'

'The backgrounds are too different,' said her mother, cutting her off. This was the only thing that her mother and mother-in-law had in common with each other. They were both very good at cutting her off mid-sentence! 'I mean, look at his mother for instance! She's positively obnoxious! And look at us!'

She spread her hands out as though stating the obvious and Lisa groaned as she realized where this discussion would inevitably lead.

'What does his mother have to do with anything?' asked Lisa feeling a little defensive, even though she knew that she too had been dragging his mother into every issue recently. She didn't understand why she felt the need to defend her husband considering how upset she herself was with him.

'Come on, Lisa!' Her mother looked at her in surprise and shook her head impatiently. 'It's his roots. What do you expect?' She wagged a finger at her daughter as she spoke: 'I did warn you about this. The families are as different as chalk and cheese. I mean, did you see the age of the girl who was working in their house as a maid the last time we visited? She was barely twelve! I would have reported her at once if she hadn't been Karan's mother. Doesn't the woman know that child labour is illegal? Doesn't she know that all children are entitled to free and compulsory education till the age of fourteen? Appalling!'

'I don't think that has anything to do with what I'm saying,' muttered Lisa, trying to get a word in.

'Oh, but it does,' said her mother 'it points out a basic difference in thinking. See how I treat the lady who works here! I treat her like an equal; I even insist that she reads the newspaper every day.'

Lisa suddenly wished that she hadn't told her mother about her recent arguments with Karan. It had been several days since the night she'd returned from Mumbai and even though there had been no more fights after that, the tension between them was still palpable. As much as she hated admitting it, it bothered Lisa a lot and she'd been meaning to talk to her mother about it, hoping to get some advice on how to deal with the situation. But now she suddenly regretted bringing it up. All that her mother had done since Lisa had mentioned the issue, was to go on and on about these dominating men and how women were the equal of men in every way – why even the constitution said so – and in conclusion proclaimed how Lisa should set an example for the women of the world by standing up for her rights.

'It's no wonder then that Karan is behaving like this,' continued her mother as Lisa sighed in resignation. 'The men in such families are always the chauvinistic and dominating type.'

'I don't think Karan is dominating,' interrupted Lisa's father, putting his book down. 'He's a very intelligent and capable boy. And a good husband.' It was time he stepped in.

'I'm not saying that he isn't,' said Katherine Singh. By then she looked as though she was in the middle of a very heated debate. 'But there are certain things that are a part of his basic upbringing which he just cannot change.' She shook her head and a lock of dark brown hair tumbled out onto her forehead from the tight bun. 'Look at his sister, for instance. Zero ambition! And his mother! Happy in her little pond, totally oblivious that there's a world beyond her crepe suits and kitty parties! Mother and daughter, both cut from the same cloth!' She gave Lisa a grim look and shook her head. 'Thankfully, Karan was sensible enough not to join his family business and chose to work as a professional instead. That's some consolation at least! I'm actually amazed that he turned out so level-headed and aware! He's so different from the rest of his family. Are you sure he's not adopted?'

Lisa almost choked on her soup and her father patted her on the back as she spluttered and coughed.

'That's completely out of line, Katherine,' he said to his wife. 'Lisa is upset enough as it is. She needs you to advise her.'

'That's exactly what I'm doing.' Katherine Singh looked disapprovingly at her daughter. 'I would have expected you to be stronger than this, Lisa. Look at you, letting him get the upper hand like this.' She stopped to take a sip of her green tea. 'Anyway, I'll speak to him when he visits next. But you be very clear about what you will and won't accept.'

Lisa nodded again and finished the last of her soup. She was suddenly in a hurry to leave. She loved her mother very much but she could be extremely overwhelming at times. It was a lovely Saturday and she didn't want to waste it, sitting there and listening to her mother go on and on about Karan and his family. She was supposed to be meeting Sameera for lunch at Khan Market anyway, and she didn't want to be late. She was looking forward to meeting her best friend. It always did her good.

'I have to go now, Mum,' she said as she rose from the sofa and picked up her bag. She kissed both her parents and then smiled regretfully at her father. He looked at her helplessly then and she almost laughed out loud as they exchanged a conspiratorial smile. She'd been looking forward to chatting with him a bit but they'd hardly spoken to each other. Still, that wasn't surprising. When Katherine Singh was in a mood like this, not a lot of people were lucky enough to get a word in.

The rest of the day was pleasant and enjoyable. As planned, Lisa and Sameera met for lunch at Khan Market. It was such a lovely place to spend a Saturday afternoon with all the young crowd, the cozy little cafes that dotted its sides, and narrow cobbled streets. The moment they settled down at a corner table at The Big Chill, Khan Market's legendary restaurant, Lisa's mood changed for the better. As usual, the restaurant was packed to the gills, but even the noise and chaos did nothing to deter her. It was actually great to be out, and after last week's fight with Karan, this morning's lecture from her mother, not to mention how much Milind had kept her nose to the grindstone all week, she felt she deserved a break. The day stretched out in front of her, long and lazy and happy. She didn't have any plans for the evening anyway. Knowing Karan, he'd probably be working late and she was in no hurry to get home.

Lunch was uneventful and fun as always. The girls chatted about work, friends and Lisa's Mumbai trip. It was only when Sameera ordered two generous slices of the house cheese cake that Lisa sensed that something was a little amiss. Sameera's dietician had put her on a low glycemic index diet plan which didn't permit any refined sugar in any form at all. Sameera had been very diligent about the diet and now the fact that she was ordering something so rich and laden with sugar and calories could only mean that she was feeling low and needed to talk.

'Sam, you look a little down. Everything all right with you?' Lisa asked solicitously.

Sameera stirred her coffee and sighed.

'Well, not really, but it's not the end of the world I guess,' she admitted as Lisa listened. 'I just broke up with that guy I was dating.'

'The banker? Why? I thought things were going really well.' Sameera had been going steady with him for a while now, and even though it was too soon to arrive at a conclusion, Lisa had thought it would last longer than this. 'I thought he was totally your type.'

'He was until I found out that he already had another girlfriend,' confessed Sameera wearily. 'I thought I'd surprise him with a couple of movie tickets the other day, but I was in for a surprise myself. I saw them leave his office together, arm in arm. He even kissed her as they got into the car together. And when I confronted him about it, he told me that it wasn't any of my business because he hadn't made any commitment to me; we hadn't talked about being exclusive and that I shouldn't be sneaking around, spying on him.'

'What a shit!' exclaimed Lisa, furious about what had happened to her friend. She couldn't believe anyone could be that nasty with someone as nice as Sameera.

'I guess I should have asked him whether we were exclusive,' sighed Sameera. 'It seems to be a prerequisite these days, particularly since people seem to have very strange moral standards. Anyway, don't worry. I'm not heartbroken. He wasn't the love of my life. I just liked him a lot.'

'Forget about him,' advised Lisa, getting up to give her friend a hug. 'He's not worth it.'

'I know,' agreed Sameera, 'it just leaves a bad taste in the mouth. Not to mention that it makes you a lot less trusting about your future relationships. Anyway, let's talk about something else. Ah, here's a reason to be happy. The pièce de résistance!'

She smiled as the waiter placed the cheesecake in front of them.

Not surprisingly, the two girls had a wonderful afternoon together. It was the perfect girly outing and just what they both needed. It was lovely to just amble around the shops and watch people languidly strolling past. Saturdays were always very relaxed. The temperature had risen considerably by the afternoon, but in spite of the heat, the market was packed and there were a lot of people sauntering around, couples arm-in-arm doing a spot of shopping or eating ice cream, groups of friends catching up over cups of coffee, and foreigners in light summer clothing and huge designer sunglasses sitting around the cozy cafés. The two girls checked out all their favourite stores, had coffee in one of the little cafés on the sidewalk and afterwards, even stepped into their favourite lingerie store and tried on all kinds of sexy nightwear. It was great fun.

'That red and black lace chemise is really nice on you,' commented Sameera to Lisa in the trial room. 'And look, you get this black thong free with it.'

'Oh, I don't need it.' Lisa shook her head and slipped off the chemise hurriedly. 'Karan and I aren't exactly very intimate these days anyway.' It was amazing how frankly she could talk to Sameera without a twinge of embarrassment. But Sameera did not look amused at Lisa's confession.

'That doesn't sound like a lot of fun,' she said seriously, 'besides, it's not healthy for a relationship. You should do something to amend that.'

'Like what?' asked Lisa, pulling on her skirt. 'He doesn't seem too bothered about it.'

'Well then, all the more reason for you to be bothered,' said her friend reprovingly. 'Actually, maybe you really should buy that thing. Hell, you never know, it may liven things up a bit.'

'Six grand!' exclaimed Lisa, looking at the price tag. 'And I doubt it will really help. Karan is too busy with his proposals and reports and clients these days.'

'I can't believe you're saying this.' Sameera looked really surprised. 'Physical intimacy was never a problem between the two of you. Do you remember the first time he returned from a trip?'

Of course, she did! But if anything, the memory only made the current situation even more depressing.

'Yeah, well, things change,' she muttered gloomily.

'Then maybe this is exactly what the doctor ordered.' Sameera waved the lacy chemise under Lisa's nose and walked over to the cashier decisively.

□

A dinner date and a surprise

When Lisa got home that evening, Karan was already there. He'd been working late every day for the past few days, and she didn't know what to make of it as she pushed open the bedroom door. There were times when she wondered if he stayed late in office simply to avoid an argument or confrontation with her, particularly when they were going through a difficult period. She knew that she did; after all, no one wanted to come home after a gruelling day to a nagging, complaining spouse. In spite of the fact that it was Saturday, she was admittedly surprised to see him home so early. Maybe he simply wanted to work from home. He had mentioned some proposal that was due on Monday, hadn't he? That was probably it.

He was sitting in front of the TV, watching a lawn tennis match when she entered the bedroom. She closed the bedroom door softly behind her and he smiled at her as he turned off the TV.

'Hi! I didn't hear you come in.' He couldn't help noticing that she looked particularly elegant today. She was wearing a purple silk shirt with a black, pencil skirt, and high heels; her hair was swept off her face and pulled back into a chignon, and she looked every bit the senior editor of one of the country's leading fashion magazines. As he watched her surreptitiously, Karan couldn't help but admire her, albeit a bit involuntarily. But even he couldn't deny that she certainly was a very remarkable woman.

'Would you like a cup of coffee?' he offered then, but she shook her head and asked Rama to bring her a glass of water instead.

'I'm parched!' she declared, settling down in the recliner chair in their bedroom and kicking off her shoes. She hoped Karan wouldn't notice that they were new again. 'It's hot today, isn't it?' she remarked, hoping to distract him.

'Yeah,' agreed her husband, 'it's like an inferno out there in fact!' It was amazing how well the topic of the weather worked if you wanted to steer someone away from a particularly inconvenient conversation. 'Were you at work?' he asked as Rama came in with a glass of water for Lisa and she gulped it down thirstily. 'It's almost six.'

'No,' said Lisa, shaking her head, 'I was at Khan Market with Sameera and the traffic was crazy on the way back. Oh, and I went to visit my parents in the morning after my Pilates class.' She didn't mention that she had stopped at Galleria market to pick up a bottle of sparkling wine on her way back and that had taken almost half an hour since the wine shop had been totally packed. She wasn't even sure whether they would even get to use it or the chemise. The way things had been the past few months, she didn't want to get her hopes up and have them dashed later. It was just smarter to play it by ear.

'So, how are they?' Karan's voice snapped her out of her thoughts and she quickly steered herself back to the conversation.

'My parents? Oh, they're fine. They were asking about you.'

'I haven't met them in ages,' said Karan with a frown. 'Things have been so busy. I feel terrible about it.'

'I understand,' said Lisa with a smile. 'You've been up to your eyes in work lately.' She was actually surprised that they were having a congenial conversation without getting into another inexplicable argument.

'Why don't we invite them for dinner next weekend?' suggested Karan but Lisa was quick to shake her head.

'Next week my Mom's going to Mumbai to speak at a conference for the rehabilitation of victims of child abuse. And she's starting an important case right after that. Rape and attempt to murder.'

'Sounds ugly!' remarked Karan. 'But knowing her, I'm sure she'll do a fabulous job. Actually, I can't think of a better lawyer than her for something like this.'

'I'll tell her you said so,' said Lisa, touched at his honest praise for her mother, 'and now I'd better check on dinner. I don't want Rama serving us baingan ka bharta and moong ki daal on a Saturday night.'

'Would she dare?' laughed Karan.

'You never know with Rama,' smiled Lisa.

'Well, I have a better idea,' said her husband then. He stroked his chin thoughtfully as though working something out, and Lisa couldn't help noticing that he looked particularly handsome that day. In fact, for no specific reason, she suddenly wished he would just take her in his arms. It was what she would have easily expected a year ago, but the last few months seemed to have created such barriers between them that spontaneous, affectionate gestures weren't as common as they had been once. Lisa pushed the unpleasant thought away and tried to concentrate on what Karan was saying.

'I was thinking, it's been a while…why don't we go out for dinner?'

The suggestion was followed by a short silence as she wondered what to say to him. It hadn't just been a while – it had been way too long! There had been a time when sitting home on a Saturday evening would have been unthinkable, but now she couldn't remember the last time they'd gone out for dinner.

'I'd love to,' she said at last and Karan heaved a sigh of relief. He was glad that she'd been receptive to his suggestion. Actually, she seemed to be in a better mood than she'd been in a long time. Maybe it was good that she'd spent the afternoon with Sameera who always had a positive effect on her.

'But don't you have to go to the gym?'

He shook his head in answer to her question. 'No, I thought I'd skip it today. I've been almost every day this week. Besides, I'd really like to go out with you tonight.'

She smiled at him then and Karan noticed how pretty she looked when she smiled.

'Did you have something particular in mind?' she asked and he nodded eagerly.

'Yeah! I was thinking about that Thai place – the one in Mehrauli.'

'Banyan Tree?' Lisa was pleased with his suggestion. Banyan Tree was one of her favourite restaurants. The ambience was wonderful there as was the food. But the most important thing was that it was a perfect place to have a conversation. And a proper conversation was exactly what they needed tonight. It wasn't a loud or noisy restaurant; in fact, it was perfect with its elegant décor and soft piped music.

'That's the one,' nodded Karan. 'In fact, I already took the liberty to call them and reserve a table. I remembered how much you like it.'

'Sounds great!' She was surprised that he'd even made the reservation. Usually she was the one who did that. 'What time's the reservation for?'

'Eight-thirty,' confirmed Karan. 'Is that too early for you?'

'No, it's fine.' She gulped down her water and rose from the chair. 'But I'd better pop over to the salon then. I need to get my eyebrows done.'

They were both ready to leave by a quarter to eight. Lisa looked absolutely lovely and Karan smiled admiringly when he saw her. Skinny jeans that had always been a bit tight but now fit nicely thanks to the weight she'd recently lost, teamed with a form-fitting white silk shirt that had been presented to her by one of her designer friends. It gave her the kind of glamorous, sexy look that would reduce most men to near distraction.

'You look beautiful.' He took her in his arms then and surprised her with a sudden kiss on the lips. He didn't want to spoil her make-up so it was just a light peck, but she was pleasantly surprised. His admiration was genuine she knew, and she revelled in it. It felt good to be complimented and wanted. She was glad she'd made a special effort tonight.

'Hey, I hope your lipstick is smudge proof.' She laughed at his words and gently drew back from him.

'Let me check.' She whipped out a hand mirror from her bag and carefully surveyed the result. 'Seems okay!'

Karan grinned at her as she put the mirror back into her bag and clasped it shut. He noticed the bag was new again but he didn't comment. It wasn't the right time anyway and he had to admit that Lisa looked great. But then she'd always been a very stylish woman.

'Ready?' he asked and she nodded. He was looking good too in a pair of crisp, black trousers and a deep purple shirt that he'd left open at the neck. It wasn't the kind of shirt he usually wore – it was a lot less formal than the white and blue shirts he wore to work – this one was dressier and the kind she would have picked up for him. She noticed that he was wearing the Omega she'd given him for their first anniversary, and she realized that he'd put it on for the first time in months! She knew he kept it for special occasions which meant that he must be in a particularly good mood tonight. Lisa had a feeling it was going to be a good Saturday evening after all. She felt decidedly more cheerful as she tucked her hand into the crook of his arm, and even though neither of them realized it, they made a very handsome pair as they walked out of the house together.

Strategically located somewhere between the Delhi Greens and the Qutub Minar, Banyan Tree was a lovely Thai restaurant with an excellent view of the historic red sandstone and marble structure. Due to its proximity to the airport, every few minutes you could see a plane whizzing past above. The lighting was soft and muted, the music mostly romantic piped, and the ambience tranquil and soothing. The restaurant was famed for its mouth-watering Thai delicacies and it really was a great place to sit back and enjoy a glass of wine and a good conversation. In fact, it was prefect for couples and small, intimate groups of close friends or even family. Karan and Lisa had always agreed that it was one of the best restaurants in Delhi and a personal favourite with both of them. Karan was glad he'd picked this restaurant for tonight. He couldn't think of a better place to surprise her with his big announcement. He'd waited long enough and this was the perfect opportunity to do it.

They entered the restaurant at exactly eight-thirty-five and Karan was pleased. He never liked to be late for anything. They were greeted at the entrance by the maître d' who led them to one of the best tables in the restaurant with an excellent view of the Qutub Minar. Even though it was warm, there was a pleasant breeze blowing and most people were sitting outdoors. Karan noticed that the restaurant was full but that was expected since it was a Saturday evening. He was glad he had made a reservation. He smiled at his wife as she sipped her water and the waiter brought them the beverage menus.

'Should we order a bottle of wine?' he suggested. He knew that Lisa liked wine, but most of the wines she liked weren't usually available by the glass and she had never been known to finish a bottle by herself.

'Sure.' She looked pleased at the suggestion and Karan turned the page to the wine list.

'White or Red?' he asked and she laughed.

'Red of course. You know I don't drink white wine. It gives me acidity. But maybe you don't remember any more.'

It was said lightly but Karan was hurt at her comment. Of course, he remembered. He'd just wanted to give her the option. 'I do remember,' he remarked, trying to conceal his feelings. 'I just thought that you might want to try something different, you know; everyone says that white wines pair better with Thai food and . . .' 'It's okay Karan,' she smiled, 'don't take everything I say so seriously.'

He smiled back at her then, wondering if that was true. Did he really take everything she said too seriously? He went back to studying the menu then and they finally settled on a Rioja that the sommelier confirmed was light and would go well with the food. Lisa suggested that they order an appetizer with the wine since it was too early for dinner and they were both feeling peckish. So they ordered the Chicken Satay with Peanut Sauce and a Steamed Basa with Tamarind. 'And please don't make it too spicy,' said Lisa to the waiter as she placed the order. Karan didn't say it but he was touched that she'd remembered that he couldn't eat spicy food. These were the little things that despite everything, had kept them going after all.

'So, how's work?' asked Lisa as the waiter poured the wine into delicate crystal glasses. Karan took a sip and nodded approvingly to him, confirming that he liked the taste and temperature. The waiter poured them each a glass and then discreetly placed the bottle in an ice bucket and left the couple to chat. That was another thing they both liked about the restaurant – the service was good but unobtrusive.

'You don't really want to know, do you?' he teased his wife then as she grinned sheepishly.

'Of course, I do. I know how important your work is to you. Just don't go on and on for hours.'

They laughed together and Karan sat back in his chair as a plane whizzed past right above them. He was glad to see her looking so relaxed. Things were still not completely normal between them and there were still frequent, awkward silences, and stilted bits of conversation that took them both by surprise considering that other than the past few months, they'd always felt more than comfortable with each other. However, tonight things were definitely looking up. 'Don't worry, I won't,' he said then with a laugh, 'I don't want to talk about work either.'

'Well, what do you want to talk about?' asked Lisa with a laugh.

He looked at her for a moment and then shrugged. 'I don't know,' he said, 'you tell me. Us?' he added thoughtfully.

'What about us?' she teased as he smiled at her and she felt her heart skip a beat. He really did have a wonderful smile. In fact, it was his smile that had instantly attracted her to him when they'd first met. As they sat there looking at each other, long forgotten memories of happier times came rushing back to both of them, and it was suddenly impossible to believe that they were the same people who'd been going at each other's throats just a couple of days ago. Karan was just going to reach out across the table for her hand when the waiter appeared with the first course and the spell was broken. He smiled ruefully to himself and then turned to the waiter.

'We'll help ourselves, thank you.' The waiter nodded as he placed the food on the table, re-filled their water glasses, and disappeared. There were a few moments of silence as they helped themselves to the food and then Lisa looked at Karan with a pensive smile.

'We'll talk about us some other time,' she said gently, 'but seriously, tell me about your work. I really do want to know about it. I know how hard you've been working recently. Did you get that project you were working on?' Tonight, she was in a good mood; they were being nice to each other after a long time and she wanted him to feel that she still cared about things that were important to him.

'Not yet,' he answered as he tasted the fish and nodded approvingly. 'Good stuff!' he remarked, helping himself to some of the tamarind sauce that had come with it. 'But we're among the three companies that have been shortlisted for the job,' he continued. 'They'll have a decision for us by next week. Their Managing Director's meeting with Vivek is on Tuesday and we're keeping our fingers crossed… '

'Karan!' Lisa almost dropped her wine glass in surprise at the sudden scream. She had barely had a moment to process where it came from before a girl in a very short dress flung herself on Karan like a thunderbolt. 'Karan! Is it really you? Where in hell have you been all these years?'

Lisa couldn't see her face – only a pair of extremely well-toned legs in a dress that was now riding even higher up as the girl bent down to hug Karan. Karan, on the other hand, was looking extremely taken aback and somewhat embarrassed as he tried to untangle himself from the girl and stood up.

'Well! How are you Anoushka?' He gave her a sort of half smile and turned to his wife who was still sitting there looking as astonished as ever. 'Lisa, this is Anoushka. We used to study together years ago.'

'Oh, dear! What a way to introduce your ex-girlfriend!' The girl pretended to look furious and then laughed. 'But I guess you've forgotten all about that, haven't you? It's literally been a lifetime!' She smiled at him, showing perfect teeth and Lisa had to concede that she was certainly striking. Other than the fact that she'd been blessed with a gorgeous face and lustrous hair, she was tall, skinny and sophisticated. She was a little too thin for Lisa's liking, but admittedly, the printed mini dress she was wearing did look marvellous on her. It was by one of Lisa's favourite designers and she had accessorized it beautifully with a pair of very high black pumps and a simple gold clutch. She was extremely well put together and she seemed delighted to see Karan as she rose to kiss him on the cheek. The kiss however landed somewhere in between his cheek and his lips – actually it might have been closer to the lips!

'Oops! Sorry! Old habits die hard, I guess.' At least her lipstick was good enough not to leave a mark. Some consolation! She threw her head back and laughed and Karan looked helplessly at Lisa. 'So darling, what have you been up to these last few years?' Anoushka pulled out a chair and sat down. She obviously didn't think she needed an invitation, but Lisa was amazed at her confidence. 'Really, I have a bone to pick with you for disappearing like that, Karan! I haven't seen you in ages! I tried to contact you on Facebook and...'

'Um... Anoushka, this is my wife.' Karan managed to utter the words before Anoushka could say any more. Lisa had composed herself by then and tried to look as nonchalant as she could. With as much grace as she could muster, she held her hand out to Anoushka, who, in turn, had the grace to look visibly flustered at the introduction.

'Oh... I'm sorry... I didn't know... when did you get married?' It wasn't the appropriate thing to say and congratulations might have been more in order, but Anoushka suddenly looked mortified.

'Well, I guess we've been out of touch far too long,' said Karan at last, trying to say something appropriate. 'It's been more than seven years.'

'Yeah, yeah I know. It's been so long!' Anoushka smiled again but this time at Lisa. 'Well, it's lovely to meet you Lisa. But I'd better go now. We were leaving anyway.'

She got up just as quickly as she'd sat down and picked up her clutch. Just as well, thought Lisa grimly to herself as she nodded and took another sip of wine. Anoushka smiled at both of them, said a hurried goodbye to Karan sans kiss or hug this time, and ran off to join her girlfriends who were waiting for her at the exit and were all as skinny as her. She waved to Karan and he waved back awkwardly before finally turning back to his wife.

Smiling at her apologetically, he shook his head. 'Well, well, well! So where were we before we were interrupted?'

Lisa was surprised to see the usually well-composed Karan looking so flustered. He normally didn't turn a hair at most things so this was quite an interesting reaction. She raised one perfectly shaped eyebrow questioningly at her husband. 'Quite an interruption I'd say.'

'Yes, well, Anoushka was always like that. You know, spontaneous and gregarious and….'

'Was she?' Lisa looked unimpressed and Karan shook his head again and hurriedly took a sip of wine. 'Stop teasing me, Lisa! I was as surprised as you were.'

Lisa's lips twitched a little and she tried to keep a straight face as Karan watched her intently. Suddenly, they both burst out laughing and Lisa shook her head disbelievingly. 'I can't believe you never told me about her.'

'Like I said, it's been a really long time,' said Karan, enormously relieved that his wife had decided to take it sportingly. 'And frankly, I didn't think it was important. I dated her –yes – but we were just students then. I'm sure you have a fairly interesting past too.'

'Depends on what you would call interesting,' said Lisa, 'I don't really have any skeletons in the closet for you to discover.'

'Well, neither do I.' Karan looked sheepish and Lisa laughed at how obviously mortified he had been. At least he'd had the grace to be embarrassed.

'Well, I have to say that I'm impressed,' she said magnanimously. 'She's very pretty.'

'Very generous of you to say so,' said her husband, looking embarrassed again. He'd been surprised to see his ex-girlfriend after all this time and he had to admit that even though she was as pretty and charming as he remembered, she couldn't hold a candle to his wife. She had neither Lisa's effortless grace or elegance, nor her intelligence or wit. And he wasn't unaware of the number of heads that turned every time Lisa walked past. 'Anyway, enough about that already! Can we please go back to what we were discussing before we were interrupted?'

'Sure.' Lisa shrugged her shoulders and sat back in her chair. She tucked a stray strand of hair behind her ear and cocked her head to one side. 'You were telling me about that project.'

'Yes, that's right,' said Karan, glad to be on safe territory again. 'It's a critical project and –yes – it's been a bit of a haul recently. Believe it or not, there are mornings when I just don't feel like going to work but there's always something that just has to be done.' He sighed and took a sip of his wine, all thoughts about his ex-girlfriend now clearly forgotten. 'But if I want to be the youngest vice-president our organization has ever known, I'm going to have to slog it out.'

'You were always very ambitious.' She was actually touched that he was sharing his innermost feelings with her.

'I know you think that all I do is work these days,' continued Karan with a wry smile, 'you probably feel that I'm the most boring person to be around.'

She was taken aback at the candidness with which he had spoken and shook her head, feeling embarrassed. 'That's not how I feel,' she murmured, looking awkward. She knew she'd been giving him a hard time about being too busy. 'I understand that you've been under pressure.'

'Do you?' He was teasing her by then and she smiled.

'I try. But you can't blame me completely.' It was good to be having a proper conversation after what seemed like ages, good to be honest with each other about their feelings. 'After all, look at how things have been, Karan. No time for each other even on weekends, ages since we went on a vacation and…'

'Not ages!' interrupted Karan, but Lisa was quick to shake her head.

'Come on, Karan! It's been ages and you know it. The last we went anywhere was... um... I don't even remember. Now you know what I mean?'

'Well, I remember all right,' said Karan with a firm nod.

'You would!' laughed Lisa blithely but he wasn't amused.

'Of course, I do. We went to Jaipur and...'

'You call that a vacation!' exclaimed Lisa, looking amazed. 'It was three measly days including a weekend!'

'But we enjoyed ourselves and...'

'And we spent half a day driving back and forth anyway,' continued Lisa. 'Nope! That certainly wasn't a vacation.'

'If you insist,' relented her husband, not wanting to get into a disagreement. They were having a good time and he didn't want to spoil it over a petty argument. So he held his tongue and didn't say anymore when she shook her head and repeated it again, even more firmly this time. 'No way! That was just a weekend.'

Just then the waiter appeared to take their order for the main course and Lisa's stomach rumbled. She remembered she hadn't eaten anything substantial since lunch and it was almost ten o'clock.

'Let's order first,' suggested her husband as though reading her thoughts. He beckoned to the waiter and after some deliberation, they ordered the main course. The waiter clucked sympathetically when Lisa asked him to keep the food mild since her husband couldn't tolerate spices, nodded approvingly when they ordered the restaurant's signature dish on his recommendation, and then refilled their wine glasses before finally leaving them to continue their conversation.

Karan closed the menu and leaned back in his chair. 'Anyway, let's not argue about whether the Jaipur break was a vacation or not. Actually, I wanted to talk to you about something rather important, something that's been on my mind lately.'

His tone was casual but she was suddenly alert. Had this dinner been a ploy to break some unpleasant news to her? Maybe her mother-in-law had thrown a tantrum again and he wanted them to move in with his parents? Well, that was something that she wasn't even willing to consider. Or maybe he was having an affair! That would certainly explain the lack of intimacy between them but she would be devastated if that was the case. Or perhaps he had one of those excruciatingly long trips coming up and wanted to prepare her for those lonely weekends and solitary nights. Well, at least she had Sameera and Ayesha and her parents and...

'So, like I was saying, I know I've been busy lately but so have you.' His voice snapped her out of her thoughts and she turned her attention back to him. 'Needless to say, I feel really bad about how little time we've spent with each other recently. I mean it Lisa.' Karan took a sip of wine and looked at Lisa out of his clear, brown eyes. She couldn't help noticing how guileless and almost childlike his expression was. Despite the maturity, he still had that boyish, unassuming quality that had drawn her to him when they'd first met.

'I really feel terrible about it. Don't think I don't remember that I was out of town on your birthday last year and you were in Milan on our anniversary. I understand that we've been going through a difficult time lately. I know there are issues between us that have cropped up over the last few months that need to be resolved; I know that sometimes you think I'm insensitive and you even feel that I basically don't love you anymore.'

She didn't know what to say to that but could feel the tears beginning to form at the ends of her eyes. Damn! She should have worn her waterproof mascara. She blinked back the tears resolutely. She didn't want him to think she was a weepy wimp. 'Trust me, there are times I've felt the same. Very hurt, very lonely,' he said then. He placed his hand on hers and smiled gently. His palm was firm and dry. 'But believe me Lisa, our marriage is very important to me. I would do anything I could to set things right. And so, I've been planning a vacation for the two of us to Bali. I think we need to spend some time together, just the two of us and I know how much you've always wanted to go there. I've already spoken to Vivek and he's agreed to give me two weeks off right after that European client goes back. I have to get the team started on the project but Mayank's going to handle it after that. So, what do you think?'

'Are you serious?' Lisa looked at him incredulously. 'Is this a joke?'

'Of course not, Lisa!' Karan looked indignant as she continued to stare at him in amazement. 'I've been checking out possible hotels and flights. I've even managed to build up a tentative itinerary. But will you be able to take time off? I know you've been pretty busy too at the office. And what about the Paris couture show?'

'Oh, Milind's going for the Paris show this year,' said Lisa in answer to his question. 'And since other than that measly Jaipur trip, we haven't gone anywhere this year, I do have a lot of leave saved up.' She had a twinkle in her eye as she spoke and Karan smiled sportingly. 'But seriously Karan, how could you not tell me? Wow! Bali! This is the best news I've heard in a long, long time.' She was almost incoherent with excitement as she pushed back her chair and came around the table to fling her arms around her husband. 'I really can't believe it!' Barely noticing anyone else, she kissed him on the lips. Slightly shocked at first – after all it had been a while since she'd done something as spontaneous as kiss him in public like that – he then smiled as he kissed her back with relief. At that particular moment, he was sure that after a long time, he felt the same sizzling chemistry between them that had been there at the beginning of their relationship. All in all, he was ecstatic with the way things had turned out and he truly believed that tonight was going to be a new start to their relationship.

Their lovemaking that night was as natural and effortless as it had always been. Lisa was amazed at how exciting his touch was even after five years of marriage. The instant attraction that they'd experienced towards each other almost as soon as they'd met hadn't died out. Truth be told, it was an enormous relief to both of them that they'd been able to rediscover everything that they'd forgotten about their relationship in the past few months. Lisa was actually glad since she'd been worried about it; the distance she'd been fretting over had just melted away between them. And she had been able to use the chemise after all! She smiled to herself and secretly thanked Sameera for talking her into buying it. All in all, it had been the perfect evening. Later as they lay in each other's arms, whispering like children in the dark, Lisa couldn't remember the last time she'd been so happy. Admittedly, she'd missed him. She'd missed being close to him, lying contentedly in his arms after they'd made love, sharing little secrets, talking in bed for hours. She'd missed him so much. Now she could hardly wait for their holiday to Bali. She'd always wanted to go there and given what she'd heard about the place, she had a feeling it was going to be a deliriously romantic holiday. She was still astounded at the way Karan had planned everything. This was literally the first time he'd taken the initiative and she had to say that she was impressed.

'What are you thinking about?' he asked her as she traced her finger down his chest. It felt so wonderful to be back in his arms and she smiled contentedly to herself as he drew her closer.

'Us,' she said in answer to his question, 'I'm thinking about how wonderful tonight was. Thank you for doing what you did.'

'You don't have to thank me, sweetheart.' She noticed that he had used the endearment after a long time. He kissed her then, first on the forehead and then on the lips. Planning this holiday was probably the smartest thing he had done in a while. 'I was desperate to set things right between us. The last few months have been agony. But let's not talk about all that now.'

'Yes, let's talk about Bali,' laughed his wife. 'Let me warn you that this holiday is going to put a dent in our accounts for sure.'

Karan shrugged nonchalantly. 'Oh, let's throw caution to the winds for once. Live a little, you know.'

Lisa looked at the usually frugal Karan in surprise. 'You must be in a really good mood. Ok then let's treat ourselves to a really decadent holiday. Go get your laptop and let's figure out the hotel and flight.'

□

Holiday planning works its magic

When Lisa skipped into the office on Monday morning, she felt relaxed and happy after what had been a blissful weekend. She was early that morning; it was only a quarter to nine after all, but she noticed that quite a lot of people were either already at their desks or just walking in. As she waited for her computer to start, she got herself a cup of coffee from the cafeteria and brought it back to her desk.

'Morning, Lisa! You're looking good! That color's radiant on you.' Preeti gave her a thumbs up from her desk and Lisa smiled at her as she mouthed a Thank You. She knew that it wasn't just the crimson red of her dress that looked good – it was her vibrant mood that reflected visibly on her face that morning. She had a feeling it was going to be a good day, and was just about to settle down at her desk with her coffee, when her mobile rang suddenly. She pulled it out of her bag and almost instantly winced when she saw the number. She hadn't felt this happy in a very long time and the last thing she wanted to do was to get into some sort of an argument or altercation with her mother-in-law which was bound to happen. But she might as well talk to her now and get it over with or she'd have to call her back later anyway. She took a deep breath and answered the call.

'Hi, Mom. How are you?' she asked, trying to keep her voice low. Milind had just marched in and she didn't want to invite his wrath. It was common knowledge that he did not approve of personal calls in the office, particularly on a Monday morning.

'I am fine, thank you for asking. How are you, Lisa?'

'I'm fine too, Mom. What's new with you?'

'Oh, nothing special, Puttar. I met an old friend yesterday at the mall and she has not changed a bit. Still looks so young. I couldn't believe she is a grandmother now. She was buying her grandson an ice cream when I spotted her. Lucky woman!'

Lisa knew where the conversation would go from there on and she looked heavenwards as her mother-in-law continued: 'So, well, God knows when I'll be able to take my grandson to the mall. Anyway, that is up to the two of you to decide. Who am I to interfere? But my mother is already 89 and it would be lovely if she would live to see her great grandchild.'

'I'm sure she'll live to be a hundred, Mom,' said Lisa with a smile. Karan's grandmother had always been sweet to her and she was fond of the old lady.

'From your lips to God's ears, Puttar. But I feel you should think about what I've just said. You know, these days couples are having all sorts of problems in conceiving and you have already been married five years or is it six and…'

'Mom, if you're that keen on a grandchild, why don't you talk to Amisha?' Lisa couldn't help retorting. 'I mean, she's been married four years too.'

'Oh, Amisha's no more than a child herself,' laughed Anju Chopra. 'She is not prepared for the responsibilities of motherhood yet. Let her enjoy herself for a while.'

'Anyway, I may as well tell you that Karan and I have no plans to have children anytime soon.' She knew her tone was cold but she couldn't help it. This subject was too private for her and she didn't like anyone interfering.

'Why not?' Anju Chopra sounded appalled. 'You should be talking about it at least. How old are you, almost thirty, isn't it? That's old enough if you ask me. You don't want to be one of those geriatric mothers, do you now?'

Geriatric mother! She was barely thirty! And anyway, what was wrong with geriatric mothers? Someone show her Bridget Jones' Baby, please! Such an endearing film too!

'Tsk, tsk! I have seen some of them, all of forty and having kids at that age. Embarrassing, it is! Not to mention the problems you may have in conceiving if you wait too long. No, no you must plan soon.'

'Well, I do have a career and…'

'Career? Career! Don't career me, Puttar. Nothing is as important as having your own child at the right time. Is it that you've been trying and nothing is happening? Don't be disheartened, Puttar! There are a lot of treatments these days and infertility is a common problem and… '

What! Lisa couldn't believe her ears. How could she explain to her interfering mother-in-law how careful they'd been over the years to make sure that they avoided an unwanted pregnancy because they just weren't ready for the responsibility and commitment? How could she explain that despite the stomach cramps and skin breakouts, she still waited anxiously for her period every month and how terrified both of them got every time it was even a day late!

'Anyway, whatever you want.' Anju Chopra finally sounded defeated. 'It was my duty to advise you. The rest is up to you and God. You have always been headstrong and…'

'Mom, I'll have to call you back,' interrupted Lisa then, before she lost her temper and lashed out. She didn't want to be goaded beyond endurance. 'I've just entered the office and I have to start work.' She glanced at the emails that had started loading on her laptop, and then almost immediately, groaned as she saw the mail that Milind's assistant had sent her early that morning. Milind wanted to see her at eleven. He probably wanted to discuss that article. 'Facts and Myths about Lip Injections', and Lisa wanted to go over her notes once before she met him.

'Sure, you can call me back any time, Puttar,' answered her mother-in-law, snapping her out of her thoughts. 'Oh, and before I forget, I wanted to check how Karan is feeling? He was sounding a little… what is that word you are always using… ah, stressed! Yes, he was sounding a little stressed when I spoke to him on the phone the other day.'

'Oh, Karan's fine. In fact, he was really sweet to me this morning. Even made me lemonade because I was too hung over from all the cocktails we had last night. I think the Rusty Nail must have done it. It can be lethal sometimes!' There! Take that! Lisa chuckled to herself as she imagined her mother-in-law's horrified expression.

'Rusty Nail! What is that?' Anju Chopra sounded appropriately shocked.

'Oh, it's a cocktail, Mom. Didn't you know? One and a half ounces Scotch, three-fourth ounce Drambuie and...'

'I do not wish to know of such things.' Anju Chopra's voice had taken on a rather sanctimonious, pious tone, and Lisa had to fight the urge to laugh. 'Well, I hope your hangover is better now.'

'Oh, yes, I'm right as rain now. Like I said, Karan made me lemonade and even served me breakfast in bed this morning.'

There was a long, pregnant silence on the other end and it was well over half a minute before her mother-in-law found her tongue again.

'Well, I guess there is no more to be said then. And you had better get back to work, Lisa. I will talk to you some other time.' She put the phone down even before Lisa could answer. She must be furious! Lisa, in turn, burst out laughing as she slipped the phone back into her bag and turned to her laptop. It was going to be a good day after all!

It certainly was. Other than the article, Milind had a bit of very interesting news for Lisa when she met him in his office later. The management of the magazine was thinking of starting a supplement on shoes and bags and Milind wanted her to lead the effort.

'This could be your big chance,' he said to her excitedly as she stared at him in delight. 'This can be your baby! Think about it!'

'It sounds too good to be true,' admitted Lisa then. 'But why me? There are so many other talented people around.'

'Yes, but nobody knows shoes and bags like you do. Don't be so humble, Lisa, you're enormously talented.'

'I don't even know what to say,' she said then in a shaky sort of voice.

'A thank you might be in order,' her boss retorted, pretending to look outraged. They both laughed and then Milind wagged a finger at her. 'Now, I want you to develop a great presentation so that we can completely sell this to the management of the magazine. If you do a good job, you can even present it yourself. The presentation is on 1st January. New Year's Day. Make sure you're not hung over.'

Lisa groaned and Milind grinned. 'I'm serious. I hear the Executive Managing Editor is flying in from New York for the presentation.'

She looked horrified and Milind laughed. 'You underestimate yourself. I'm sure you'll do a great job. Now get out of here before you waste any more of my time. I have work to do. And so, do you, young lady.' He nodded firmly at her and Lisa got up hurriedly. She gathered up her papers and thanked him profusely before she left the room. She wanted to whoop with joy! Wow!

The next few days flew past blissfully for Lisa and Karan. Lisa shared her news about the supplement magazine with Karan, and even though she didn't think he understood how important and prestigious an achievement it was, he was happy for her. She knew he was probably secretly wondering what all the hullabaloo was about shoes and bags, but he didn't say that of course. In fact, he took her out to dinner to a fancy French restaurant to celebrate. It was a sweet gesture, and Lisa was just happy that everything was well in their little world. The upcoming holiday seemed to have worked its magic but sometimes she could hardly believe it. After all, things had been pretty difficult the past few months. But everything was perfect now and she wasn't questioning it. Why should she look a gift horse in the mouth? She was just happy to forget the unpleasantness of the past few months and look forward to the holiday. They were happier than they'd been in a long time and everyone who knew them noticed it. Lisa would go to work looking positively radiant and return tired, but happy. More than once, Preeti commented on the glow on her face and spring in her step, and Lisa would blush slightly as she told her friend all about the romantic dinner they had shared the previous night, or the flowers he'd brought her. Even Milind was in an agreeable mood and didn't put up too much of a fight when Lisa asked for two weeks leave for her holiday. He did, however, mention categorically that he himself hadn't taken a proper vacation in two years and was only granting it to her because she hadn't taken too much time off that year. Lisa was just glad that he'd granted her the leave. She could hardly wait. Two weeks of sun-kissed beaches, mangrove trees, and exotic islands with Karan. Two weeks of absolute bliss! It would be just the two of them and they wouldn't even think about work or anything else. They would forget about all the unpleasantness of the past few months and would have the most fabulous time ever. They would go back to being the people they'd once been, and as poetic as it sounded even to her own ears, she hoped they would fall in love with each other all over again.

A Shock for Karan

'Karan, this is serious. Have you spoken to the client?'

It was a beautiful fall day in October; the air was cooler and the trees were bursting in a brilliant potpourri of reds, browns and yellows. The weather had been much more pleasant for days but the mood in the office was anything but. Karan had just returned from Mumbai that morning and had barely had time to glance at his emails when Vivek had called him into his office. Now as they sat there, discussing the interim report that had been sent to one of their major healthcare clients in Bangalore, Karan could see how worried his boss looked.

'Yes, Sir, I spoke to Parag Kulkarni this morning.' Karan glanced at his notes and shook his head. 'He's saying that some of our call reports are fabricated and many of the figures aren't adding up.'

'How is that possible? Did you tell him that we do not outsource any work and all the people who work with us are qualified professionals?'

'Yes, Sir,' said Karan. 'But he won't accept it. He's being very uncompromising.'

'I think he's deliberately trying to be difficult,' said Vivek in exasperation. This was the last thing he needed after a particularly stressful quarter. 'He didn't want to hire us in the first place, and he certainly wasn't thrilled when his country manager gave us the project.'

'I agree, Sir,' said Karan. 'But we don't have a choice. It is Parag Kulkarni who's in charge of the nitty-gritties of this project. His country manager's role is pretty much peripheral. We'll have to redo some of the interviews. If nothing else, that will at least validate our figures.'

Karan paused, wondering whether to say anymore. Vivek wasn't going to be thrilled about what else Parag had said. But Karan had to tell him. He had a right to know.

'He also said that if we don't redo the interviews, correct the figures, and analyze the data again, all within the timelines, we can forget about ever working with them again.'

'Jesus Christ!' Vivek shook his head in consternation at this and threw his head into his hands. 'He seems to have a vendetta against us! Karan, this is one of the biggest healthcare companies in the world. They spend billions of dollars on research every year. This is the first project we've ever done for them. It took all my convincing ability to get them to commission this project to us and not to their usual research agency. We can't afford to lose this client.'

'I understand, Sir. But we'll have to act very fast if we want to complete this within the timelines they want. We'll have to pull Rohit in as well and get him to do some of the interviews himself.'

'Involve that new girl too,' said Vivek. 'She's very good. Analytical and sharp. What's her name now? She's quite a looker! The one with the hazel eyes and perfect face.' He smiled slightly, pleased with his attempt at levity in spite of the seriousness of the situation.

'Esha Malhotra,' answered Karan, smiling back at his boss while he wondered how someone as busy as Vivek could even notice something as trivial as her eye colour at a time like this.

'When do they want us to make the final presentation?' asked Vivek then, and Karan quickly glanced at the project schedule in his notebook.

'Last week of November,' he confirmed and Vivek nodded. 'I'm going to be in Singapore for the plastics conference at that time. I want you to make the presentation, Karan. In fact, I want you to personally oversee and direct what's left of this project. This is now your responsibility.'

'But, Sir,' said Karan immediately, 'as you are aware, I am scheduled to go on a vacation from the third week of November for two weeks. Mayank was supposed to make the final presentation.'

'I'm sorry, Karan.' Karan could feel his heart plummeting as he listened to his boss's words. Vivek had started shaking his head even before Karan had finished and Karan was dreading what he knew Vivek would inevitably say next. 'You'll have to cancel your vacation. There is nobody else I trust enough to handle this. I know Mayank was handling this project, but he's not half as experienced as you are at competitive intelligence. You know we've already lost two big projects in the last three months to our competitors. We can't afford to lose any more. Not to mention the loss of reputation that the company will suffer. I need your help to salvage this situation now.'

'I understand, Sir,' said Karan, trying to keep himself calm, 'but I've already booked the tickets and the airline will levy a pretty hefty cancellation charge. And the hotel...'

'We'll compensate you for all that.' Vivek's voice was sympathetic but firm. 'And I promise to give you time off in a few months. But not now, Karan. I'm really sorry and I know how much you were looking forward to this, but I can't help it. I need you here.' He shook his head again and spread his hands out in a gesture of helplessness. Karan couldn't help but feel sorry for him. There was nothing he could do. Everyone knew that Vivek hadn't taken a holiday himself that year, not even during his kids' summer vacation. Things had been too difficult. There was nothing left to say. Karan slowly nodded his head as he rose from his chair and tried to smile at his boss.

'I understand, Sir. No problem. I'll speak to the airline and the hotel today and cancel.'

'Thank you, Karan,' said Vivek with a sigh of relief. 'You're the only one I can trust to sort out this mess. And do apologize to Lisa on my behalf. I know it's not going to be easy for you to break the news to her.'

'No, Sir,' said Karan with a wry smile, 'it most certainly is not going to be easy.'

Karan's mind was a muddled mess of trepidation and anxiety as he walked back to his cabin. He didn't even dare to think about what was going to happen as he collapsed into his chair and closed his eyes. For a minute his own disappointment didn't even hit him, he was so worried about how Lisa would take it. The vacation had been all she'd been talking about for the past few weeks, and he felt terrible about how disappointed she would be. Actually, furious was more like it! He knew it wasn't fair; none of this was fair, but there really was nothing he could do. And there was another thing he was very worried about. After the harmony of the past few days, the one thing he wanted to avoid at any cost was another altercation with his wife. He didn't think their relationship could take any more strain and after everything they'd been through the past few months, it hadn't been easy to bridge the gap. They'd both made a lot of effort, but he had to admit that the vacation had been the real reason for the turnabout. All Lisa spoke about these days was Bali. The other day she'd come home laden with clothes she had bought "especially for the holiday". And then yesterday she'd suggested that they buy a new camera to take to Bali, and even this morning, he'd seen her checking the weather forecast for Bali on her mobile.

And now it wasn't going to happen! In spite of how skeptical he felt and knowing that the thing he dreaded the most was inevitable; he couldn't help hoping that she would somehow miraculously understand.

'Ooh! Flowers! Again! I must have done something right!' Lisa looked at him lovingly as she accepted the huge bouquet of red carnations that he'd picked up from Ferns and Petals on his way home. She rose on tiptoe to kiss him on the lips and he tried his best to smile at her, wondering how much longer this friendly exchange was going to last. He sighed and took off his jacket and she poured him a cup of coffee.

'Tough day?' she asked sympathetically, glancing at the clock. It was a quarter to ten and he must be exhausted.

'Consulting is a tough business,' he said, trying to set the base for what he had to say. Procrastination wasn't usually a part of his nature and he wanted to get it over with. 'Vivek's going crazy too these days. He agrees to just about anything that a client demands.' He smiled wearily and loosened his tie, and she nodded and handed him the coffee.

'I know. I had an exhausting day too. In fact, I was completely beat when I got back. But I just fixed myself a margarita and thought about the vacation, now see how relaxed I am.'

He tried to smile at her but his heart was beating faster with every word. He was amazed she hadn't sensed his unease yet. And they said men were dense!

'You need to relax,' continued Lisa solicitously. 'Go take a shower and I'll get dinner ready for you. Then let's just put our feet up and talk about our big holiday. That should cheer you up all right.'

'That was great! I enjoyed it. Thanks!' Karan gave her the thumbs up and Lisa smiled at him. She'd got home a little early that evening and had decided to make his favourite dinner. They were both tired of Rama's sabzi-roti and even though Lisa was usually too beat after work to really do much in the kitchen, today she'd stopped by at Super Gourmet on her way back and picked up everything she needed for the Caesar Salad.

'Well, your mother called me earlier and she seemed to think that raajma-chaawal would have been a better choice.'

Karan laughed in spite of his state of mind and shook his head. 'Really? I'm surprised she said that. I've never been particularly fond of raajma-chaawal.'

'I tried telling her that. But she wouldn't listen. She was actually distressed that her precious son was going to be served just salad for dinner. She even said that since you are a very robust boy, you would need something more substantial. In the end, she very emphatically stated that it might be better if I left the cooking to the maid. Anyhow, I don't mind as long as you don't expect the same from me,' she chuckled. 'After all, you've always known that I'm more Coco Chanel than Coq au Vin.'

They both laughed at that. 'Don't worry about it,' she added as she picked up the dishes and carried them into the kitchen. He couldn't help noticing the unusually relaxed expression on her face and the spring in her step. And was that a new hair cut? Especially for Bali, huh? Karan slowly placed both hands firmly on the table and briefly closed his eyes. It was time to take the bull by the horns. He had to get it over with.

He pulled himself up from the dining chair and followed his wife into the kitchen. She was stacking the dirty dishes on one side of the sink and talking to Rama about what to make for lunch the next day. 'Gawd! I just hate all this menu planning,' she remarked in exasperation. 'Monday – daal-chaawal; Tuesday – chole-chaawal; Wednesday – kadhi-chaawal. It makes me sick! Sambhar-chaawal bana lena!' She nodded to Rama and then turned to Karan. 'I don't know about you, but I'm dying to get out of here! Nothing to worry about, no menus to plan, no responsibilities, no calls, no work! Just you and me and two whole weeks in gorgeous Bali! I just can't wait any longer! I wish we could take off now!'

Karan took a deep breath before he finally spoke. 'I have to talk to you about something,' he said softly.

'Really? That sounds like something important.'

'I suppose it is,' he said as they walked out of the kitchen together. 'Maybe we should go inside,' he suggested, leading her into their bedroom. Lisa followed her husband into the room and shut the door behind them as he turned to look at her. She couldn't help noticing the somber expression on his face and it unnerved her as she tried to gauge his mood. What could it be? Was he upset with her about something?

'What is it Karan?' she asked at last as they sat down on the bed together. 'Why are you looking at me like that?'

'Like what?' asked Karan in a shaky sort of voice. He wished she was psychic and would just guess so he wouldn't have to tell her.

'Like your world is coming to an end. Nothing can be that bad.' Lisa cocked her head to one side and placed a hand over her husband's.

'Can't it?' he asked softly as she punched him playfully.

'Stop it, Karan! Why are you behaving like such a nervous Nellie? You're making me nervous too!' For a brief second, she wondered if he was having an affair or if it was something to do with his health. Both scenarios were unthinkable, and her heart almost stopped for a moment.

'Are you in love with someone else? Is that what this is all about?' She almost choked on the words.

'Jesus! Of course not!' How could the thought have even crossed her mind? That too after the way he'd made love to her last night! 'And before you go any further, let me remind you that I got a clean chit from the doctor last week,' he continued, 'we all went for an executive health check at the office, remember?' She was amazed at how well he knew her, but he still hadn't answered her question.

'So, what is it? Is it something you want me to do for your mother? That's what usually makes you behave this way. Well, don't worry if that's it. I don't mind. I'm too happy about Bali to get upset about anything. So, you have nothing to worry about.'

Karan's heart sank at her words and he didn't know where to look. No, this wasn't right. After all, she was his wife! He had to be honest with her and she had to understand. He couldn't avoid it any longer. He took a deep breath and took both her hands in his, all the time wishing for a miracle.

'Actually sweetheart,' he started, 'I know this is terrible but there is no easy way to put it. There's been a crisis at work and we were going to lose a major client. We may still lose them. The client is a huge healthcare company, one of the biggest in the business.' He paused, barely glancing up to look at her, but he couldn't read her expression. If anything, she looked… well, concerned. Not angry. Yet. 'And,' he continued, wondering for the hundredth time how he'd managed to get himself into this mess. 'I'm really very, very sorry, but Vivek has cancelled my leave for the vacation. It's not his fault and there's nothing he can do. This was so damned unexpected and sudden, and nobody could have thought something like this would happen. But it's not just you sweetheart, I'm terribly disappointed about this myself. But this job is very important to me and I've worked so hard for it. Vivek's promised me that as soon as this project is over, he's going to give me leave and we can plan something then but…' Karan knew he had started rambling but now that he'd said it, the words just seemed to be tumbling out. 'I'm really, really sorry about this!'

He stopped, took another deep breath and glanced at his wife, willing her to see things from his point of view, willing her to understand. But he was shocked when he saw the expression on her face. Somehow, he hadn't expected this. She wasn't just angry, she looked furious! Bitter disappointment was etched across her face and he could see that she was trying hard not to burst into tears. He felt wretched as he watched her and wished that he had the courage to take her into his arms. But he didn't dare, particularly when she pulled her hands away from him and then, without so much as a word, got up and walked out of the bedroom. She looked as though she was in a daze.

Karan didn't try to stop her or follow her. He knew that this was a huge disappointment and he wanted to give her a little time to digest the news. Besides, he was exhausted himself. He sighed heavily and closed his eyes. His mind was a blurred mess and he couldn't think straight. Between the pressures at the office and the tension of telling Lisa about the cancelled vacation, he was now too drained to even think straight. All the pent-up tension and stress of the day had taken its toll and somehow, he didn't quite feel the wave of relief he'd thought he would now that he had told her. On the contrary, his head was throbbing painfully, and he just didn't want to think anymore. He wished he could get out of the house for a while – just go anywhere – maybe even get in the car and just drive around for a bit. But he didn't want to leave Lisa alone when she was obviously so upset. He wondered what she was thinking, and wished she would at least come and talk to him about it. He was going crazy just sitting there, thinking and wondering. He needed to do something, anything, to keep his head from bursting from the stress of it all. He looked around and the first thing he saw was the TV remote. He automatically picked it up and flicked on the TV, barely understanding what he was doing. It was tuned into a South Indian music channel, but Karan didn't even notice as he sat there, staring into space, feeling almost numb. His mind had finally reached a point when he couldn't think anymore.

'So, you're watching TV.'

Karan was so lost in his thoughts that, for a minute, her voice sounded like it was coming from somewhere very far. He slowly turned his face to look at her, and at first, he didn't understand. She was standing in the doorway, arms crossed across her chest and just as he'd expected, she still looked furious.

'Sorry?' he asked as she stared at him. 'Did you say something?'

'I said that it seems a little strange that while I'm sitting there crying my eyes out over this huge disappointment, you're doing something as insensitive as watching TV. I can't believe you, Karan.'

Karan stared at the South Indian music channel on the TV screen, wondering how it had got there and shook his head. 'No, I'm not, I…'

'You've got to be the most insensitive and selfish person around,' she continued, cutting him off as he tried to fathom what she was saying. 'Don't you care about anything at all? I can't believe you! I can't believe that even at a time like this, you're sitting there doing something as moronic and insensitive as watching TV!'

'I'm not!' He suddenly got up from the bed and shouted. He had come to the end of his patience. Why, he was as disappointed about the vacation as she was! 'Can't you see that it's tuned into a Tamil music channel and I can't even understand a single word, let alone watch it?'

'Don't you shout at me, Karan,' said Lisa incredulously. 'I can't believe your nerve after what you've done.'

'All I'm saying is that I wasn't watching TV.' He had lowered his voice now as he fought hard to control his temper. He was trying to be as patient as he could, even though he didn't feel particularly patient, but it just wouldn't do if both of them lost it. 'I don't even remember when I switched it on,' he tried to explain, 'I guess I was a little lost.'

'Well anyway, what do I care? You can do whatever the hell you want. I couldn't care less!' She glared at him. He sighed and slowly walked towards her as she stood there, looking more hostile than ever before. He knew it was going to be a very long night when all he wanted was to go to sleep. He was so tired; he could barely keep his eyes open. But he couldn't just ignore it. He had to at least try to explain. He owed her that much. He tried to take her into his arms but she would have nothing of it. Again, and again, he tried to pull her close but again and again, she pushed him away. He tried to speak to her but she cut him off almost at once, and shook her head angrily when he offered to make them both coffee and suggested that they sit down and talk sensibly. There was nothing he could do to get through to her, and after innumerable attempts, he finally threw his hands up and shook his head.

'Look, I'm really sorry about this. It's the last thing I expected when I planned the vacation, and believe it or not, I'm as disappointed as you are. But there's really nothing I can do. Vivek...'

'I don't believe you,' she snapped at him as he stared at her. Her eyes were as hard as rocks. 'You knew how important this vacation was to me, you knew how much I was looking forward to it. I even cancelled my London plan with my mother for this vacation! How could you do this Karan?' Her voice was rising steadily, and he almost cringed at the harshness of her tone. 'After everything we've been through, this was like a thread of hope I was hanging on to. I hate you, Karan! In fact, at this moment, I hate the very sight of you. You and your work and your insensitive attitude and your mother with her stupid, horrible comments and...'

'This has nothing to do with my mother. So, I'd appreciate it if we could leave her out of it,' said Karan coldly but she wasn't prepared to be reasonable.

'No, I will not. I'll bloody well say what I want to.' By now she was shrieking so hard that her voice was reverberating around the room. Karan's head felt like a ton of bricks; he had to fight the urge to tell her to just shut up as he stood there waiting for her to finish her tirade. It seemed as though all the tension, the stress, and the uncertainty of the past few months were coming out now in a great tidal wave. But what about the last few weeks? They'd been so wonderful! Had all that been a lie? Or a wonderful illusion which could never last.

'Can't you even understand that it's not my fault,' he asked her then, looking helpless. He didn't say it but he was very, very hurt. Even though he'd imagined the worst since Vivek had broken the awful news, he'd never thought that she would talk to him like this. How much everything had changed over the years! They'd been so compatible back then; it was actually hard to believe they were the same people.

'No, I can't understand. I don't want to understand. I'm sick and tired of you! I'm totally fed up!'

'Of course, you don't understand. Have you ever?' he retorted, finally losing patience. He couldn't take it anymore. This was not his fault. 'You can only see things from your own point of view, Lisa. You are the most selfish, most…'

'That's it!' she screamed, as he stopped mid-sentence and stared at her in mute amazement. She looked almost hysterical as she stood there clenching and unclenching her hands. Hot tears were streaming over, leaving a black trail of her volumizing, high definition mascara, all down her face in the process. 'That's it, Karan! I've had all the shit that I'm going to take from you. I don't want to live with you anymore. I don't want to see you anymore. I want a divorce!'

When Karan rang his father-in-law's doorbell at 1:00 am, he wondered how things had reached this point. This was ridiculously extreme; couldn't they have waited till the morning? But one look at Lisa's tear-stained face and angry eyes convinced him that this was the best option. He didn't trust either of them to do the right thing anymore. After all, the word divorce had never been a part of their vocabulary before this. Something had definitely gone very wrong. The amazing thing was that in spite of everything she'd said, in spite of the accusations she'd hurled at him, the distraught look on her face tore at his heart, and he wished he could do something to set things right for her.

'I'm sorry, Lisa,' he said finally, for what seemed like the hundredth time that night. 'I'm sorry about everything. All the disappointments, all the times when I've let you down.'

The tears started falling then and she turned away from him as he sighed.

'I just don't know how to deal with this anymore, Lisa. I believe in my heart, that what you said before were just meaningless words said in a fit of anger.' She knew he was talking about the mention of the word divorce, but what could she say? Even she herself had been shocked when the words had tumbled out of her mouth. Everything else notwithstanding, neither of them had ever been careless or reckless about saying something so extreme before. She knew plenty of couples who threatened to leave each other at the slightest reason, but despite all the fights and arguments, that was something neither of them had ever done. But the words had been said; she couldn't unsay them, could she? She didn't know that the mere mention of the word divorce had almost broken his heart. Admittedly, for a moment, he had wondered too whether it was the only solution now, after all who could have imagined that things would come to this point, but he had pushed the thought away and willed himself to believe that she hadn't meant any of it.

'I just know that we both need to do some serious thinking before we cause irreparable damage to our relationship. There was a time when we couldn't live without each other and now it seems as though we can't live with each other.' There were tears in his voice and Lisa's eyes were welling up again. Despite everything, she wanted to reach out to him, but once again, her pride seemed to be getting the better of her. She didn't answer and he shook his head resignedly as he pressed the doorbell again.

Half a minute later, they heard hurried footsteps and the sound of a key being turned at last. The door was opened a crack but the safety chain was still firmly in its place. Dr. Singh's worried face peeked out and the shock on his face was palpable when he saw his daughter and son-in-law standing there.

'What the… is everything okay?' he asked as he fumbled for the chain and removed it from its lock. He swung open the door and Lisa stepped in, followed by Karan.

'Terribly sorry to have bothered you at this time, Papa,' mumbled Karan, looking and feeling very embarrassed at having woken them up like this.

'Oh, my God! Lisa! Are you okay, darling?' Katherine Singh hurried towards her daughter before Dr. Singh could respond. She looked at Karan questioningly as she took her crying daughter into her arms. 'What happened?' she asked, looking directly at Karan while he struggled with how to respond. What could he say? He was actually mortified.

'Mom... actually... Lisa's very upset and...'

'I can see that,' interrupted Katherine Singh, clearly very distressed at the way Lisa looked. Despite her state of mind, Lisa couldn't help berating herself for causing her parents so much stress. 'What I want to know is, what could have happened to upset her like this?'

'Why don't we all sit down and talk about it?' suggested Dr Singh, shooting a warning look at his wife. He knew she could be a little biased sometimes. 'I'll make some coffee.'

'No, really Papa,' interrupted Karan at once, 'please don't bother yourself. As it is, I feel terrible about disturbing both of you like this. Besides, I have an early start tomorrow morning and I have to get home.'

'Why don't you stay here?' suggested Dr. Singh as Lisa's mother poured out a glass of water for her daughter. 'It's much too late to go all the way back.'

'I wish I could,' said Karan apologetically, 'but I have to be in the office early tomorrow and the traffic will be terrible in the morning. Besides, I left my laptop at home.'

By then Lisa had started crying again and her mother had taken her in, mumbling something about 'don't appear weak in front of men!' as Karan looked at his father-in-law and sighed.

'I'm sorry, Papa. We had an awful fight. She's very upset.'

'Well, you take care of yourself,' said Dr. Singh as he walked his son-in-law to the door. He was worried about his daughter but he knew Karan well enough too and could vouch for his decency. 'And drive carefully please. Don't forget to call me when you reach home.'

'I will,' promised Karan, stopping to give his father-in-law a quick hug. 'I'm really sorry about waking you up like this but it couldn't be helped. Good night, Papa.'

'Good night, Karan. And don't worry too much.' He smiled at Karan understandingly. 'These things happen. After all, which couple doesn't fight sometimes? I'll talk to Lisa in the morning.'

□

Friends to the rescue

Karan was exhausted when he woke up the next morning. In fact, when the alarm clock went off at seven-thirty, he felt as though he hadn't slept at all. He groaned as he turned it off and hauled himself out of bed. The first thing he noticed was the empty space on the other side of the bed, and for a minute, he was confused. Then suddenly the events of the previous night came rushing back like a jolt, and he almost wanted to cry as he remembered what had happened. Trying not to think about it, he put on his slippers and threw open the curtains to let in some sunshine. The birds were chirping cheerfully as usual outside the bedroom window but with so much on his mind and hardly any sleep, Karan felt far from cheerful. His head was pounding and he felt disheartened and depressed as he walked into the living room and switched on the percolator. Rama had brought the newspaper in, but for once, Karan didn't feel like reading it. He wished he could take the day off, but they had a client coming into the office that day, and then he had a lot of work to finish on the healthcare project. He dragged himself to the bathroom as he thought about what a stressful day he had ahead.

Despite everything, he was dressed and ready for breakfast by eight-thirty, and he had to admit that he was proud of himself as he sat down at the table. Anyone else would have surely taken the day off and gone back to bed. He shook his head ruefully as he glanced at the still unread newspaper which Rama had now placed on the dining table. She'd set the table for one, and even though Lisa's absence was extremely conspicuous, she didn't ask any questions as she brought in his quinoa and grapefruit. She'd heard the yelling and crying the previous night. But she'd got used to their frequent fights. Most of the time she didn't even understand what was being said since they spoke mostly in English, punctuated occasionally with a smattering of Hindi. The last few days had been a welcome respite though. But it hadn't lasted long, had it? Maybe his mother had done something again. Rama didn't like Karan's mother either; the woman was always rude to her too. Rama had, on many occasions, overheard her telling Lisa Didi to reduce her salary and not to give her the same food that they ate themselves. Not that Lisa Didi ever listened to her. And Lisa Didi was such a nice person too: she was always kind and considerate and treated her so well, unlike some of the other Didis. Rama couldn't, for the life of her, imagine why Bhaiya was always doing something or the other to upset her. But even Rama knew that yesterday had been serious. She could swear that she'd heard the word divorce in their conversation. She felt sorry for Lisa Didi and hoped things would work out, for even Rama could see how much they genuinely loved each other. But it was none of her business, and to give her opinion or ask any questions was unthinkable. She couldn't do anything about it anyway and she had too many worries of her own to deal with. There was her younger brother to educate, and her elder sister had to be married off this year, and her father had taken a huge loan again. These rich people knew nothing about problems anyhow; their lives were so easy but they were still always complaining. Rama sighed as she set the quinoa and grapefruit down, asked Karan if he wanted anything else, and returned to the kitchen.

Lisa wasn't as dedicated as Karan that day. She'd spent a sleepless night tossing and turning in bed, her mind a battleground of questions, doubts and denial. The result was that she was completely exhausted when she woke up that morning and had to call in sick. In fact, her head felt like a ton of bricks when she sat down to breakfast with her parents at eight-thirty. Groaning, she held her pounding head in her hands as her mother poured her a cup of black coffee and her father looked at her gravely over his newspaper.

'Did you speak to Karan this morning?' he asked as she slowly sipped her coffee. Her mother had forgotten to add milk to it but Lisa didn't even notice. 'Did you check whether he had breakfast before he left for work?'

'Karan's not a child,' said her mother sharply before Lisa could answer. 'Besides, it's not her job to check on trivial things like that! I'm amazed you're thinking about Karan even now. Can't you see how upset Lisa is?'

'Well, he's her husband,' said her father quietly. 'I have to worry about both of them. Lisa has us but right now he doesn't have anyone to take care of him.'

'Well, the least he could have done was to be a little apologetic. After all, it's his fault! Is this the way to treat his wife?'

'All I'm saying is that they're probably both to blame and…'

'All you men are the same!' said Katherine Singh in disgust. 'Why can't you ever see things from a woman's point of view? After all, what's sauce for the goose is sauce for the gander!'

'We are not at one of your women's liberation meetings, Katherine,' answered her husband, 'and neither is this about women's rights! And I still think Lisa should call him. He's obviously under a lot of pressure. The least she can do is be a little supportive. You, as her mother, should encourage her to do the right thing.'

'Why should she call him?' demanded Katherine Singh, staring daggers at her husband. 'Just because, like all men, he's too egocentric to call himself? And, I know my responsibility as her mother. I don't need you to tell me. I go around teaching the women of the world to be independent and strong and self-reliant, and you want me to encourage my own daughter to become a doormat!'

'That's not what I meant,' said Dr. Singh with a sigh. 'All I'm saying is…'

'Mom, Dad, please,' said Lisa at last, tired of the argument between her parents. It was the last thing she needed. 'I don't want the two of you to start fighting,' she pleaded, 'I'm an adult and I can handle this myself.' She picked up her cup of coffee and got up. 'In fact, I think I'll get out of the house for a while. Maybe I'll meet my friends. It'll make me feel a bit better.'

'So, we're not going after all!' Lisa sighed and looked gloomily out of the window. 'I can't tell you how disappointed I am.'

The three girls had decided to meet at a pub near Sameera's school. Both Sameera and Ayesha had taken extended lunch breaks from work as soon as Lisa had called.

'I can't believe he cancelled!' exclaimed Ayesha, signalling to the waiter. 'He knew how much you were looking forward to it.'

'Well, obviously it wasn't as if he could help it. He's under a lot of pressure.' Sameera shot a warning look at Ayesha as the waiter came over to take the order. Lisa was angry enough without being made angrier.

'Three vodkas, please. Straight up!' ordered Ayesha as Sameera stared at her.

'Ayesha! It's one-thirty in the afternoon on a working day! Why are we ordering vodka?'

Ayesha looked at her in amazement. 'Don't you understand? Look at Lisa! She needs it. Do you expect her to handle a situation like this with… with… fruit punch?'

'I don't think a vodka is going to solve her problem,' said Sameera firmly, cancelling the order. 'Besides, I don't know about you but I have to get back to work.' She turned to the waiter. 'Three iced teas and two portions of chicken tikka, please.' Shutting the menu, she looked at Lisa and sighed: 'Look Lisa, I know you were looking forward to this vacation. I know you're very upset. But… I'm sure, so is Karan. You have to be fair about this. What if Milind hadn't agreed to give you time off? There's really nothing you can do if the boss says no. This is hardly his fault.'

Lisa sighed and shook her head wearily. 'I don't know what to believe anymore, Sameera. I'm just so disappointed. After all the effort I made, after everything I did the last few days…'

'All the effort you both made,' corrected Sameera, 'you told me yourself how wonderful he's been to you these past few weeks.'

'I still can't believe he told me we can't go,' said Lisa, tears welling up in her eyes. 'It was the only thing I've been thinking about. I know this sounds like an exaggeration but after everything we've been through recently, this vacation was like the light at the end of the tunnel, like a reminder of the better times we've had before things started going wrong. When he told me about it, I felt there was finally something to look forward to, something that was going to set everything right in our life. And then last night, it was as though all that just came crashing down. I can't believe how naïve I was to believe that things would work out between us after all.' She allowed the tears to fall as Sameera groped for something reassuring to say to her friend, but this time, even she couldn't come up with anything.

'I'm so disappointed!' continued Lisa, then as she wiped her eyes with a tissue, 'I feel as though everything's over.'

She didn't tell her friends that she'd been so upset that she'd even mentioned divorce. Somehow the next day, in a saner state of mind, she couldn't help wondering if she'd overreacted the previous night.

'I need to use the loo,' she muttered then, getting up from her chair. Picking up her bag, she headed in the direction of the lady's washroom as her friends watched her, concern etched on their faces.

'Poor thing!' whispered Ayesha to Sameera, 'she's totally shattered! Say Sameera, do you think Karan's having an affair? I mean, things have been a bit erratic between the two of them haven't they – first the hostility, then the sudden lovey-dovey stuff, then this change of plan. You know I was reading the other day that the first indication of an affair…'

'Are you out of your mind, Ayesha?' Sameera glared at her furiously and shook her head: 'Karan! An affair! He barely gets time to eat and sleep!'

'That's what he says to Lisa but how do we know? Men can be very discreet when they want to be, and Lisa was telling me that there are a lot of pretty women in his office, and he does travel a lot…'

'Don't you dare mention something like that to Lisa! She doesn't need this from you right now. As it is, I don't know why she even called you. You're not exactly the best person to turn to for advice at a time like this. Why don't you stop reading all that crap?'

'It's not crap! And I think you're being very rude, Sameera.'

'Anyhow, I'm worried about Lisa. She's teetering on the edge of a breakdown. She's emotionally spent.'

'Shh! She's coming back.'

They turned to smile at their friend as she sat down at the table, still looking as miserable as before.

'Preeti called. I have an article due tomorrow, and I don't know how I'm going to focus on writing. As it is, I can't even believe I write articles on relationships and give advice to our poor, unsuspecting readers, when the most important relationship in my own life is in such tatters. I'm a total fake.'

'You're not! And frankly, if that's the general rule, then I can't believe Ruchi is your resident Health and Fitness girl,' said Ayesha, trying to lighten the atmosphere. 'I saw her when I came into your office the other day, and I could bet that she's put on at least ten pounds. Why, she was positively popping out of her dress! And I distinctly remember that guy – what's his name – Probir or something, well, didn't he write an article on breast implants? If anything's fake, then that certainly is!'

Even Lisa had to smile at that, and she felt grateful for her friends' support as Sameera patted her hand comfortingly.

'All couples argue and fight sometimes,' she said, 'it doesn't have to mean anything.'

But Lisa shook her head stubbornly and looked at her friend with teary eyes: 'Aman and Preeti don't. They never fight. They're so perfect together! They're so…'

'No couple is perfect,' interrupted Sameera gently, 'and as far as Aman and Preeti are concerned, wait till they're married! Right now, the only bone of contention between them is whether to eat Chinese or Italian on Friday and which club to go to on Saturday. Wait till they start talking about mothers and finances and household chores and who spends more. They haven't even got there yet. No relationship is perfect, Lisa. I know things haven't been great, but this isn't the end of the world.'

'I can't help it,' said Lisa as the waiter came over with their iced teas and chicken tikka. 'I feel as though he's let me down.' Sameera nodded understandingly and Ayesha patted Lisa's hand. 'Comfort food,' she said, offering the chicken tikka to her friend. The girls helped themselves to the succulent kebabs and mint chutney as the waiter placed the tall glasses of iced tea garnished with slices of lemon and orange in front of them.

'Thanks,' muttered Lisa as she bit into a piece of chicken tikka. She looked more lost than ever and Sameera got up to give her a hug.

'I think you need a break, Lisa. After all, even love needs a break sometimes. Yes, that's exactly what you need. A break from love! I have a suggestion.'

Lisa was decidedly more cheerful after Sameera had talked to her about her plan. They all agreed that it would be the best thing to do.

'We'll have to figure out the dates though,' said Sameera thoughtfully, 'I won't be able to take time off after the second week of November. My parents are visiting me for Eid and I'm sure Lisa would want to be here with Karan for Diwali too.' Lisa didn't answer and just looked noncommittal. She didn't want to talk about Karan right now. Even the mention of his name brought tears to her eyes, and the last thing she wanted to do was to start crying again.

'So, I was thinking…' Sameera had noticed Lisa's expression and quickly tried to change the subject, 'can we go next Saturday? The weather will be pleasant enough.'

'Sounds great,' agreed Ayesha, 'I haven't taken much leave recently, and frankly, I think my Dad will be more than happy to get rid of me for a while. Can you believe, he actually accused me of spoiling the discipline in his office the other day? He said I keep the office lines busy with my personal calls; I'm always on social networking sites instead of working; my boyfriends drop in all the time, and I'm a bad example for the other employees.' She made a face and the other two laughed.

'I'll have to speak to Milind too,' agreed Lisa. 'But I don't think it should be a problem. If anything, the previous dates were closer to a couple of very important celebrity interviews, so I have a feeling he's going to be pleased about this change. But we'd better pick a hotel immediately. I just hope we get bookings at this eleventh hour.'

'It's not peak season or anything,' shrugged Sameera. 'They'll probably lay out the welcome mat.'

'It's always peak season in Goa,' laughed Ayesha. 'Come on, now that that's settled, let's order something a little more cheerful than iced tea. Come on Sam, don't be a party pooper.'

'No thanks,' Sameera shook her head resolutely. 'I have a lot of papers to correct and grade when I get back, and I don't want to give A's instead of D's.'

'Gawd! You're such a grouch!' Ayesha made a face and signalled to the waiter. 'Well, suit yourself. We're having some beer.' She ordered a round of beer for Lisa and herself, and Lisa smiled. She was feeling much better and was glad that she had two best friends she could always count on.

'Thank you, girls.' She smiled at both of them. 'For being there for me.'

□

Marriage and Manipulation

The week flew past more quickly than ever, and before they knew it, Goa was upon them. It was the day before they were due to leave and Lisa had just got home after a spot of last-minute shopping. As she walked into the apartment, she was surprised to see Karan already there. He was working intently on his laptop as usual but looked up when she entered the living room. She dropped her bag on the dining table and pulled off her hair band, her hair tumbling around her face in silky, dark brown curls. As always, she looked very beautiful to him, and Karan was aware of the fact that whatever the state of their relationship, he always felt hopelessly attracted to her. He ignored the stirring he felt in his body as he tried not to think about the fact that they hadn't made love since the night before he'd told her about the cancelled vacation. But then, they hadn't exactly sorted things out after that terrible night. She'd stayed at her parents' house for a couple of days and things had been distinctly awkward between them when she'd returned. He'd been feeling very hurt too and try as he might, somehow, he couldn't get it out of his head that she'd mentioned divorce. They hadn't spoken about it again but it had been like the elephant in the room. Neither of them was confident about where things stood between them, which was never a good sign. It was as though their marriage was in limbo with both of them uncertain about what to do. But on the bright side, at least they hadn't had another fight. That was some consolation. Yes, things had definitely been calmer after she'd told him about the Goa plan, and despite his disappointment, he'd been encouraging about it. He'd even taken her shopping and bought her some gorgeous beach wear, a new swimsuit and some other things that she needed for the trip. Lisa had been surprised at his peace offerings but she had accepted them as graciously as she could, given the circumstances.

'So how was your day?' She smiled tentatively at him now as he put his computer away and ran a hand through his hair.

'Stressful! Ashish and Rohit are threatening to quit.'

'Why is that?' She looked genuinely surprised. 'I thought they were two of your best guys.'

'They are but they say they can't handle the pressure. Everyone can't,' he added with a wry smile as she nodded. 'Anyway, let's not talk about my work. So, did you go to see your parents? How did it go? What did they say?' asked Karan.

'The usual,' sighed Lisa, 'Mom thought it was a good move, particularly since it reflects well on the liberated and modern Indian woman, but my dad looked extremely disapproving about the whole thing and sighed in resignation when I told him that you don't have a problem with my going. Oh yeah, and Kriti's appalled that I'm doing something quite so preposterous, by the way.'

'Sounds like her,' smiled Karan. 'I don't think she ever goes anywhere without her husband and children, does she?'

'Only to meditation class,' laughed Lisa, examining her nails.

'I wonder how you get along with her at all,' asked Karan with interest. 'You have nothing in common with her.'

'Oh, I believe in maintaining good neighbourly relations.'

'Yeah, that's something you Delhi women are great at.'

She made a face at him and they laughed together. For a brief moment, Lisa was surprised to discover how strangely reassuring the sound was. It was as though they could pretend that everything was fine and they were just another normal couple sharing the evening twilight together, compatible enough to laugh at the same things. Not two people who'd been arguing and fighting incessantly for months, and had even mentioned divorce when it had become particularly bad.

'So, are you finished packing?' asked Karan as Lisa blinked back the tears that threatened to emerge at the drop of a hat these days. God, but she was becoming weepy!

'Yeah, all done,' she said, looking the other way so he wouldn't see her expression. She didn't know it, but it tore at his heart to see how sad and forlorn she looked.

'Well, make sure you take enough cash,' he said gently then, 'sometimes one can't find an ATM, and it's important to have enough cash when you're out of town.'

'I know.' She managed a watery sort of smile. 'I do have my credit cards. And Sameera and Ayesha will be with me, so you don't have to worry.'

He was silent for a minute as Rama came in with a cup of tea for Lisa.

'I do worry about you, you know, whether you believe it or not,' he said a moment later. His voice was tender and she looked at him then as their eyes met and held for a long time.

'I know that,' she said at last, and he walked up to her and took her into his arms.

'Do you?' he whispered, tracing a finger down her cheek. 'Sometimes I wonder. What's happening to us, Lisa? We never used to fight. Do you remember how blissfully happy we were?' She turned the other way then, painfully aware of the fact that he had used the past tense. The past few weeks had been a respite from the tension of the last few months but it hadn't lasted.

'I'll miss you,' he said simply and she couldn't help but wonder if he even meant it.

'Why is that so difficult to believe?' He looked at her intently as though reading her thoughts.

'It's just that you looked so relieved when I told you that I was going. I thought you were happy to be rid of me.'

'Yes, I was relieved,' he admitted with a slow nod, 'but not because I was happy to be rid of you. I was just happy that you would still be able to go somewhere nice with your friends. Come on, Lisa, you really think that I wasn't disappointed about our holiday? You know how much I wanted to, needed to, get away. But it really couldn't be helped. I'm just glad that you're able to go. I want you to be happy.'

They looked into each other's eyes then, and for a moment, Lisa wished he would just tell her not to go because he couldn't bear to be without her for a single instant. She would have cancelled her trip in a heartbeat if he'd said that.

'So, you still haven't given me your hotel numbers,' he said instead. 'Where are you girls staying? Coconut Grove isn't it?'

The moment passed and Lisa sighed as she nodded in answer.

'Yeah, it's supposed to be one of the best resorts. It was even featured in that travel magazine.'

'Actually, I was surprised that you guys booked there. I thought the south was way too sleepy for you girls.'

'Well, despite Ayesha's protests, Sameera was insistent we stay in the south. Ayesha swore that nothing ever happens in the south, and Sameera said that that suits her just fine.'

They both laughed and Lisa picked up the cup of tea that Rama had brought her earlier. She took a sip and instantly made a face, 'God! How many times have I told her not to put so much ginger in my tea! Why can't she remember something so simple? Maids, these days!'

'Well, I doubt we'll get any decent help around here a few years from now, so make the most of it while it lasts. Did you read that article about all those call centres that are opening up in all the neighbouring villages these days? They're primarily for the women. You know – to give them a better life. That's where all our domestic help is headed in a few years.'

'Don't let my mom hear you talk like that,' said Lisa with a smile. 'Liberation of the rural Indian woman is practically her dream! Anyway, I hope Rama won't give you a hard time while I'm away.' She glanced at Karan and he laughed.

'Don't worry about that. She won't get a chance. I'm not going to be staying here.'

'Really?' asked Lisa in surprise. This was news to her. 'Where will you be?'

'At my Mom's,' he answered simply, as Lisa stared at him. 'Your Mom's?' she whispered, not wanting to believe it. She was desperately trying to quell the sudden feeling of panic that had instantly started rising up inside her.

'Yeah,' said Karan with a shrug. He didn't seem to notice the anxiety in her voice. How could he be so dense? 'No point staying here on my own. Makes sense, doesn't it?'

Lisa was speechless as she nodded at him. Suddenly feeling very queasy in the pit of her stomach, she didn't know what to say to him. It would hardly sound fair to suggest that he stay alone while she was away on a holiday with her friends just because she didn't trust her mother-in-law. That sounded selfish and paranoid even to her. Karan trusted her enough to let her go away with her single friends, but she didn't trust him enough to let him stay with his mother. Well, but of course she didn't! It wasn't her fault that her mother-in-law was the way she was. But she didn't want to sound insecure and mean spirited so she held her tongue. She was actually a bit surprised at how much the news had bothered her considering that she'd declared only a few days ago how little she cared about what Karan did. Now she acknowledged dejectedly that she did care.

'So, whose idea was this? Yours?' she asked, trying to sound casual.

'No. I've been so busy at work I haven't had time to even think about it. My mom suggested it. In fact, she insisted. Surprisingly, she wasn't at all upset about your going away like this,' he said as Lisa shuddered.

'I'll bet she wasn't,' she thought to herself, fighting the urge to tell him exactly how uncomfortable she was with this arrangement. Maybe her dad and Kriti were right after all, and this was a really terrible idea.

'So, when do you leave?' she asked as calmly as she could.

'Tomorrow. I'll go there straight from work. Rama can take a few days off too. She's been pestering you about it, hasn't she? And now I think I'll take a shower.'

Lisa watched him as he rose from the sofa and walked into their bedroom. Shaking her head incredulously at what he'd just told her, she reached for her tea, but it had gone cold. She hadn't wanted it anyway. Too much damn adrak. Damn Rama! Oh, everything was absolutely hopeless! Lisa suddenly felt drained and slumped into the sofa, throwing her head into her hands. Now what was she going to do?

'Wow! That's really thoughtful of you, Lisa. Karan will be thrilled.' Mayank sounded delighted at the suggestion.

'Then you'll arrange it?' Lisa was glad that Mayank couldn't see the expression of relief on her face over the phone. She wondered when and how she had become so insecure. She'd never been like that earlier. She was sure that confident women who were sure about their marriages and husbands never felt insecure. She actually found it unbelievable that she was being so manipulative – it was so unlike her. Karan would call her Machiavelli if he knew.

'Of course!' Mayank's voice jerked her out of her thoughts and back to the conversation. 'I know he's not working that Saturday. Nor am I. I'll speak to a couple of other guys in the office and we'll all go over to Dam

Dama Lake. They even have water sports there.' Nothing like sports to keep him away from his mother!

'You can even stay the night,' suggested Lisa. 'They have a lovely resort and why attempt to drive back after …um…one too many drinks, you know.'

'Absolutely,' laughed Mayank. 'Lovely of you to suggest this, Lisa. Most women wouldn't encourage their husbands to bond with their friends like this, let alone take the initiative to plan things. It's incredibly nice of you.'

Lisa bit her lip. Mayank was right of course. Everyone knew how guys behaved when they were with their friends, particularly the married ones who didn't get that opportunity often enough. They got drunk, they flirted around, they misbehaved, they did everything that they couldn't normally do. But at least this was one weekend taken care of. She knew he would be too busy during the week anyway for her mother-in-law to play any tricks.

'Well, Karan has been so supportive about my holiday with my friends. It's the least I can do.' She hoped she sounded convincing enough.

'That's true!' agreed Mayank enthusiastically. 'It'll be a refreshing change for all of us after all the slogging in the office, particularly for Karan who's been working the hardest. It doesn't always pay to be the boss's favourite. He barely gets time to eat lunch.'

Lisa didn't know what to say to that. The truth was that she was feeling a tad guilty about giving Karan such a hard time. Maybe he was right after all. Maybe she really hadn't been as understanding as she should have been. Lisa shook her throbbing head as she tried not to think about it. It was very difficult and confusing, swaying like this between feelings of guilt and anger. The emotional surges had such a draining effect on her these days that sometimes she found it impossible to even handle her basic tasks like making her coffee or getting to work.

'Oh, and by the way,' added Mayank then, 'I just wanted to say I was really sorry about your cancelled vacation. Karan was really looking forward to it. He was awfully disappointed.'

'Thanks, Mayank. These things happen, I guess.' She smiled wistfully into the phone, not knowing what else to say. She couldn't explain to anyone what the vacation had meant to her. It had been a hope, a granted wish, an assurance, that despite everything, things would turn out all right after all. Even her best friends didn't completely understand.

'I'm glad you're taking it in your stride. Most women would have thrown the worst possible tantrum. Some particularly unreasonable ones would have even threatened divorce. But I knew you would be understanding about it. You're the best!'

Lisa almost choked on the glass of water she was drinking. Yeah well, best or not, everyone has to be manipulative sometimes, she thought to herself as they said goodbye and hung up.

Later as she showered, Lisa thought about what Karan had said earlier. Was he really going to miss her? All she'd been doing lately was fight with him, so it was a little difficult to believe that he'd miss her that very much. Why was it so difficult to believe and accept some of the simplest things in their relationship these days? Had things come to such a point? Even though her initial reason for planning this vacation had been to get back at Karan and prove a point to him, Lisa didn't quite experience the feeling of triumph or satisfaction that she'd thought she would. All she felt was – well – just sad that things had been so difficult for both of them lately. She'd thought everything would be okay after they'd made the Bali plan, but things had only become worse. Would they ever get better? She didn't know what to think or believe anymore, and she couldn't help but remember all the blissfully happy times they'd spent together over the years. All those weekend mornings spent cuddling each other in bed while the sun streamed in through the windows, all those crazy nights spent dancing the hours away in each other's arms as though nothing else mattered, the playful teasing, the confiding in each other about the smallest and biggest things, the feeling of returning after a hectic trip knowing that someone special was waiting at home, the impromptu weekend trips to Jaipur… it had all been so perfect! And then things had started going wrong. They'd become busier – the practical pressures of surviving in a difficult world had taken over – the disagreements, the fighting, the hurtful words, the disappointments. This time she couldn't stop her tears as she closed her eyes and turned her face towards the shower. Tears came too easily these days. At least crying in the shower had its advantages: she didn't need to wipe the tears away; she could just let them flow down with the water.

□

Goan beaches

'Why do they put us on the flight if they're not going to take off for hours? We haven't even started moving yet.' Ayesha stuck out her lower lip and pushed her seat back as far as she could. 'I could have gotten a coffee. I haven't had a single decent cup and I've been up since six! On a Saturday morning, for crying out loud!'

'Well, I'm sure the air hostess will get you some coffee,' suggested Sameera with a shrug. 'Yeah, but I hate in-flight food. It's terrible!' Ayesha made a face and pressed the service button above her seat.

An air hostess with a very bright smile and lots of make-up on her face, appeared a minute later.

'Hello! Can I get you something?'

'Yes, I'd like a coffee.' Ayesha pressed a finger to her temple to indicate a headache, 'and make it black please,' she added for good effect.

'I'm sorry, Ma'am, but we haven't started our in-flight service as yet. All I can serve you right now is water. And could you please straighten your seat to an upright position? We're going to be taking off any minute.'

'That's what you've been saying for the past twenty minutes,' snapped Ayesha, straightening up her seat and scowling at the air hostess.

'I'm sorry, Ma'am,' said the air hostess without looking the least bit sorry. 'But it's a government regulation that once the seat belt sign is on, you must have your seat in an upright position.' She flashed her a professional smile, and then promptly turned to attend to another passenger who was threatening to throw up. Ayesha looked at her friends incredulously.

'This airline sucks!' she exclaimed. 'No wonder air travel is supposed to be so stressful these days! I mean how can they be so mechanical? Even their stupid smiles are so artificial!'

'Well, you be careful, Ayesha.' Sameera looked up from the magazine she was reading. 'People are being offloaded from flights these days for misbehaving with the staff. Don't get into any altercations with anyone.'

'That's disgusting! What happens if the staff misbehaves with us? I mean that's just plain unfair!' Ayesha shook her head in exasperation and opened the book she had brought to read on the flight. Just then, the captain made an announcement and the plane finally started moving slowly on the runway. Ayesha exhaled in exaggerated relief, as Sameera flipped through the in-flight magazine, and Lisa stared out the window.

'Well! You seem to be very far away! What are you thinking about?'

Lisa turned towards her friend and smiled at her wistfully as the air hostess poured them both coffee. They'd been flying for over half an hour, and other than the initial delay, it was turning out to be a relatively smooth flight.

'Just… this and that,' answered Lisa with a shrug.

'What sort of this and that?'

'That's the problem with close friends. They want to know everything.'

They both laughed and Lisa stirred her coffee. How could she explain to her friend how desperately worried she was about her marriage, about everything that had gone wrong between them? How could she explain to her how much she felt the need to anchor her relationship, to solidify it once again like earlier? The feeling of uncertainty was almost too much to bear, and the loneliness literally seemed to consume her these days.

'Well, if you want to know the truth, I was thinking about Karan,' she admitted at last. 'I was thinking how far we seem to have drifted from each other. Somehow, this holiday doesn't seem like such a great idea to me anymore.'

'But I thought you wanted this,' said Sameera in surprise. 'That's why we planned it.'

Lisa sipped her coffee thoughtfully and sighed. 'Yeah, I know I did. I know I was fed up with everything – work, our fights, even him. But that doesn't mean that I'm not distressed about the way things have been between us these last few months.'

'Well, that obviously means that you still love him enough to care,' pointed out Sameera, as Lisa stared at her.

'Of course, I care. This is my marriage we're talking about. How can I not care? That's why I'm so hurt in the first place.'

'Why don't you give it some time,' suggested her friend. 'I'm sure all couples go through phases and …'

'I'm not sure it's as simple as that.' Lisa looked serious as she shook her head. 'We've said some pretty awful things to each other the past months. Do you know I even mentioned divorce the night he told me about the cancelled vacation?'

'Well, did you mean it?' Sameera was nonplussed, but she tried not to show it. Mentioning divorce was certainly a little extreme.

'I don't think so,' said Lisa with a sigh. 'Maybe it was just something said in a moment of anger. But it's a warning sign, don't you think? The word was never in our vocabulary before. It's never, ever happened before,' she added emphatically.

'Well, worrying about it like this is not going to solve anything,' said Sameera sensibly. 'Maybe somewhere you two aren't cooperating and communicating. After all, every marriage needs commitment doesn't it?'

'Come on, Sameera,' interjected Ayesha, looking up from her book. 'Why are you always so sensible about everything?'

'Because I do not get all my life's directions from mushy romance novels.' Sameera raised her eyebrows pointedly as she stared at the book Ayesha was reading. 'Knight in Shining Armour? Does anyone still read that stuff? No wonder you're still waiting.'

'Oh, sod off,' said Ayesha irritably, going back to her book. Lisa stifled a giggle, and Sameera shook her head in exasperation before turning back to her.

'Look, Lisa, let me just say this. Karan is a good man. He's a sensible person with a good head on his shoulders. In fact, they don't make them as nice as him anymore. You should meet some of the guys I've dated recently. Maybe then you'll realize. And whatever may have happened, you still love each other, any fool can see that.'

'Well, love isn't always enough to make a relationship work.' Lisa looked at her friend bleakly and sighed.

'Love is what makes the world go round, Lisa.' Sameera smiled at her friend. 'Anyway, for now, I think the best thing to do would be to just sit back and relax. Enjoy the holiday. You've been looking forward to it and it would be a real shame to waste it, wouldn't it?'

'I guess you're right.' Lisa pushed her seat back. 'There's no point worrying incessantly about it.'

'And you never know,' added her friend, 'this vacation may prove to be a blessing in disguise. You know, distance makes the heart grow fonder and all that.'

They both laughed, and Sameera squeezed her friend's hand as the air hostess came around with the food trolley.

'Vegetarian or Non-Vegetarian, Ma'am?' she asked with a practiced smile.

The rest of the flight was smooth and uneventful. The girls chatted, read magazines and napped, and before they knew it, they were looking out of the cabin window and gasping at the vast expanse of deep, blue sea.

'It's gorgeous!' breathed Sameera. 'Oh, I'm so glad we came.'

'It is beautiful,' agreed Lisa, 'but then being an Aquarian, I'm a little partial to water anyway.' She smiled at her friends and buckled up her seat belt. The flight was about to land and the seat belt sign was on again. 'Oh, did I tell you guys? Aman's taking Preeti to Las Vegas for their honeymoon. He's booked one of the best hotels there, and after that they're going on an Alaskan cruise. In fact, Preeti told me she didn't have to do a thing. He made all the arrangements himself. Hotels, tickets, visas everything!'

'Wow! Las Vegas!' Ayesha looked visibly impressed at the news, 'that's fab!'

'Yeah, Aman is one sweet guy. Preeti couldn't have done better. I'm glad they're finally getting married. They're such a perfect couple!'

'I think it's a little early to pass a sweeping statement like that,' said Sameera carefully. 'They're not even married yet. Things do change a lot after marriage. All the same, I wish her all the best of course.'

'Well, if he's taking her to Vegas for the honeymoon, he must be a keeper,' declared Ayesha as she leaned over in her seat and peered down the empty aisle. 'Hey, what's happened to the air hostess? The service on this airline is appalling! I need another coffee. This is the second time I've rung for her.'

'The seat belt sign is on, you dummy,' laughed Sameera. 'You should have called her ten minutes ago. Besides, she must be sick of you. Anyway, you'll have to wait till we land.'

The hotel was as beautiful as it had looked on the website. A guitarist greeted them at the entrance with a jovial Goan song and the three girls laughed and sang along with him as their luggage was unloaded. It was certainly a great way to start a holiday and they said as much to each other as they were led up a flight of stairs to the reception. It was a brilliant day and sunlight was streaming in through the big French windows of the open reception. The reception led out to beautifully landscaped, verdant gardens on all sides where groups of people were sitting in the sun, sipping tea or coffee. The hotel looked busy, there was a crowd of people heading towards the multiple tourist buses that were lined up to take people sightseeing. A group of foreigners in tiny shorts and huge sunglasses were also just checking in. Everyone was chattering and laughing loudly, there was a happy, touristy atmosphere around and one could hear a jumble of different languages being spoken.

'Sounds like bedlam here,' Lisa commented as the pretty receptionist returned their ID's. The check-in happened quickly and smoothly enough and afterwards they stood in the lobby, breathing in the fresh, salty air and sipping the fruity welcome drinks they'd been given.

'There's something so lovely about a beach holiday!' exclaimed Ayesha brightly as she sipped the mocktail. 'Even the welcome drink is so, so... well, so beachy!' She pointed to her non-alcoholic Pina Colada that had been served in a tropical cocktail glass with a slice of pineapple and a cocktail umbrella neatly mounted on the side and nodded enthusiastically. 'Know what I mean?'

Sameera and Lisa laughed at her description.

'We know exactly what you mean,' agreed Lisa. 'So, what are we waiting for? Let's get to it. I can't wait to see the pool!'

'And you might also want to try out the seafood shack we have on the beach,' volunteered the friendly looking receptionist. 'It's recently won an award for the best seafood in Goa. It's very romantic at dinner and the sunset is absolutely perfect.'

'Well, romance is actually the last thing I'm interested in,' muttered Lisa with a sigh. She gestured to her friends to finish their drinks quickly so they could get to their room and settle in. It was already lunch time and they didn't want to waste a single minute standing around. The holiday had finally started and she was looking forward to it. Needless to say, of course she couldn't help wishing, for what seemed to be the hundredth time, that the Bali plan had worked out instead.

After lunch in the hotel's all-day dining restaurant, the three girls strolled back to the room. Milind had helped them with the reservation, and thanks to all the corporate bookings their company made every year, the hotel had upgraded them to one of the best suites and they were absolutely thrilled. It was a great start to their holiday. The suite was luxurious with two plush, well-appointed bedrooms, two elaborate bathrooms with built in jacuzzis, and a private patio with a gorgeous view of the swimming pool that looked almost like it was merging into the open sea.

'Fabulous!' Sameera flung open the patio door. 'Please convey a big thank you to Milind, Lisa! I'm glad we decided to stay in the south. It's so much more peaceful and the resorts are much better. Well girls, do you want to unpack now or later?'

'Oh, let's get it out of the way, please,' said Lisa. 'I hate living out of a suitcase.'

'Good idea,' agreed Ayesha, hauling hers onto the bed. They were soon sorting through their stuff, bickering over who needed more closet space.

'No, you can't have this drawer too, Ayesha,' grumbled Sameera. 'It isn't our fault that you've brought so much! I thought you said you were traveling light this time. And look at what you've done! You've mixed up your bras with mine.'

'Well, that shouldn't be a problem, Sameera. Some of us happen to be better endowed than others. You're a 32 B and I'm a 36 C. No chance of a mix-up.' She smiled sweetly at her friend.

'Thanks for pointing that out,' glared Sameera then. 'Anyway, this side of the closet is mine so make sure you don't encroach.' She nodded her head firmly, shut her suitcase with a final thud, and slid it under her bed. 'Time to hit the beach girls.'

The hotel had its own private beach which promised to be cleaner and safer than some of Goa's notorious public beaches. The hotel staff had even offered to organize parasailing and other water sports for them if they wanted, but there was plenty of time for all that later. They were tired after the flight and it was only their first day after all. All they wanted to do now was relax, and as they languidly strolled on the beach together, the breeze felt wonderful on their faces. Lisa smiled at her friends and walked a little ahead of them as she watched the waves curl gently into the shore and then disappear into the sand. She shook her hair back and breathed in big gulps of the fresh, salty air. She felt miles away from Delhi, miles away from her life there, miles away from Karan. She was still furious with him for what he'd done of course, but try as she might, she just couldn't stop thinking about him. It was difficult not to wonder what he was doing right this minute. Was he thinking about her at all? Was he missing her, even a little bit? There was something very evocative about the sea, it seemed to bring a lot of suppressed thoughts to the surface. Dangerous, particularly these days when she wasn't really in a great frame of mind! She sighed and was about to turn back when she saw a couple walking hand in hand just ahead of her. They were obviously newly married because the girl was still wearing the customary red and white bangles on both wrists. The guy had a camera slung around his neck and he smiled indulgently as he clicked endless photographs of his wife. They seemed to be completely lost in each other, oblivious to everyone else around as he playfully pulled her into the water and she squealed in delight. Lisa stood there, looking at them and the girl suddenly noticed her and smiled at her brightly.

'Hi!' she called out. 'Do you mind taking a picture of my husband and me? We're alone and we never seem to get enough pictures together.'

'Sure,' said Lisa spontaneously. She smiled back and held out her hand for the camera and the guy came around at once to put an arm around his wife. He drew her close and Lisa felt a pang inside even as she clicked their picture and they thanked her and walked away. Feeling pensive, she strolled back to where her friends were watching from a distance and Ayesha shook her head and made a face.

'Honeymooners, I tell you! They just don't miss an opportunity to catch whoever they can to click their photographs.'

'Well, those two did look pretty cute together,' remarked Lisa then.

'Wait till they go home.' Sameera sounded confident. 'This is the honeymoon stage, remember? Everything looks absolutely perfect doesn't it? The way he's got his arm around her, the way she looks at him so adoringly. Well, wait till they go home and she discovers that he leaves dirty socks everywhere, snores and gets fed up of her shopping and complaining. Oh yeah, then we'll see.'

'Why are you always so cynical, Sameera?' asked Ayesha. 'Anyone would think you were completely against the idea of love.'

'Oh, I'm not against love,' clarified her friend. 'Just the false illusions it creates in some people's minds.'

They all laughed at that together as they turned back to walk up the path that led to the resort.

□

Separation blues

I hope you guys don't mind. I invited Vinny and his gang to join us.'

'Vinny? Who's Vinny?' Sameera stared at Ayesha in surprise.

'Gawd! Sometimes you guys can be so thick! Vinny and his gang! The guys we met at the reception when we were checking in this morning – the ones with the Louis Vuitton luggage!'

'Don't miss the Louis Vuitton,' grinned Lisa as Sameera looked at Ayesha with amazement.

'Them! But we don't even know them!'

'Of course, we do,' said Ayesha with a shrug. 'We spoke to them, remember?'

'Yeah, like two words,' retorted Sameera. 'Why did you go and invite them to join us? Without checking with us too! I thought we came here to have a nice, quiet holiday by ourselves.'

'Quiet holiday! Who comes to Goa for a quiet holiday? What are we, ninety? You're never going to get a guy with that attitude, Sameera. I mean, we have to grab every opportunity we get to meet suitable guys.'

'And how do you know this, this – what's his name now – this Vinny is suitable?' demanded her friend.

'The Louis Vuitton said it all naturally,' put in Lisa with a grin. She didn't have to be a part of this. She was happily married – well, not completely happily these days – but married nevertheless. Anyway, this was not her problem. It was up to Ayesha and Sameera to decide.

'Besides, what about Hemant?' Sameera asked Ayesha. 'I thought you were going steady with him. Would he be okay with you having dinner with this …this…?'

'Vinny! I wish you would remember his name!' Ayesha looked annoyed as she put finishing touches to her make-up. 'Anyway, I already broke up with Hemant before we came here.'

'You did?' exclaimed Sameera. 'I don't remember you mentioning it. What happened?'

'Well, you know I dated him for a year and he was this close to proposing,' Ayesha gestured with her index finger and thumb. 'But thankfully I discovered in the nick of time that he was the most miserable miser I'd ever seen. You know being rich isn't enough, you need to have the spine to spend a little too. I wanted to ask him whether he intended to take all that money to his grave.' She shook her head disdainfully and sighed. 'Anyway, I'm just completely done with him.' She snapped shut her lipstick and reached for her handbag. 'Come on you two. I promised Vinny we'd meet him at the pool at eight forty-five and I don't want to keep him waiting.'

'Of course not!' Sameera winked at Lisa as they walked out of the room together. 'After all, he's the guy with the Louis Vuitton suitcase!'

'Eat up Puttar, eat up. As it is you have become so weak.' Anju Chopra heaped more rice onto Karan's plate and he groaned.

'Mom! This is too much. I never eat such a heavy dinner!'

The Chopras were eating dinner together in the dining room of their two-story bungalow in Sainik Farms. Surrounded on all sides by lush green gardens, it was a sprawling house that could have been extremely elegant had it not been for Karan's mother's insistence to decorate it herself. His father had tried to convince her to hire a professional decorator but she had insisted that she was perfectly qualified to do so herself. Besides that, it was a lovely house with an expansive dining area for family-style meals, a large country kitchen done in earth tones, an elaborate living room big enough to welcome as many guests as the Chopras wanted, and gorgeous garden vistas that one could enjoy from any one of the four colonial-style bedrooms. There were, however, the obvious downsides that came with living in a farmhouse in Delhi. Frequent power cuts, for instance. Even now the air conditioner was on, but the room was warm and heavy with humidity since the electricity had been gone for several hours that day and had only just been restored. Karan, who was particularly sensitive to the heat and not used to the power cuts in Delhi after having lived in a building with power back up for over five years, had lost his appetite and didn't find the chicken curry and daal makhani his mother had prepared for dinner as appetizing as he usually did. But he didn't want to hurt his mother's feelings and so had dutifully joined his parents at the dinner table. He was bone tired after a grueling day and hadn't even been able to talk to Lisa for more than a couple of minutes when she'd called earlier to tell him that she'd reached Goa. Just as well she wasn't here. He really was up to his eyes.

'Heavy! It is only daal-chaawal! What is heavy about that?' His mother looked shocked at his remark.

'Mom, daal makhani is not just daal! And I must confess that I prefer steamed rice to this.'

He pointed to the dry fruit pulao his mother had served and she stared at him in consternation.

'Steamed rice!' she exclaimed, 'who eats steamed rice? We're not poor people. What dreadful habits have you developed, Karan? Lisa should know better and she should…'

'Mom, this has nothing to do with Lisa,' retorted Karan as his father chuckled. 'Furthermore, steamed rice is better for health. Some people are even shifting to brown rice because of its health benefits.'

'Brown rice! That awful thing that tastes like cat food!' Anju Chopra screwed up her nose and made a face.

'It's a lot healthier than white rice,' continued Karan firmly. 'They even serve it at weddings these days. And look at this chicken! Why have you put so much butter in it?'

'Butter! Where is the butter? I swear there is no butter in the chicken. You can go and look in the kitchen if you like and if you find any butter anywhere…'

'Of course, there is no butter in the chicken,' agreed Prakash Chopra with a dry smile. 'Only a heap of desi ghee.'

His wife glared at him and pursed her lips: 'desi ghee is good for health,' she said firmly. 'Even the health magazines say so. It took them years to discover what we always knew.' She wiped her eyes with the end of her dupatta and turned back to her son: 'Eat up Puttar, eat up. God knows when I'll be able to cook for you again.'

Lisa took a sip of wine and leaned back in her chair. It was a lovely, balmy night, and she could hear the roar of the distant waves rolling onto the beach. The dinner that the hotel had organized for all its resident guests was lovely; there was a lavish, multi-cuisine buffet laid out by the pool, and a live band was playing merrily on one side; the atmosphere was festive and cheerful. Lisa had to admit that she was enjoying herself. She had been skeptical about the way the evening had started. Ayesha had latched onto Vinny the moment they'd reached the restaurant and was even now, laughing wildly at one of his jokes. Sameera, despite all her talk about not being interested in having dinner with these guys, seemed to be happy enough to talk to Vinny's friend Gautam who was also apparently single. The fact that he was a professor as well didn't hurt of course. Sameera and he seemed to have a lot in common, and had been talking nineteen to the dozen about the IB education system as opposed to the CBSE education system for the last hour. They seemed to be getting along like a house on fire. That left Lisa and the third guy, Ronit, to entertain each other and after talking to him for twenty minutes, she had to grudgingly admit that he was both interesting to talk to and down to earth. He was younger than her but seemed mature for his age. Surprisingly, they discovered that they had quite a few common interests. He was also good-looking and charming and Lisa couldn't help thinking that if she hadn't been married, she would have liked to get to know him better. She realized with a jolt that it wasn't the most appropriate thought, particularly given her current situation, and she was a bit disconcerted that the thought had even crossed her mind. Somehow it seemed disloyal and she did feel a tad guilty. She picked up her phone to check if there were any messages from Karan and was instantly disappointed that there were none. She couldn't help but feel a bit annoyed too. Here she was, beating herself up about merely talking to another guy, when Karan was seemingly too busy to even send her a message. Resolving not to let it bother her, she dropped her phone into her bag and turned back to her dinner companion.

'Did you try the balchao? It's delectable.' Ronit smiled at her, showing perfect teeth.

'No. I'm not really a huge fan of spicy food.'

'I like to try most things once,' he continued, 'I'm a travel photographer so I've had the opportunity to travel a fair amount. The best part of travelling is that you get to experiment with food. I'm seasoned now, so nothing makes me squeamish.'

'What's the weirdest thing you've ever eaten?' Lisa smiled back as she took a sip of wine.

'Trust me, you don't want to know.' Ronit threw his head back and laughed. 'Can't decide between the White Ant Egg Soup in Laos or the Black Pudding in Ireland. Believe it or not, I didn't find either of them revolting.'

'It must be interesting to travel to exotic places all the time,' commented Lisa. 'Quite a life!'

'Doesn't leave much time for family though,' smiled Ronit. 'Just as well that I'm single.'

Lisa wondered if that was a deliberate attempt to let her know that he wasn't married. She noticed he wasn't wearing a wedding ring, so at least he wasn't fibbing.

'Well, my husband travels quite extensively too, so I know what you mean.'

There! That was crystal clear! Now if he felt that it wasn't worth his while to talk to her, she was perfectly fine with it. She didn't need any unnecessary complications in her life either. After all, she did have a husband even if she was mighty miffed with him at the time.

'So, what did he say?'

'I suppose he turned his back to her after that and concentrated on that sexy foreigner in the backless dress,' answered Ayesha before Lisa could.

All three girls laughed as they staggered back to their room. It was only ten-thirty but they were tired. It had been a long day and even though the evening had been enjoyable, all three of them wanted to turn in for the night.

'No, actually he didn't really react.' Lisa unlocked the door and they trooped in. 'In fact, he invited me to have dinner with him.'

Sameera looked taken aback and shook her head. 'That's weird! Why would you have dinner with him? He's a complete stranger!'

'I think he was quite nice.' Ayesha looked impressed. 'Good looking and all.'

'That doesn't make him nice,' pointed out Sameera. 'And who cares if he's good-looking? Lisa's married, remember?'

'Well, I'm not suggesting that she should have an affair with him. Dinner sounds harmless enough. Good for a few laughs if nothing else.'

'When are you going to grow up?' Sameera looked exasperated with Ayesha and Lisa rolled her eyes.

'Whoa! Easy girls! It's not like I'm going to have dinner with him, so you don't have anything to quibble about.'

'I guess you're right,' agreed Ayesha. 'Anyway, speaking of Vinny, I really like him. He's totally my type!' It was more a declaration than a mere statement and Sameera raised her eyebrows in surprise.

'Isn't it a little early to say that? Why do you always rush in where angels fear to tread, Ayesha? No wonder you make such awful mistakes with men.'

'No, I don't.' Ayesha stuck out her lower lip obstinately which made her look like a petulant child. 'Vinny really is my type. I don't think I have ever said that about anyone else before and…'

'You said the same about Hemant,' pointed out Sameera, 'and about Sumer. And…'

'Oh, okay,' said Ayesha, reluctantly giving in. 'I don't feel like arguing with you right now, Sameera. Anyway, Vinny's asked me out for lunch tomorrow. He's taking me to this amazing Goan restaurant. He says they have the best seafood in town. Their jumbo prawns are the most…'

'Don't you think that's a little fast?' Even Lisa was surprised at Ayesha's haste. 'You only just met him.'

'Yeah, but if I want to find my rich, handsome husband soon, I have to start working on it. You don't understand, Lisa. I'm twenty-nine! I don't want to be on the shelf forever! Besides, my parents aren't going to wait any longer. Mom's already started talking to her friends and relatives about an alliance. An arranged marriage! Me! I would rather die!'

'Why are you so against arranged marriages?' asked Sameera curiously. 'What's wrong with an arranged marriage? As long as the guy's nice, what difference does it make whether you meet in a club or your parents introduce you?'

'That's straight out of Monsoon Wedding! How many times have you seen it?' Ayesha shook her head impatiently. 'Thanks for the gyaan, but that's not how I want it. Even plain Janes like Sumita are having love marriages! Get this: she met him right in her house! He's her niece's French tutor. And now they're getting married. And she's only twenty-five, for God's sake! Maybe I should hire a tutor too. I've always wanted to learn French.'

'Now there's a novel thought,' laughed Lisa. 'Don't worry darling! You'll find the right one eventually. Just have patience.'

'Easy for you to say that, Lisa. Particularly since you have a great guy yourself.'

'For once I agree with Ayesha.' Sameera smiled at Lisa. 'In spite of your current circumstances, I'd still say you're lucky. Like I said before, they really don't make them as nice as Karan anymore.'

□

Monday morning male bonding

'Can you believe she's done that?' Mayank looked visibly outraged as he puffed his cigarette furiously. It was Monday morning and they were all understandably stressed out. There was heaps of work as usual and it had been an endless three hours since they'd entered the office. There were two major proposals to be sent to clients and a critical interim presentation that was scheduled that week. Karan was thankful that he'd managed to get a part of his work done over the weekend. Now, as he glanced at his watch and decided that a fifteen-minute break was the maximum he could afford to take, he patted his friend on the back, urging him to calm down.

Mayank had been irritated since he'd stepped into the office and he'd dragged Karan and Sameer out for a smoke at the first opportunity, saying that he couldn't possibly wait till lunch. Incidentally, Sameer had broken off with his environmentalist girlfriend, and the first thing he'd done after the break-up was to light up for the first time in weeks. Now as they all started on their second cigarette, Mayank glared around at no one in particular and shook his head irately.

'How could she do that to me? It makes me feel like such a loser!'

'Come on, Mayank. What's the big deal? Matrimonials aren't such a bad option and…' started Sameer as Mayank gasped.

'Don't even say the word! Someone may hear you. Do you want everyone to know that my mom has put my profile up on a matrimonial website?'

The last two words were said in a hushed whisper and Mayank looked around nervously to make sure no one was listening.

'So what?' asked Karan, with a casual shrug. 'What's so awful about that?'

'Everything.' Mayank's tone was emphatic. 'Everyone will think that I simply can't find a girl on my own. That in this day and age, when people are meeting droves of girls in gyms and clubs and on vacations abroad, I have to register on some dratted matrimonial site to find a girl. My cousin met his fiancée in Vegas. How much more perfect can it get?'

'Nothing is perfect,' pointed out Karan sensibly.

'Well, at least he'll have a great story to tell! And what would I say? That we met on a matrimonial site and my mother arranged it for me. Do you know she's even called me fair skinned in the profile? Who, I ask you, who, in their right mind would call me fair?' Mayank looked heavenwards as his friends laughed.

'Everyone's fair in the world of matrimonials, Mayank. At least she didn't call you "Milk White," remarked Karan, making air quotes with his fingers. 'That's the usual term.'

'I thought that rubbish was reserved for girls,' objected Sameer.

'Don't let any of the ladies hear you pass a sexist remark like that, Sameer.' Karan looked amused at his friends' aghast expressions. 'Look at the number of fairness products for men! They're practically flooding the market right now! Fair & Lovely Menz Active, Fair and Handsome Fairness Cream, Garnier Men Power Light, Nivea Men Advanced Whitening Oil Control Moisturiser...'

'Jesus! Did you recently do a project on the subject?' asked Mayank sarcastically. 'It's all very well for you to tease me like this. Particularly when you have a lovely, gorgeous wife waiting for you at home.'

'Not exactly waiting for me at home, remember?' muttered Karan. Not that he begrudged her or anything for that. In fact, he really couldn't blame her for getting so frustrated; after all, he'd hardly had any time for her the past few months. He had to confess though that he couldn't help but feel a bit resentful that she was sitting in sunny Goa having a whale of a time with her friends while he was burning the midnight oil. How he would have loved to go to Bali with her! How could she even have imagined that he hadn't been disappointed about the vacation? The truth was that he hadn't had the opportunity to even think of his own disappointment. He bit his lip and tried not to dwell on it as he turned his attention back to his friends.

'Yeah well, she's still gorgeous and she's still your wife.' Mayank lit another cigarette and took a long drag, blowing little smoke rings in the air as he exhaled. Karan wanted to point out that it was his third one in less than fifteen minutes but it didn't seem like the right time.

'On a serious note, to be perfectly honest, this matrimonial experience is just too superficial, too practical, too devoid of emotion for me. I'm sure it works for some people,' added Mayank, 'but not for me. I'd like to feel a bond, a connection with the woman I marry. I actually do happen to believe in love even if I'm not yet in love myself. I want to feel it here,' he said, gesturing to where he thought his heart should be. 'Is that crazy?'

'No,' said Karan with a slow smile. 'It's not. If you ask me, I think that's how it should be. That's how I felt about Lisa when I met her.' He realized that Mayank was right. That was what love was all about, wasn't it? Emotions – good and bad, joy and sorrow, expectations and disappointments – but emotions nevertheless. After all, Lisa and he had experienced every possible emotion in the five and a half years that they'd been married – intense love, overpowering passion, bitter disappointments and deep dejection.

'Thinking about Lisa huh?' Sameer laughed, reading his friend's thoughts. 'Well, even I have to agree with Mayank that you're lucky, Karan. Lisa's a great girl.'

'The grass always looks greener on the other side, Sameer,' said Karan, trying to keep his tone light. 'You're not the one dealing with her when she flies into one of her Godawful temper tantrums.'

'Well, wait till you hear what I have to tell you,' said Mayank, nudging him. 'You may feel a bit differently then.'

Ten minutes later, there was a definite spring in his step as he walked back to his office. And why not, it had been such a pleasant surprise. A weekend away with his friends sounded just like what the doctor had ordered. Damdama would be perfect this time of year and what made it even better was that the suggestion had come from Lisa. Karan had to admit that he'd been astonished when Mayank informed him that not only had Lisa called him specially to suggest the weekend, but she had practically insisted on Mayank following it through.

'She said you've been working too hard and you need to let your hair down a bit,' Mayank had said. 'I think she was very concerned about you. Like I said before, nice wife you have there.'

Karan had smiled then, and even though he hadn't said anything, he was touched to the core by Lisa's thoughtfulness. It was the sweetest gesture and he made a mental note to remember to give her a call later to thank her. He hadn't realized how concerned she'd been about him. Never would he ever know what her real motive had been!

Later that day, he met Vivek for a quick update on business development and on-going projects. As they sat in the conference room together, he couldn't help noticing that Vivek had started looking particularly stressed these days. He knew that there was pressure – they were all feeling it after all – but he had never seen his usually calm and cheerful boss looking so harried. He waited quietly as Vivek took off his glasses and leaned forward to talk to him, peering at him intently as he spoke.

'Karan, I'm very worried. Raman sent me his resignation yesterday.'

'Raman!' exclaimed Karan. He was amazed. Raman Bajaj was a bright and enthusiastic guy, and one of their best associate directors. He'd been as excited as a child when he'd joined their company a year ago and he'd always assured Karan that he absolutely loved his job. 'Why?'

Vivek spread his hands out in a helpless gesture. 'Says he can't handle the pressure. Says he doesn't have a personal life anymore. He recently got married and I had to cancel the leave I'd sanctioned for his honeymoon. That must have done it.'

'A honeymoon's a honeymoon, Sir,' said Karan, shaking his head. He remembered now. Raman had applied for two weeks leave for his wedding but all he'd got was four days. In fact, he'd been in the office till six o'clock on the day before his wedding and had been sending out emails even the next day. What was happening in the office these days?

'We're not in an easy business, Karan,' said Vivek as though reading Karan's thoughts. 'And the buck stops with me. I need to get the proposals and reports out on time. You know how uncompromising clients are these days. And Richard and Mark start questioning me the moment we don't meet our targets.' Richard Elliot and Mark Logan were their joint venture partners in the US. Vivek looked heavenwards as though he couldn't understand how he was supposed to survive between uncompromising clients, demanding partners, and uncooperative, stressed-out employees.

'Anyway, I've spoken to him and he's withdrawn his resignation for the time being. But we have to create some sanity out here. People can't work under this kind of pressure. Why haven't you recruited those project managers you were talking about?'

'I spoke to Mallika about it,' said Karan. 'She said she hadn't been able to find anyone suitable yet.'

'Well, she'd better find them soon,' said Vivek brusquely. 'I've had enough of this! I don't want to lose my best people. We need two project managers, one of whom must have experience in the healthcare area.'

'Yes, Sir,' said Karan. 'I have a couple of bios with me too. I'll ask Mallika to set up the interviews urgently.'

'One more thing, Karan. I want a daily report on that healthcare project from here on. I want things to start looking better before I leave for Singapore.'

'Sure, Sir.' Karan nodded and rose from his chair to go but Vivek put out a hand to stop him.

'I'm sorry Karan, I should have mentioned this earlier but I forgot. It's been so crazy around here. I wanted to apologize once again for cancelling your vacation. I hope it didn't disrupt the peace in your house?' Vivek looked genuinely contrite.

Karan smiled and shook his head. He couldn't possibly tell his boss that the cancelled vacation had not just disrupted, but absolutely ruined the peace in his house and in his life, and that his wife had even threatened to divorce him in a fit of anger.

'Of course not, Sir. Lisa was understandably disappointed but she's a professional too and she understands that sometimes these things happen,' he said instead.

'Get her a new diamond ring,' suggested Vivek with a grin. 'I'm a seasoned man, I know. It always works like a charm.'

Karan smiled at his boss and shook his head. 'Oh, I did better than that, Sir. I sent her on a vacation to Goa with two of her best friends.'

'Smart move,' agreed Vivek with an appreciative nod. 'Very good. Now that the wife has gone, you can really put your head down and work.'

□

Just dinner, not a date!

'If anything's a holiday, this certainly is one.' Ayesha crossed one shapely leg over the other and smiled smugly to herself as she noticed a group of Russian guys staring admiringly at her. And why not? She was looking pretty saucy in the black swimsuit she was wearing today, even if she did say so herself. She sat back in the sun chair and sipped her fresh watermelon juice. It was their fifth day in Goa, the weather was beautiful, and the palm trees were swaying gently in the morning breeze. The vacation had been great so far. They'd gone to the famed Leela Beach Resort for lunch the day before, and had ended up spending the day there. Today, the three of them had agreed to stay in the resort and spend a lazy day by the pool. The water had looked very inviting and they'd been there since eight o'clock in the morning. It was a balmy day and the girls were enjoying the luxury of doing nothing at all except lounging around, reading, and occasionally taking a dip in the cool water. In fact, the pool was completely packed today and as Ayesha looked around at all the people sitting around, sipping their tall drinks and soaking in the sun, it seemed as though most of the hotel was there.

'I hear there's going to be a Michelin starred chef at dinner tonight,' remarked Sameera, sipping her virgin coconut mojito. 'He's supposed to be renowned for his crab claws with garlic butter. And speaking of dinner,' she added then, looking at Lisa pointedly, 'we forgot to ask you what happened with Ronit. You mentioned that he asked you to dinner. What did you say?'

'What could I say?' Lisa sighed in answer to her friend's question and shrugged. 'It was just a dinner invitation after all. I reminded him that I'm married and all, but he just laughed and said that it wasn't a big deal, and he'd still like to be friends.' She rummaged in her bag for her sunscreen as she spoke. The sun was strong and her skin tanned much too easily. 'He said it didn't matter these days and that he has a lot of married female friends.' She began to apply the lotion all over her exposed skin liberally before proffering it to her friends.

'Is it appropriate to ask a married woman out on a date like that? Besides, he's younger than you!' Sameera looked disapprovingly at Lisa and Ayesha groaned.

'Jesus! You sound like my mother!'

'Not a date,' clarified Lisa emphatically. 'Just dinner. Anyway, I'm thinking of accepting.' She looked amused, almost gleeful, and Sameera looked at her in surprise. 'It could be worth a few laughs if nothing else.'

Sameera didn't say it, but she personally didn't approve of this. She had very conservative ideas about these things, and she knew Lisa well enough to understand that her friend was bored and lonely and looking for some excitement. Sameera, however, didn't think having dinner with a strange guy was the answer.

'Are you seriously considering going out with this guy? It's not like you to go out with a total stranger, Lisa. Besides, will Karan be okay with it? I mean…'

'Oh, don't be such a grouch, Sameera.' Ayesha rolled her eyes. 'So what if she's a married woman? That doesn't have to change everything. It's always interesting to meet people and make new friends. Anyway, I'm going out with Vinny for dinner tonight.'

'I think you should probably think about it,' said Sameera to Lisa, ignoring Ayesha. 'Karan really may not be comfortable with it.'

'Well, he's not here to object, is he? After everything that's happened, I don't think he has the right to be upset about anything. And frankly, I don't think he'd even care.'

Lisa's eyes glistened as she spoke and Sameera looked at her uncomfortably. It was evident that she was still very sore about everything that had happened with Karan.

'That's not true and you know it. Of course, he cares. He cares very much.'

'Anyway, he isn't that narrow-minded,' interjected Ayesha again. 'Doesn't she go out with Abhishek? And Milind? Karan doesn't mind.'

'Abhishek is her childhood friend and Karan knows him very well. Hell, he's as much Karan's friend as Lisa's. And Milind is her boss and probably gay. This Ronit is a complete stranger.' Sameera glared at Ayesha who just shrugged.

'Stop it, you two!' Lisa was tired of the conversation. She was amazed at how they were bickering over her choices and decisions as though she wasn't there at all. 'I'm a grown woman,' she said to Sameera, 'I can take care of myself. I just feel like talking to someone new for a change. I'm not going to do anything stupid. Despite the fact that I haven't been exactly thrilled with Karan's attitude recently, I do respect the holy vows of matrimony,' she added caustically but her friend wasn't convinced.

'How would you feel if the roles were reversed, Lisa? If Karan went out with another woman while you're out of town? After all, what's sauce for the goose is sauce for the gander, right?'

'I don't want to talk about it anymore. We've discussed this enough. I'm starving! Club sandwiches anyone?'

And that was that. Lisa's face had taken on a rather stubborn, petulant expression, and Sameera knew it was no use arguing with her. She seemed to have made her decision anyway. It must be the attention this guy was giving her. Yes, that must have done it. And the tension between Karan and her couldn't have helped either. But Sameera wasn't usually the kind to give unsolicited advice and she had already said what she wanted to. Lisa was an adult after all. Besides, she knew Lisa could be impulsive and did strange things sometimes, but she was basically a level-headed person and usually knew how to take care of herself. So despite all her misgivings, Sameera held her tongue and didn't say anything more. She just hoped that given how insecure her friend was feeling right now and the troubled state of her marriage, better sense would prevail and she would use her judgement.

They decided to meet in the hotel lobby at eight o'clock. Lisa got there five minutes early, which was more than a little surprising since she wasn't usually a very punctual person. Karan was in fact, always nagging her about the importance of being on time, but today she hadn't taken too long to get dressed. Afterwards, there hadn't seemed any point in hanging around the room, particularly since Ayesha wasn't around and

Sameera had been holding her head and complaining about a severe headache since five-thirty. As she sat down to wait for Ronit in one of the lobby's comfortable leather couches, she noticed that the lobby seemed very crowded even at this hour of the evening. There were quite a few people checking in: families with young children, groups of friends all dressed up and going out to dinner, and several couples too, both young and old. You could always tell the honeymooners apart from the others though, and it wasn't just the customary red and white bangles that the new bride usually wore on her wrists or the intricate patterns of henna that adorned her hands. It was also the palpable starry-eyed look that they had as they strolled around hand in hand, sharing intimate jokes, talking and laughing together. Lisa suddenly felt a pang inside as she watched them and memories of her own honeymoon in Bangkok so many years ago, came rushing back to her. She smiled wistfully as she thought about it. It had been the perfect honeymoon and she'd never been happier in her entire life. In fact, she could easily say that it had been the best ten days of her life. They'd spent so much time together, just the two of them, away from everyone else. They'd returned home ecstatic, tanned and very much in love with each other and...

'Hey!'

Her thoughts interrupted, she looked up to see Ronit walking towards her, an apologetic smile on his face. 'Sorry I'm a bit late. One of their elevators broke down. I waited a couple of minutes and then took the stairs.'

She smiled at him. 'It's ok. I haven't been waiting long.'

'So, shall we head out? I took the liberty of making a reservation at a restaurant of my choice. I think you'll like it. By the way, you look lovely.'

She had to admit that he was charming. And chivalrous, which was a rarity these days. In fact, he was disturbingly like Karan had been during their dating period. His charming manner, his natural good looks, his easy smile. He was even dressed like him in a pair of crisp black trousers and a dark blue shirt. His shoes were well polished, his cologne smelled good and his hair was combed to perfection. A little yuppie perhaps but it suited him. In fact, he hardly looked like a travel photographer – more like a young corporate lawyer or executive. Lisa said as much to him and he laughed out loud.

'I was born into a quintessential business family. I'm the odd one out. My father's a businessman, as were both my grandfathers and great grandfathers. I guess that's where the dressing style comes from.'

'It suits you,' smiled Lisa as they walked towards the porch and hailed a cab.

'Thanks!' Ronit grinned back at her and then turned to the driver. 'The Fisherman's Wharf, please,' he said and they sped off. Lisa looked out the window and tried not to feel guilty about going out with Ronit. After all, this was just dinner, not a date.

'Nice!' Lisa looked impressed as the maître d' led them to a corner table with an excellent view of the waterfront. 'Good choice.' She gave him a thumbs up as she settled down in her seat and he looked pleased. The restaurant was full and he was just glad that he'd had the good sense to make a reservation. It was a pretty restaurant on the bank of a river with fairy lights all around and live music.

'I always make it a point to come here when I'm in Goa. The atmosphere is lively and cheerful and the music is the best in south Goa.'

'So it is,' agreed Lisa. The waiter came over to take their drink orders and after some debating, they both decided on beer. Somehow it seemed too warm for wine.

'So, Lisa.' Ronit looked at her mischievously as his dark brown eyes twinkled. 'Why did you agree to come out with me? After all, you're a married woman. You clarified this very categorically the other night.'

'And yet you asked me to dinner?' shot back Lisa immediately. 'I thought that would have been enough to deter you, but apparently not.'

'Touché!' Ronit laughed and put his hands up. 'I concede. To tell you the truth, I like meeting new and interesting people. I enjoy talking to different people, sharing opinions, experiences. And I have to admit that you seemed like a very interesting person. I promise you I wasn't trying to get a free invitation to next year's Paris Couture Week.'

They both laughed and Lisa realized that he seemed like a nice man. And it was certainly interesting to talk to someone new.

'I guess that's why I accepted your invitation,' she remarked. 'I enjoy meeting new people too.' She didn't confess that she was enjoying the attention as well. It was certainly flattering to be invited out to dinner by a good-looking, charming man, and to be treated so nicely. Their drinks arrived then and the music got a bit louder. The weather was balmy but there was a gentle breeze blowing which kept it pleasant. They chatted very amiably after that and Ronit kept the conversation very lively with interesting tales about his travel experiences. It was only when they had finished their appetizers and the waiter appeared with the main course that Lisa realized how quickly the time was flying.

'This looks delicious,' she commented, helping herself to Pork Vindaloo. 'I'm glad I asked you to order. You certainly know food.'

'I live to eat!' he declared expansively before taking a bite from the aromatic Beef Fry, one of the legendary Goan dishes that he loved. 'This is sublime! Call me irreverent if you like since I am a Hindu, but beef is my undisputed favourite meat. There's a unique flavour to it that you can't find in anything else. In fact, I'd go as far as to say that for me, if I have to eat a burger then it's got to be a beef burger – with a double layer of beef, no less!'

'I agree with you,' nodded Lisa as she tasted the Beef Fry. 'This is superb! I must say Goan food is pretty flavourful.'

'Oh, you haven't eaten Goan food till you've tried the Pork Sorpotel,' laughed Ronit with a wicked look. 'But mind you, it's not for the faint hearted.'

'That, I think I'll pass on, thank you very much.' Lisa made a face and sipped her beer.

'Oh, it's not always boiled in the animal's blood,' grinned Ronit. 'All you have to do is ask.'

'Can we change the subject please? I don't fancy ruining my appetite!'

Ronit laughed good-naturedly and Lisa ran her finger around the rim of the bottle, wondering if she could be honest with this man. She didn't really know him but he seemed straightforward enough.

'And now I have a non-food related question,' she said as she decided to be candid. 'It's a bit personal but please don't get offended.'

He looked at her quizzically, wondering what she was going to ask him. He wasn't worried, just curious. He had nothing to hide.

'I wanted to talk to you about Vinny. I mean, my friend Ayesha seems to be quite enamored, but I don't want her getting hurt. I know she looks frivolous and like she's just having a good time, but there's more to her than meets the eye.'

He looked thoughtful for a minute as though weighing his words. Lisa understood that this was a tricky situation for him, sandwiched between a strange woman he hardly knew, and his friend whom he wanted to be loyal to.

'Well, let me just put it this way,' he answered finally. 'Vinny's a good friend and a nice guy, but he's not someone your friend should get too attached to. I could be wrong, but I don't think he's looking for anything serious right now. He's not had a single serious relationship yet and he's almost twenty-seven.'

'Thanks for being so honest. I really appreciate it.' Lisa looked at him gratefully and he smiled.

'Just don't quote me. I don't want him to misunderstand me but I don't want your friend to get needlessly hurt.'

'Don't worry, I won't.' She knew she had to warn Ayesha but she'd have to do it tactfully.

'It's just that, quite frankly, marriage is the last thing on his mind. He's focused on his work right now and when he's not working, he's having fun. I, on the other hand,' he continued, smiling mischievously, 'am looking for something serious. But just my luck to be out with a married, albeit lovely, woman. Trust me, I was quite heart-broken when you told me about your husband.'

They both laughed and the conversation moved on to other things. Lisa hadn't taken his comment seriously, it was just friendly banter after all, and he didn't mean any harm. Actually, she couldn't help but feel flattered. Anyone would. He'd been so attentive to her and in other circumstances, it would have been the perfect date. But this wasn't a date, it was just dinner with – what was he – he wasn't a friend; she didn't know him after all. He wasn't even an acquaintance. Just a charming stranger who'd crossed her path and made her feel special. She smiled wistfully to herself as she realized how young and carefree she was feeling. The parallel thought that ran through her mind was that her husband wouldn't be too thrilled about it. Which man would, after all? Perhaps Sameera had been right; it wasn't appropriate and Karan wouldn't understand it. In fact, he may even be downright upset if he got to know about it. It wasn't a date – she was still very clear about that, but she wasn't comfortable telling Karan about it. Somehow, however platonic the interaction had been, the fact that she couldn't be honest with her husband made the whole thing feel clandestine. However little they may be getting on these days, she knew that he trusted her which made it even more mortifying. She decided that she couldn't possibly see Ronit again. Her mind made up, she decided to enjoy what remained of the evening, and deal with it after dinner.

□

Love and guilt

The next day was warm and sunny, and the three girls set off soon after breakfast. They were going to Panjim for a spot of shopping and sightseeing and had hired a car and a driver to take them. Lisa was a little quieter than usual and it didn't go unnoticed by her friends. They knew that she'd spoken with Karan that morning but hadn't told him about the previous evening. She was feeling a wee bit guilty about the whole thing since she was usually upfront and honest with him, but they didn't want to pressurize her into talking about it. They figured she'd get over it eventually. It really was a gorgeous day and she did seem to cheer up a bit as they all sat back to enjoy the drive and the car sped past white sandy beaches, narrow country lanes lined with palm trees, and huge coconut plantations. Now and then they would hear bells chiming in the distance and then quite suddenly, the tall gleaming steeple of a church would appear and the girls would strain their necks to see it. Some of the churches were from the prehistoric colonial era with magnificent Portuguese architecture. Such was the beauty and grandeur of some of the churches, that the girls were tempted to go in and explore them right away. Their driver, however, advised them to keep it for another day if they wanted to get to Panjim in time. It was actually a very pleasant drive and even the driver, who had been recommended by the hotel, was a nice, unobtrusive guy, and the girls felt comfortable with him.

'So, Ayesha,' said Lisa as she unpacked a chicken and cheese sandwich. The hotel had given them sandwiches and muffins to keep them going until lunch. 'How was your date with Vinny last night? You got back so late, we never got around to asking you about it.' Ronit's warning about

Vinny rang through her head and she wondered if her friend would be receptive to some well-meaning advice.

'Oh Vinny!' exclaimed Ayesha, her expression brightening. 'He's just the most amazing guy I've ever met! Just too good to be true!'

'That probably means it's not all true,' said Sameera sardonically as she smirked.

'That was rude, Sameera Quereshi! I'm not going to talk about it if you're going to make fun of me. I'm sick and tired of your cynicism.' Ayesha looked livid.

'Stop it, you two,' interjected Lisa who was getting tired of their constant squabbling. 'Come on, Ayesha! Don't be so touchy. We just think that maybe you're rushing into things and it may be better to try and take things slow and easy. But of course, we want to know about your evening. Sameera won't say another word, I promise.' She shot Sameera a warning look and Sameera threw her hands up in resignation.

'Okay, okay, I won't say anything.' She smiled at Ayesha and squeezed her hand. 'Come on, we're all ears.'

Ayesha still looked a little sulky but she couldn't resist talking about her date, so she gave in.

'Well, it was a lovely evening and I had a wonderful time. He took me to his aunt's house for a drink.'

'His aunt's house?' exclaimed Lisa. 'We didn't know he has an aunt here.'

'Neither did I,' admitted Ayesha. 'Well, technically she's not really his aunt. She's actually his mother's old college friend. But the two families are very close. Anyway, so he took me there for dinner which obviously means he's serious about me. Otherwise why would he introduce me to his family?'

Sameera had to resist the urge to point out that it was too ridiculously soon to be even talking about how serious he was, but instead the two of them just nodded politely and waited for Ayesha to continue.

'So, his aunt lives in a gorgeous villa on Miramar Beach. That, by the way ladies, is one of the most affluent areas of Goa.' She looked at them smugly and Lisa wished she could be honest with her friend. She didn't want to see her getting hurt.

'And get this! They have this huge villa, with a private pool and the most gorgeous, perfectly manicured, landscaped gardens,' continued Ayesha fervently, totally oblivious of her friends' expressions. 'Oh, and they have about half a dozen helpers in the house, including a butler and a diving instructor. His aunt was really nice too: she was wearing a lovely Satya Paul saree and the most enormous solitaires you have ever seen. Very chic and...'

'Ayesha, we don't want to hear about his mother's friend for God's sake,' said Sameera, unable to control herself any longer and wondering why on earth Ayesha was rambling on about all this. 'Tell us about him!'

'Oh him!' said Ayesha as though the thought hadn't even struck her. 'Well, after a round of drinks at his aunt's place, he took me to this really exclusive seafood restaurant right on the beach and we had lobster and champagne for dinner. Just like Hollywood.' She grinned at them and sighed. 'Then we went for a walk on the beach. He's really romantic,' she added dreamily, 'and loaded. He's from Delhi too and he works in the family business. You see his father's a business tycoon. He's got stakes in various businesses, pharmaceuticals, real estate, steel – you name it! His mother's very well known in Delhi's social circuit and is a regular on Page 3. They have a huge bungalow in Vasant Vihar and Vinny's paternal grandfather...'

'We don't want to know about his paternal grandfather, Ayesha! We want to know about him!' interrupted Sameera again as Ayesha stared at her as though she was quite a dimwit.

'I am telling you about him!'

'I mean him. Not his family history.' Sameera tried not to roll her eyes.

'Well, if you mean what colour underwear he wears and whether he snores when asleep, well, I don't know yet, okay!' She looked exasperated. 'Suffice it to say that he's one of the best guys to have crossed my path recently.'

'Well, I still think it's too early for you to pass a sweeping statement like that.' This time Sameera couldn't stop herself. 'Anyway, since we don't seem to be agreeing, let's change the subject please. How was your evening, Lisa? Did Ronit show you a good time?'

There was a short, awkward silence before Lisa answered her friend's question.

'It was a very pleasant evening,' she admitted at last with a sigh. 'He's a thorough gentleman. But I can't help feeling guilty about the fact that I concealed it from Karan.' Lisa seemed distressed and her friends looked at her in concern. 'That's the one thing I've never done before. We may have had fights; we may not have always agreed with each other, but we've never lied to each other. Karan and I have always had a very transparent relationship, and even though this was just a casual, completely platonic dinner, somehow, I don't think I can tell him about it. I don't think he'd understand.'

'I hate to say I told you so, but I told you so.' Sameera smiled at Lisa and shook her head.

'Do me a favour Sameera, will you?' Lisa pushed her half-eaten sandwich back into the brown paper bag and wrung her hands together as though she were pleading. 'Please don't give me a hard time. I've been beating myself over it enough already, and of course, concealing it from Karan makes it even worse. But no, guilty as hell though it makes me, I won't be telling him about this.'

'But Lisa, why not?' persisted Ayesha. 'You didn't do anything wrong. All you did was go out for dinner. You've got nothing to hide. Karan is a progressive, open-minded man. I'm sure he'll be reasonable about it.'

Lisa sighed and looked out of the window at the passing fields.

'You don't understand. I don't want to upset him.' She turned back to her friends and even through her sunglasses, they could clearly see the distress in her eyes. 'I've been agonizing over it, wondering what to do since last night! We've been going through such a rough time lately that the smallest thing seems to trigger off a misunderstanding. Things have been so stressful and strained recently. Telling him about this dinner would be pushing it too far.'

'I guess I see your point,' said Ayesha. 'Anyway, research says that only about twenty-seven per cent couples are even remotely honest with each other. Don't fret so much, Lisa. It's not a big deal.'

'I know.' Lisa dusted the sandwich crumbs off her clothes and smoothed down her skirt. 'It's just that, whatever research says, we're usually honest with each other.'

'Well, I agree with you. It may be better to say nothing at this stage. But then, I guess love and guilt usually go together. But don't be so hard on yourself. You didn't do anything wrong.' Sameera squeezed her friend's hand as the car suddenly screeched to a halt and the driver turned around in his seat to smile at them.

'Panjim,' he announced as he swung open the door and jumped out. They didn't know it but he'd quite enjoyed listening to the friendly banter between the three friends. It was a welcome change from the usual tourists who couldn't stop asking endless questions about where to eat and where to shop and which beach was the least crowded. It had been a very pleasant drive.

As Karan waited for Vivek in the bar at the Crowne Plaza hotel that evening, he wondered what was taking his boss so long. Vivek was usually a stickler for punctuality and he was rarely, if ever, late. Karan glanced at his watch and clicked his tongue impatiently as he realized that he would probably miss the better part of the match. It was an India-Sri Lanka final match and he'd been looking forward to watching it. He'd even made arrangements to stay at the house in DLF that night so that he could get home early and watch the match in peace. When his boss had called him in and said that he needed to discuss their strategy for the next quarter that evening, Karan had assumed that they would do it in the office. But then Vivek had mentioned that he needed to go home first and had suggested that they meet for a drink somewhere. Vivek liked to take his core team out occasionally and usually Karan enjoyed it, but today he just wanted to go home, kick his shoes off, and watch the match. Well, it seemed like that wouldn't be happening tonight he thought, as he switched on his laptop and asked the waiter to bring him a glass of chilled water.

When Vivek finally walked into the bar, it was almost eight-thirty and he was nearly an hour late. Karan had given up the plan to watch the match by then but he still wanted to go home and relax. It had been a long day. But Vivek was so sorry about being late and he apologized so profusely that Karan just smiled and waved off his apologies. In fact, Karan appreciated Vivek's humbleness and knew that a lot of bosses wouldn't have apologized at all. He smiled at Vivek warmly and ordered a stiff Martini for him. He knew it was his boss's favourite drink. He asked for a glass of red wine for himself and then the waiter handed them the food menus as Vivek chuckled.

'This will probably ruin my appetite for dinner and then I'll never hear the end of it from Ria. But I am kind of peckish, so let's order something light. What will you have Karan?'

'Anything, Sir. As long as it's healthy.' Karan grinned at his boss and Vivek laughed again as they studied the menus carefully.

'Yes, well it never hurts to be a bit careful about food choices. How about a Mezze Platter? And a portion of this Smoked Salmon with Asparagus?'

'Sounds great!' agreed Karan, enthusiastically. They placed the order with the waiter, closed the menus, and sat back in the comfortable couches to begin their discussion.

Their meeting went on for about an hour and a half and when they finally wound up, Vivek was very pleased with their discussion. They'd discussed their manpower planning for the next three months as well as sales target and key clients to focus on. Karan had made some pretty interesting suggestions, and Vivek was happy that they'd come out instead of doing it in the office. He said as much to Karan as they paid the bill and got up to leave.

'Coming here was a good idea. We should do it more often,' he commented as they made their way to the hotel foyer. 'It can get pretty stifling in the office.' They asked for their respective cars and Vivek smiled at Karan warmly as they waited.

'You're one of my best guys. I usually don't say it to anyone but I know I can trust you enough to be upfront with you. Mark my words, one day you're going to be the youngest vice president in this industry.'

'Thank you, Sir,' said Karan, looking a bit embarrassed at his boss's lavish praise. 'I appreciate it. I try to put in my best.'

'I know you do,' agreed Vivek at once. 'I really value your sincerity. I'm sorry you had to wait so long today. Actually, my wife was at work and I needed to pick the kids up from a birthday party.'

'That's fine, Sir,' smiled Karan. 'It's nice to see a father who's so involved with his kids. What does Mrs. Khanna do?'

'Oh, Ria's a jewellery designer. I'm sure you've heard of Ritu Bhalla. Well, she works with her. They get featured on NDTV Good Times very often. Not your typical corporate job but very interesting and challenging, nevertheless. Ria works very hard and she's very talented and enormously creative. My life would be dull as dishwater if it weren't for her. I would be stuck in boardrooms and conferences all day but thanks to her, I do get to go to some of the best parties in town and meet some of the biggest celebrities in the country. I'm very proud of her.'

The pride was palpable in his voice and suddenly, Karan couldn't help thinking about Lisa and his awful comments about her job a few months ago. How could he have been so insensitive? He'd made rude and thoughtless comments about her work; he'd dismissed her talent just because he didn't think it was what a proper job should be like. But then, he'd always been a quintessential corporate guy. His father was a businessman; all his uncles were businessmen or in conservative professions, and Karan had grown up amidst conversations on profit and loss, conferences and meetings. After completing his Bachelors in Commerce, he'd done his MBA from one of the best business schools in the US, and landed a perfect job with a multinational healthcare company soon after. He'd worked in the US for a couple of years and moved back to India when his mother had started complaining about being too lonely. He'd tried working with his dad for a bit but that hadn't worked out, and he'd gotten into consulting right after that. It had been the perfect decision. He was made for consulting. He loved the deadlines, he was passionate about the pressure, and no one felt the adrenaline like he did when they got a new project. But he'd never been able to understand unconventional professions like music, writing or art. Ironically, he'd fallen in love with Lisa. Lisa with her eccentric ways and her unusual habits. She would get up in the middle of the night and listen to a song that she insisted had been on her mind all day; she would stop in the middle of a dusty street to admire a piece of pottery that seemed quite ordinary to Karan. Lisa was one of the most extraordinary people Karan had ever met and he'd instantly fallen head over heels in love with her. They'd been the perfect example of opposites attracting. And yet he'd failed to understand and admire her for the very thing that had attracted him to her in the first place. Karan felt very guilty as he thought about it now, and he suddenly wished that Lisa was around so he could run home and apologize to her immediately. He was hardly listening to his boss anymore and he nodded mutely at something he was saying about some project he wanted to send a quote for.

Just then Vivek's black Mercedes appeared up the driveway followed by Karan's silver Toyota Camry. The drivers got out and saluted smartly as Vivek turned to pat Karan on the back.

'Well, Karan, I enjoyed our evening. I'll see you in the office tomorrow. Say hi to Lisa when you speak to her. How is she by the way?'

'Having fun in Goa,' answered Karan as Vivek got into his car and grinned.

'Things have certainly changed. My wife and I can't even fathom going on a vacation without each other. But I guess you young, modern couples are different. Well, good night!'

□

A healthy debate

The next day dawned bright and sunny again. The sea was a bit rough though so the girls had to drop their plan to go parasailing, and after a bit of conferring, they decided to relax in the hotel that day. They were all tired out after the sightseeing of the previous day, and didn't feel like doing anything too strenuous. Some downtime was always a welcome respite. That was the best part of staying in a good hotel; there was always enough to do. Sameera and Ayesha wanted to go for a swim in the pool and just laze around, but Lisa was keen on checking out the spa. She enjoyed getting a massage every now and then and the spa at their hotel was famed for its Aromatherapy massage. So she called the spa manager immediately after breakfast to make a reservation. Luckily, they managed to squeeze her in for an eleven o'clock slot despite such short notice. She was glad she was getting the opportunity to relax a little since she hardly ever got time for such luxuries in Delhi.

At a quarter to eleven, she changed into her dressing gown and a comfortable pair of slippers, and took the elevator to the lower level of the lobby where the spa was located. The welcoming sound of water trickling down from a fountain and the heady aroma of jasmine and sandalwood were almost instantly relaxing. A soft-spoken, serene-looking therapist in a spotless white uniform, led her into one of the softly lit massage rooms and offered her a cup of mint tea. It was all so wonderfully calming and tranquil that it was hard to believe that there was a bustling world that existed beyond all this serenity. As she took off her dressing gown and lay down on the bed, Lisa couldn't help thinking about the massage Karan had given her when they'd gone to Bangkok years ago. He was always so gentle, yet knew just the correct amount of pressure to apply, and she had teasingly told him that he had magic in his hands. It had been a very sensual experience and she smiled as she remembered their ardent love-making afterwards. That had been the perfect grand finale. Breaking her reverie, the therapist entered the room and dimmed the lights. This was going to pale in comparison, she thought as she closed her eyes and sighed.

She joined her friends back at the pool at twelve-thirty after the massage. There hadn't been any grand finale obviously but she did feel admittedly more refreshed and rejuvenated, and for the first time in weeks, she really felt that she had absolutely no knots in any part of her usually exhausted body. She laughed to herself as she thought about it and then waved to her friends when she spotted them. They were lounging around in the comfortable deck chairs by the pool and sipping fresh orange juice.

'Hey you,' said Sameera, waving her over to where they were waiting, 'the massage seems to have done you a world of good! You're looking positively radiant!'

'I know! The spa was amazing! After the massage, they even did a Body Composition Analysis for me and a Dermalogical Face Mapping Analysis…'

'Okay, okay! Don't go on for hours, will you?' interrupted Ayesha. 'Speaking for myself, I have to admit that I prefer lounging around here and checking out all the hot guys in their swimwear to lying face down on a massage bed, allowing some random woman to practice her tricks on my poor, unsuspecting body. Really Lisa, haven't you heard of all the awful cases of infections that are caught in spas? Why, according to a survey…'

'You and your surveys!' Lisa pretended to look outraged and then grinned sportingly at her friend. 'Well, my research says that pools are the worst breeding grounds for infections. Yet you spend hours here.'

'How about some lunch?' Sameera intervened before they could get into an argument. 'It's almost a quarter to one and I'm famished. I haven't eaten anything besides the measly bowl of cornflakes I ate for breakfast. Now that Lisa's had her massage and you've checked out all the available hot guys around, can you please do something about feeding this undernourished, starving friend of yours?' She pretended to swoon and they all laughed.

'Let's try the Chinese restaurant today,' suggested Ayesha as they collected their things and picked up their bags. 'Oh, we forgot to ask you Lisa! What happened with Ronit? I saw you talking to him this morning.'

'Yes, we bumped into each other on the way to breakfast and he asked me out again.' Lisa looked matter-of-fact as she put on her sunglasses. 'He's a nice guy and harmless enough, but I told him I couldn't go out with him anymore. I know he was just being friendly; after all he knows I'm married. Yes, hurt and disappointed with the current state of my relationship and even a bit cynical and bitter perhaps, but married nevertheless. And you guys know that I would never deliberately do anything to hurt Karan.'

'What did he say then?' asked Ayesha curiously.

'He said he knew I would turn him down.'

'Why ask you out then?' asked Ayesha in surprise.

Lisa smiled, 'he said it's bad manners not to ask a lady out again the second time and I would have been offended if he hadn't.'

All three girls started laughing. 'That's so adorable. He really is charming,' admitted Sameera then as they started walking towards the restaurant.

Back in Delhi, when Karan got home at eight-thirty, he was in good spirits. It had been a productive day at work and he'd managed to squeeze in a great workout in the gym later. His father waved to him from the living room. He was pleased too since he'd managed to bag an important order that day and he said as much to his son who congratulated him warmly with a hug and a thumbs up. He then stopped to greet his mother. She was in the dining room, bickering with the maid.

'Why have you taken out this old dinner set?' she admonished. 'My Puttar is staying with us after so long; take out that new Donna Karan dinner set that my sister had brought. And remember we are business people, we have a certain standard, and do not use such old things in our house. You should know better! That crook of an agent told me you were trained!'

The maid looked at her employer sulkily and then disappeared into the kitchen, muttering to herself.

'Maids these days, I tell you!' exclaimed Anju Chopra, looking shocked at the girl's impudence. 'Totally ungrateful! This girl came here with two suits and now look how much she has accumulated, thanks to me. I saved her from a life of penury! And see how she behaves! Oh, for the days when maids were subservient and humble. Oh, hello Puttar!'

She turned to smile at Karan who was staring at the food spread out on the dinner table, looking horrified. The crumb-fried chicken, creamy potato salad and thickly buttered garlic bread looked like it was all laden with calories and saturated fats. The sight of it almost made him shudder.

'Are you happy now, Puttar? Look I made salaad for you!' She waved to the potato salad with a flourish. 'I don't even know how to cook this continental stuff that you seem to have become so fond of but I tried for you, Puttar. Mrs. Luthra's daughter was visiting and she gave me these recipes.'

Karan sighed. It was no wonder that his father had a cholesterol problem. 'Mom, potato salad layered with cream and mayonnaise is not healthy,' he explained, trying to stay patient. 'This is not just about me. You need to take care of Dad and yourself too. Look at how much weight you've put on! You need to be more careful.'

'I am careful. In fact, I am very careful. I have even been going for a walk everyday like you told me.'

'Well, that's rather astonishing since you don't seem to have lost any weight,' commented Karan, looking surprised.

'It takes time, Puttar,' said his mother with a beatific smile. 'It takes a lot of patience and perseverance.'

'Yes, but you should have lost some,' persisted Karan. 'Look at Neelam Chachi, for instance. I hear she's joined a gym, and she goes for yoga thrice a week. She's lost a lot of weight recently.'

'Neelam! She hasn't lost all that weight just by exercising. She's obviously been doing something else,' said his mother, looking extremely irritated. She never had liked that Neelam. She was always trying to outdo her in that sweet, oily manner of hers.

'Doing something? Like what?' asked Karan in bewilderment.

'How should I know!' snapped his mother. 'Pills, liposuction. The options are limitless these days. Now will you please stop complaining and eat your dinner? I have tried my best and you all know that this maid is completely useless!' She moaned on then for a few minutes about these untrained girls who didn't even know how to say "Good Morning" and "Good Evening" or make a decent cup of tea, but expected to be paid whatever they demanded. 'Oh, ho, himmat toh dekho! Utterly useless!' she repeated, even more emphatically this time.

'No, she isn't,' disagreed Karan's father then. He couldn't stop himself anymore. 'She's a good, honest girl but you practically treat her like a slave! These days you can't treat your house-help that way. You have to be kind and considerate. That's the only way to earn their loyalty and respect.'

'Acha?' demanded Anju Chopra, furious at being openly criticized in front of Karan, 'Name one person who does that.'

'Well, Lisa for instance,' said her husband without hesitation. 'She treats her maid well. Lisa's much younger than you Anju, but I have to say that she manages her house and a career very well. You could actually learn quite a lot from your daughter-in-law but I guess that goes against your pride. Anyway, I'm fed up of calling the agency and requesting that idiotic Babloo, who calls himself the manager, to send a maid every time you throw one out or she decides she can't endure your slavery anymore. So, you'd better watch yourself.'

'Anyway Mom, I can't eat this,' said Karan, trying to get a word in. 'I can't undo all the good I've done in the gym. Can you make me a banana milkshake instead? And please remember to use skimmed milk.' For a moment, he couldn't help thinking about the fit he'd thrown when Lisa had forgotten to stock up on quinoa a few months ago. Why had he been so difficult? It had been a minor oversight but he'd created such a scene.

'Skimmed milk! Tastes like dishwater, it does!' His mother's voice snapped him out of his thoughts.

'Anju, stop it!' Karan's father looked at his wife with exasperation. 'Karan is right. You do need to lose a lot of weight. Now make him his milkshake and stop this squabbling.'

Anju Chopra glared at him and heaved her ample self up from her chair. 'Don't lecture me! First look at yourself. Who goes to the club and eats lachcha parathas and gulab jamuns every Friday? Theek hai, from tomorrow you will only get cornflakes and dry toast for breakfast. I will also show you what I can do.' With that, she wagged her finger at her husband, made a face at both of them, turned on her heel, and stomped off to the kitchen to make a banana milkshake for Karan. Karan and his father looked at each other and had to stuff their mouths with their handkerchiefs to avoid bursting into peals of laughter as they listened to the angry sound of the mixer being turned on.

'Dare I remind her to use skimmed milk?' asked Karan in a whisper, but his father shook his head at once.

'I think you should just let it go for the moment,' he answered wisely and Karan agreed. He didn't want to spoil his mood either. The next day was Saturday and he was looking forward to getting away with his friends. Admittedly, he was thankful that he wasn't going to be home for the weekend. As much as he loved his mother, the last thing he wanted to do was to put up with her continuous complaining and ghee-soaked food all weekend.

Expectedly, the weekend passed by in a flash for both of them. On Saturday morning, Karan and his friends left for Dam Dama. He'd called Lisa just before they left and she'd reminded him to leave his laptop behind. She wanted him to forget about work for a couple of days. Knowing Karan, she was worried that he might go for the trip dressed in a crisp suit and tie and she said as much to him when they spoke on the phone.

'Don't worry, I've banished all my suits to the darkest corner of my wardrobe,' he assured her and they laughed. 'But thank you, Lisa. You don't know how much I appreciate this initiative of yours. It was so thoughtful of you.'

Lisa felt a bit mortified at his words as she remembered her real motive. She was still glad she'd thought of the idea of course, but she wished she could have been more upfront with her husband. Anyhow, at least her plan had worked. Karan was going to be away for the weekend, away from her mother-in-law's constant complaining, and that was all that mattered. And wasn't there a famous saying: 'The end justifies the means.'

On Saturday morning, Lisa and her friends went to see the Basilica of Bom Jesus in old Goa, the church famous for holding the mortal remains of St Francis Xavier. The architecture was in the baroque style, distinguished by richly sculpted surfaces. The church was renowned for being a UNESCO world heritage site. They spent a very pleasant morning in the church, marvelling at the marble floor inlaid with precious stones, the elaborate gilded altars, and the simple but elegant interiors. Their guide, an old and knowledgeable man with a very pleasant voice, was extremely well informed about the history of the church and the girls listened to him in rapt attention.

'The mausoleum, on the top of which is placed the silver casket with the body of St Francis Xavier, was the gift of the last of the Medicis, Cosimo III, the Grand Duke of Tuscany,' he said reverently.

Just then, they saw a group of scantily dressed women being given shawls at the entrance of the church by an austere-looking woman.

'The church has a very strict dress code,' their guide informed them.

'No shorts, for instance,' added Sameera, looking at Ayesha pointedly. They'd had a squabble in the morning about this. Ayesha had worn shorts and Sameera had flatly refused to go to a place of worship with her dressed like that. In the end, Ayesha had changed into jeans but only after a very heated argument. Now she had the grace to look sheepish and even mouthed an apology to her friend as they all trooped up to the upper level, overlooking the tomb.

'Here you will see the Bom Jesus Basilica art gallery containing the works of the Goan surrealist painter Dom Martin,' said the guide with a proud flourish. 'And after this, I will tell you where to go for the best seafood lunch in town.'

Sunday passed quite uneventfully other than a hysterical phone call from Milind who'd predictably managed to forget that Lisa was on holiday. Needless to say, he wasn't amused when Lisa reminded him that he himself had approved her leave.

'How in hell am I supposed to manage without you for two whole weeks?' he shouted on the phone. 'That famous theatre actress is arriving from London a week earlier and has agreed to an interview, God bless her! She never gives interviews and we've managed to get one! Great for our image to say the least! And…'

'Milind, Milind, relax!' Lisa almost wanted to laugh at how vague and absent-minded he was but she didn't dare. 'Don't worry! Preeti's taking care of things while I'm out. I briefed her really well before I left.'

'Yes, but that new girl, what's her name, Judy or something, she had the nerve to tell me that she didn't like the column I gave her! She wanted something more meaningful! Can you believe that? She's far from ready to be unleashed! Does she even realize how lucky she is to be given a chance to work at Diva? You'd better come and sort her out.'

In the end it took a while, but Lisa managed to calm him down and promised that she'd take care of everything as soon as she got back. 'In fact, you should take a vacation too,' she suggested to him. 'You work too hard. No wonder you're so nervy.'

'When did you say you're back?' asked Milind, completely ignoring her suggestion about a vacation. 'Next Monday, right? I'd better write it down before I forget again. And don't forget to speak to Preeti about the interview.' He hung up almost as abruptly as he'd called, and Lisa grinned at her friends who were looking on in amusement. 'Welcome to my world,' she remarked to them as she shook her head and started dialling Preeti's number.

By the time Sunday evening rolled in, both of them could easily say that they'd had a fabulous weekend. Karan, in fact, was totally geared up for the week ahead and was really glad that he'd taken the break. Even though he wished he could extend the short break by a couple of more days, he was feeling refreshed and happy. In fact, he was in such a good mood that even the bumper to bumper traffic on the highway on the way back didn't bother him, and he was actually humming to himself when he finally parked his car outside his parents' house.

□

Missing the tender touch

The next morning was unusually gloomy in Goa. There had been a thunderstorm the previous night and the sky was overcast and cloudy in the morning. And as though to match the general mood of the weather, Lisa woke up feeling hellish. She had a scratchy throat and knew it was because of all that ice-cold beer she'd had with dinner the previous night. It never did agree with her and just as she'd expected, by the time they returned to the room after breakfast, she had a runny nose, aching body and a sore throat. The three girls had made plans to go for lunch to Fort Aguada that day but Lisa knew she wasn't up to it. She shook her head weakly when they discussed it after breakfast.

'I can't,' she said, 'I'm really not feeling well.' She didn't mention it but she knew she was running a temperature as well. 'No, no, you guys go ahead,' she protested when they offered to stay back with her. 'All I need is some rest. I'll be right as rain by this evening.' She smiled at them bravely and pushed them out the door, promising to call if she needed anything.

After Sameera and Ayesha had left, Lisa took a couple of paracetamol tablets and went straight to bed. She tried to sleep but the body ache and sore throat kept her awake. In the end, she gave up and just lay there, staring up at the ceiling. Lunch time came and went. She thought about ordering in some soup but didn't feel like it. Her throat hurt too much. Her body ached too. She closed her burning eyes as she sank further into the cool comfort of the soft double duvet and turned over on her side.

She missed Karan. She missed his comforting presence when she wasn't well. She tried not to think about the time when he'd cancelled all his meetings and stayed home because she'd come down with a raging fever and stomach flu last winter. He'd made her chicken soup himself and stayed with her all day checking her temperature and bathing her head with cold towels.

She thought back to the time when she'd fractured her ankle last year. She remembered how he'd been beside himself with worry for her and how he'd made sure that he was there to help her get around, even accompanying her to the bathroom every time she needed to go. She thought about the way his brow creased with worry for her, the way he would stand by and wait so patiently and then gently try to coax her while she refused to take the medicine because it tasted nasty. She missed everything about him. She couldn't help it. After all, he was always so sweet when she was unwell and she suddenly yearned to have his arms around her. If only… she shook her head impatiently at her own childishness. This was utterly ridiculous! She was a grown woman after all, and should be able to take care of herself! Thank God her mother wasn't there, she would have just told her to grow up.

She couldn't believe she was pining for him like this. After all, she'd wanted to get away from him and so she had. This was what she'd wanted anyway, wasn't it? A break from him! And hadn't she declared just a few days ago that she couldn't bear the sight of him and didn't want to live with him anymore? Then what was this? It was so baffling! Lisa sighed and reached out for the glass of water on her bedside table. There was a medicinal taste in her mouth and even the water tasted acrid. She put the glass back on the table, turned off the light, shut her eyes and tried to go to sleep.

Mercifully, she felt almost like herself the next day. Her cold was gone, her fever was down, and she woke up feeling rested and refreshed. They had all slept in late that morning but the extra sleep seemed to have done them all a world of good. It was a lovely day and they were relieved that there was no sign of rain as they sat out on the patio, drinking tea till almost eleven. It was too late to go down to the restaurant for breakfast anyway since it had been cleared away half an hour ago. The girls were feeling lazy and didn't feel like rushing around, so they decided to indulge themselves and order room service for a change, even though it was chargeable. 'And please make it quick,' said Ayesha as she placed the order on the phone. 'We're all famished!'

Half an hour later, they were sitting around the small centre table, talking, eating and laughing, all at the same time. 'I think it's ridiculous what hotels do!' commented Ayesha as she attacked her cheese omelette. 'I mean, they should know that people come here to relax and rest and not adhere to some stupid old timetable. They should at least offer the option of a last breakfast. I mean, for God's sake, we're on holiday!'

Lisa and Sameera laughed at how indignant Ayesha sounded and helped themselves to more scrambled eggs and toast. 'So, I guess you guys had a good time yesterday,' commented Lisa, sprinkling pepper on her eggs. 'You got in quite late. What was it –almost ten – I think?'

'Yes, and I'm sorry about that, but Vinny absolutely insisted on taking us to dinner,' explained Ayesha with a sheepish smile. 'It would have been really rude to just refuse.'

'That's okay,' said Lisa, trying to be as understanding as she could and feeling very magnanimous about it. The truth was that she had felt a little hurt about being left alone all day, particularly since she hadn't been well, but since her friends apologized so profusely, she decided to be sporting about it. 'I understand. Hey, can you pass me the peanut butter please?' She held out her hand and Sameera pushed the jar towards her. Lisa dug her spoon into it and applied a generous amount on her toast. 'I'm not even hungry anymore – I had such a huge breakfast. But Karan and I both absolutely love peanut butter,' she paused to smile wistfully at her friends, 'particularly with our evening coffee. I always pack him peanut butter sandwiches when he's working late. Hey,' she said suddenly, 'maybe I should call his mother and ask her to send some sandwiches over to his office. He's working late today.'

'I think that's a great idea,' agreed Sameera. 'In fact, you should do it right away.'

'Thanks, Mom!' Karan put his laptop down and accepted a glass of water from the maid. It had been a productive day at work and he was in a decidedly better mood. He'd had a teleconference with Parag Kulkarni about the revised interim report they had sent last week and the man had finally cooled down a bit. Karan was just happy that things were looking up. In fact, he'd been feeling relaxed enough today to have even turned a blind eye when he'd caught the Business Development girls logging onto Facebook for the second time that morning. Facebook wasn't an offence in their office as it was in many other offices; it was just not encouraged. Karan, however, was of the opinion that social-networking sites were the bane of the new generation, and made it clear that the only networking site he ever used was LinkedIn. It was just one of the many things that he and Lisa, who was a self-confessed Facebook addict, strongly disagreed on.

'Thanks for what?' asked his mother then, looking up from the programme she was watching on TV. 'Even these celebrity chefs use butter,' she muttered as Karan glanced at the TV where a woman in a chef's apron was sautéing onions and garlic in dollops of butter. 'I don't even use half that quantity and yet I am always being criticized.' She shook her head, switched off the television and turned to her son. 'You were saying something, Puttar ?'

'Yes, I was thanking you. For the sandwiches.' He smiled at his mother and bent down to give her a hug. He had been feeling peckish that evening and the sandwiches had been a very pleasant surprise. 'They were super. I didn't realize that you knew how much I like peanut butter.'

'Well, then that shows how little you know,' commented his mother with a meaningful smile. 'Who knows her Puttar better than a mother?'

'That's not fair, Anju,' called out Prakash Chopra from the balcony. 'Don't take credit where it's not due.'

'What do you mean, Dad?' asked Karan as he took off his tie and his mother glared at his father. Interfering again, and that too with a cigarette in his hand! How she hated smokers! She'd vowed never to marry one, but Karan's father had charmed her with his good looks and money, and somehow smoking hadn't seemed like such a serious vice then. Besides, he'd claimed that he was more a social smoker and would give up quite easily. That day, however, still hadn't come, and Anju Chopra would never forgive him for this one thing. She gave him a disdainful look, which he chose to ignore, as he took another puff of his cigarette and looked pointedly at Karan.

'Lisa called in the morning and asked your mother to send you your favourite sandwiches. She said you always carry a snack to the office when you work late since you get hungry in the evening. So, she's the one you should be thanking.'

Anju Chopra couldn't believe her husband's unfairness. You'd think he could have shown more loyalty towards his wife! But no, he was always doing things she didn't like, always praising that Lisa, always – always!

Usually she didn't like making a mountain out of a molehill but today she was very upset with him and made up her mind to talk to him after dinner. He should know better than to always sing that girl's praises, that too in front of Karan. But what to do if apna sikka hi khota hai? Karan had always been too starry-eyed about her anyway – that's why he never saw how irresponsible and disrespectful she was. And what was so great about what she had done anyway? All she had done was to pick up the phone and call her, but it had been her – Anju – who had made and packed the sandwiches for her darling son. She had even had to request and cajole that stupid grocer to send the peanut butter since there had been none in the house. He'd flatly refused to deliver just one thing and she'd needlessly had to order all those juices and cold drinks just so he delivered the stupid peanut butter. But who cared about her effort? She was very upset and was going to make her displeasure obvious, so she pursed her lips and decided that she would not talk to anyone all through dinner. She would not even take a second helping of jelly and custard even though it was her favourite dessert.

Meanwhile, back in his room, Karan was surprised and touched that Lisa had called his mother about the sandwiches. It was a small thing, but it meant a lot to him. It meant she thought about him even when she wasn't around. It was a very sweet gesture and he picked up the phone to call and thank her as soon as he was out of the shower. She answered on the third ring and he could tell that even though she was enjoying herself with her friends, she was happy to hear from him.

'It's no big deal.' She waved his thanks away when he mentioned the sandwiches.

'Well, it was very thoughtful of you,' he remarked. 'I was just about to order something terribly unhealthy from the deli next door when the peon informed me about the sandwiches. I always get a runny stomach when I eat from that place. The sandwiches were a godsend.'

They both laughed and then chatted easily for a minute about nothing in particular. 'So how was your day?' he asked her. 'What did you girls do today?'

'Nothing much. Sameera and I spent the whole day by the pool. And then we went to the Lobster Shack at the Taj for a drink in the evening. Ayesha was out with this guy she's been dating.'

'That certainly sounds like Ayesha,' laughed Karan. 'Trust her to find someone as soon as she lands anywhere new. So, did you and Sameera have fun?'

'Oh, sure,' said Lisa. 'The Lobster Shack is lovely. I tried their grilled shark and it wasn't bad at all. It tasted just like fish – quite ordinary in fact. I don't understand what all the fuss is about. And the pool is always fun. The sun here is pretty strong though.'

'Well, make sure your skin doesn't burn,' warned her husband immediately. 'You know how sensitive it is.'

She smiled at his words and then suddenly slapped her forehead with her hand. 'Oh, no! Now that you mentioned it, I suddenly remembered! I've run out of sunscreen and tomorrow we're going to Anjuna beach. I forgot to pack a spare bottle and I've even forgotten my after-sun lotion. And my brand's not available here.'

'Oh, but I packed both for you,' replied Karan at once. 'Didn't you see them when you unpacked?'

'No,' said Lisa in surprise. 'Where did you put them?'

'In the back pocket of your suitcase. With your return ticket,' answered her husband.

'Really? Wait a second. Let me see.' She put him on hold and hauled out her suitcase from under her bed. She flipped it open and checked the back pocket and sure enough, the sunscreen and lotion were both there, neatly tucked in with her return ticket and some emergency cash. Lisa was grinning from ear to ear as she pulled them out and picked up the phone to thank him.

'I found them. Thanks Karan. You're a lifesaver!'

'No problem,' he laughed. 'After all, I still remember what happened in Pattaya.'

They were quiet for a minute as the memory came rushing back to the both of them. They'd spent the day fooling around on the beach; the sun had been scorching and she'd forgotten to use sunscreen. Her skin had slowly turned from a healthy brown to a crispy red. Her nose and back had started peeling, and even half a bottle of calamine lotion hadn't helped. She had refused to step out even to have dinner and Karan had run around like a headless chicken looking for a round-the-clock pharmacy.

'Are you there?' His voice snapped her out of her thoughts and she blinked in surprise.

'Huh? Oh yeah, sure. Why?'

'Well, I was just checking whether you'd gone all teary and nostalgic for a minute,' he teased.

'You know me too well,' she admitted. 'But really, thanks Karan. This was really sweet of you.'

'My pleasure,' he said softly, and Lisa suddenly felt goose bumps rising up on her arms and legs. There was something very sexy about the way he had said it; it was almost as if he had caressed her with his words. She closed her eyes and could almost picture him, looking incredibly sexy in his tee shirt and boxer shorts, his hair still wet and slicked back from his evening shower. He was probably wearing the Paco Rabanne cologne he always sprayed on after his evening shower and… Oh, God! What was wrong with her? But if he still had that effect on her despite all their issues and after five – no – almost six years of being married, then it was certainly something to think about. Lisa suddenly realized that her legs were feeling a bit wobbly and she sat down on the bed to steady herself, silently chiding herself for not having better control. She noticed that Sameera had discarded the book she was reading and was, instead, focusing entirely on her conversation, giving her a very meaningful smile. Lisa made a face, threw a cushion at her friend and turned the other way, trying to focus on what Karan was saying. For a moment, she found herself feeling tongue-tied and didn't know quite what to say to him. Actually, she was surprised at herself. They weren't teenagers after all! This was utterly ridiculous.

'Well, you take care of yourself and remember to use the lotion.' His voice was warm and gentle and Lisa was just relieved that he'd broken the silence. The moment had passed and Lisa sighed. She wasn't ready to admit how much she was aching for him, and how badly she wanted to just throw her arms around him right then, and pull him into one of those deep, intense kisses that drove them both into a frenzy.

'I will,' she said, with a sigh. 'So, enough about me. How was your day?'

'Crazy as always. In fact, I just got home.'

'Now? Are you trying to kill yourself? That Parag guy still giving you a hard time?'

'Oh, he's a bit of a whiner, but things are better now.' He smiled into the phone then. 'Don't worry, I'm used to it. Goes with the territory.'

'But it's almost nine o'clock!' At least she didn't sound outraged since she wasn't home waiting for him.

'Well, I'm kind of unencumbered right now. I mean, you're not exactly home waiting for me, are you?' he said then, voicing his thoughts.

'No, but your mom is,' joked Lisa and they both laughed.

'It's not the same,' he said, suddenly wishing he could take her out to dinner that night. It had been so long since that wonderful evening at Banyan Tree. Before things had all gone horribly wrong. He sighed and decided to change the subject. 'Anyway, like I was saying, things are looking up as far as work is concerned. We've bagged a couple of projects and Vivek's in a better mood now. In fact, the management has organized a party for everyone tomorrow night to celebrate the company's fifteenth year in India. Vivek made the announcement today. I haven't seen him looking so pleased in a long time. He's particularly happy that we've done better than any of the other SBUs, China included.' Lisa chuckled at his words. Everyone knew that Karan's boss did not get along well with the President of the Chinese operations and both of them were constantly trying to outdo each other.

'That's nice,' she remarked, sounding pleased. 'Well, enjoy the party.'

'I'll try,' laughed her husband. 'I'm sure Vivek will hunt me out even there and try to discuss work. Most people will be coming with their spouses though.'

'I guess I'll be missing all the fun then,' said Lisa softly. She paused and he suddenly realized that the last few days had indeed been lonely without her. There was a long silence before either of them spoke. Lisa sighed and smiled into the phone. 'Well, I'll call you tomorrow,' she promised. 'You take care and don't stay up too late. Get some sleep.'

'I will. Goodnight sweetheart.' He'd used the endearment after ages, and this time, Lisa couldn't stop the tears as they hung up, both of them lost in their thoughts.

Meanwhile, not surprisingly, things were not as cozy in the senior Chopras' bedroom. After they had finished dinner and Karan's father had retired to his bedroom, Anju Chopra had turned off the lights and sat in the dark living room, thinking of everything she wanted to say to her husband. She would certainly give him a piece of her mind. After all, you'd think he would be more grateful to her and would appreciate her more after the way she had committed herself to him, his house and the children. She had never been like the girls these days, who fought with their husbands all the time, went off for vacations without them, and expected them to do the housework too. And so, when Anju Chopra walked into the bedroom ten minutes later, she was, as expected, in a very uncompromising state of mind. She was not in the mood to agree with anything or anyone. She was a good wife and mother and that was all that mattered. So she pursed her lips, crossed her arms in front of her chest and looked at her husband questioningly.

Prakash Chopra didn't want to get into a discussion but he knew that his wife would not rest until she had her say. He sighed as he put his book away and patted the other side of the bed.

'Come, sit Anju. You look a little upset. Is everything ok?'

'Oh ho, dekho toh! You don't even know what I am talking about? I am referring to the fact that you are always taking that girl's side. She who cannot even make decent kaali daal, and who leaves her hard-working husband here and takes off for a vacation without him! As it is, Karan is enamoured with her; he thinks she walks on water! Then on top of that, you also...'

'No, Anju! This is not about taking sides,' said Karan's father immediately. He was a fair person and wasn't going to agree with her. 'Lisa is a good girl. Karan must appreciate her.'

'Acha! And have you ever appreciated me?' retorted Anju Chopra hotly. 'Double standards toh dekho!'

'Come on, Anju,' said Prakash Chopra, shaking his head. 'You should be happy that your son has a good wife. He could do a lot worse. Be fair to your daughter-in-law.'

'I am always fair to her,' answered Anju Chopra, closing her eyes. That usually meant that she was going to be stubborn and implacable. 'Never have I been accused of unfairness, never! I am always fair and just and...'

'Then you are the only one who thinks so,' interrupted her husband. 'Anyway, I don't want to get into an argument, Anju. Since you don't want to be reasonable, can we please stop discussing this?' And with that, Karan's father turned the other way and switched on the TV as his wife clicked her tongue in irritation.

'Fine! I am not interested in arguing either. I can see that it is no use trying to make you see sense. Do whatever you want but always remember that it is not good to allow your daughter-in-law to sit on your head like this. One day you will agree with me, but by then it will probably be too late.'

With that, she sighed heavily and closed her eyes again, as though resigning herself to her fate.

□

The pull of the nuptial tie

In Goa, the next day started nice and early for the three friends. After a quick dip in the pool and a hurried Continental breakfast, they set off for Anjuna Beach. The drive was smooth and uneventful, and they managed to make it in good time. It was a blazing day and the heat hit them almost as soon as they got out of the air-conditioned car. The sun was even stronger than usual, and Lisa was just thankful that Karan had remembered to pack her sunscreen and sun lotion for her. She'd remembered to slather on as much sunscreen as she could all over her face and arms before leaving the hotel, so she was in good shape and spirits as they gathered up their things and walked towards the beach. Despite the intense heat, it was rapidly filling up with locals and tourists alike, and it was clear that finding a place was going to be a challenge.

'I don't understand what's so special about Goa!' grumbled Ayesha, 'it seems the whole world is flocking to here!'

'Yeah, including you,' commented Lisa as she craned her neck to try and find a place. Sameera's sharp eyes finally spotted an empty patch and she pounced on it at once. It was a nice little shaded nook under a huge palm tree, and the girls were delighted with this stroke of luck as they spread out their things on the sand.

'We should have come the day before yesterday. At least it wasn't so hot,' remarked Ayesha, squinting in the strong sunlight. She rootled around in her bag and pulled out her sunglasses.

'It's okay,' said Sameera casually. 'Don't let the heat bother you. Speaking for myself, I'd like to just laze on the beach and maybe try out the water sports.'

So they spent the next couple of hours just lounging around, soaking in the atmosphere, and trying out the parasailing and water scooties that were so popular among the tourists. It was fun and even though Ayesha, who wasn't much of a sports enthusiast, grumbled that this wasn't exactly her idea of fun and mentioned that she would have been better off having lunch at some expensive restaurant with Vinny – all in all – it was fun to just be together and relax.

Afterwards, they went to a cozy little Italian restaurant for lunch. It was small but clean, and famous for its pastas and thin-crust pizzas. The girls ordered wine and linguine with white clam sauce, and lots of garlic bread. The food was very good, and the combination of sun and wine made them all feel drowsy. After lunch they sauntered languidly back to the beach and found another shaded spot to sit in for a while.

'Why am I so listless?' muttered Sameera, closing her eyes. 'I shouldn't have drunk so much wine. I think I'll take a nap.'

Ayesha made a face. 'Now, that's what I call a waste of a perfectly good afternoon. Don't be so boring! Hey, guess what?' She glanced at her friends conspiratorially and leaned forward. 'I hear there's a party on here tonight. You know, like a proper rave party. That firang told me all about it. Want to give it a shot?'

Sameera's eyes snapped open and she and Lisa stared at Ayesha disbelievingly. 'Not unless we want to risk getting arrested,' said Sameera at last. 'Are you crazy? There will probably be drugs and God only knows what else! We could get into trouble.'

'Oh, don't be such a fuddy-duddy!' Ayesha looked annoyed as she rolled her eyes and shrugged. 'What's the big deal? We're not making it into a lifestyle, are we now? Besides, don't we always say that we should experience everything in life? How can we come to Goa and not attend even one rave party? As it is, you guys booked us in a hotel in sleepy old south Goa where nothing ever happens!' She looked accusingly at Sameera and scowled. 'Everyone knows that only three categories of people stay in south Goa. Old people, people with small children and nuns!'

'That's not true and you know it,' retorted Sameera. 'South Goa is a lot cleaner than north Goa, and some of the finest hotels and resorts are in south Goa. It's way classier than some of the trash around here. And need I remind you that if we hadn't booked into that hotel, you wouldn't have met Vinny!'

'You have a point there,' laughed Ayesha, relenting a bit. 'But about this party, come on guys, we're here for a short while. Let's just throw caution to the winds and have fun for once.'

'We are having fun,' said Lisa firmly. 'But that doesn't mean that we have to go crazy. Speaking for myself, I'm not interested. However liberal my husband may be, I don't think he'd approve of this.'

'Well, then don't tell him,' said Ayesha with a shrug. 'What he doesn't know can't hurt him, can it? Fancy you talking like this Lisa, you're in the fashion industry after all!'

Lisa looked shocked at her suggestion and she turned to look at Sameera, who had shut her eyes again and was doing her best to ignore what she thought was Ayesha at her reckless worst.

'I'm sorry Ayesha, but Karan and I do not conceal things from each other,' she said finally. Her voice was firm. 'We have a very open, very transparent relationship, and I have no intention of lying to him for something as disgusting as this party you're talking about.'

'Really?' Ayesha pretended to look surprised and she tilted her head to one side as she spoke. 'Then why didn't you tell him that you went out for dinner with Ronit? That didn't look all that transparent to me,' she demanded.

'That was the one and only time, and I intend to keep it that way,' retorted Lisa.

Ayesha rolled her eyes. 'Come on, Lisa! It's not even like you and Karan are in the best phase of your relationship right now. He's the husband you said was unreasonable, boring, conservative.' She ticked the words off her fingers. 'Remember? You said so yourself! What's all the hullabaloo about now? Why are you playing loyal wifey when we all know that the whole purpose of this vacation was to get away from your dreary life and boring husband?'

Sameera stared at Ayesha in total astonishment. She couldn't believe that she could be as callous as to actually have uttered those words. She had always been immature and silly, but she wasn't usually this insensitive. What had come over her? She glanced at Lisa who had gone red with anger.

'How dare you, Ayesha! I can't believe your nerve...'

'You're in a fine mood aren't you, Lisa?' Ayesha tittered again. 'I've never known you to be so grouchy. What's the problem? Is it the sex deprivation? But then, I thought you weren't getting a lot of that anyway for a while now, isn't it? You couldn't even recall the last time you guys did it when I asked you, remember?'

There was a pregnant silence. Sameera glanced at Lisa to see her friend's reaction. Lisa looked like she was frozen to the spot, almost as though she was too furious to trust herself to react. She stood there, clenching and unclenching her hands, and though her friends didn't know it, she was very close to tears. She could hardly believe that her friend could have been so insensitive. Finally, she shook her head and spoke to Ayesha in a low, cold voice: 'I can't believe you said the things that you just did. Anyhow, I don't think I even want to dignify that remark with a response, Ayesha. Now if you'll excuse me, I want to be on my own for a bit.'

After Lisa had walked away towards the other end of the beach, Sameera closed her eyes and pretended to be asleep. The last thing she wanted to do was to get into.an argument with Ayesha. Ayesha, on the other hand, was just itching to quarrel and tried talking to her a couple of times, but finally gave up when Sameera didn't respond. She scowled at her friend's ostensibly sleeping face, and then, switched on her I-pod and looked out at the sea. The water was a lovely, tranquil blue; it was a calm day and the waves were lapping gently against the shore. This part of the beach was quieter and there were hardly any people around since it was the middle of the afternoon. It was actually all very serene if you ignored the tension between the three girls. A couple of seabirds circled around in mid-air and then flew down to the beach, their bright eyes darting here and there in search of fish and other food. Ayesha watched them for a few minutes and then sighing, picked up her mobile and checked it for any missed calls or messages. There were none. Even Vinny hadn't called her. How awfully depressing! She leaned back against a tree and closed her eyes too, pulling up the volume on her I-phone. 'He stopped loving her today' by George Jones was hardly cheerful music, particularly after an argument, but then she wasn't in a very cheerful mood anyway.

It was a little after six o'clock when the girls left Anjuna Beach and headed back to their hotel. The atmosphere was still very tense among them, and Sameera's feeble attempts to normalize things as she glanced nervously at both her friends were mostly in vain. Lisa was quiet and withdrawn, which was characteristic of her when she was upset, and Ayesha seemed to have developed a permanent scowl as she steadfastly looked out of the window and sat with her back to her friends. They drove down in total silence, and Sameera heaved a sigh of immense relief when they finally pulled up outside the hotel and she stepped out of the car. It had been awfully stifling sitting between the two of them and she was glad to be out in the open. It was already seven o'clock and the early evening shadows were now stretching into dusk. Their resort looked warm and welcoming, and the girls were glad to be back.

'Fancy a coffee?' asked Sameera blithely as they walked across the open-air lobby. 'I sure could use one.'

'Okay,' said Ayesha who now seemed to be in a slightly better mood. She tied up her hair into a ponytail and sighed: 'As long as it's ice cold. It's like an inferno today, isn't it?'

'I think I'll go to the room if you don't mind,' Lisa said, turning to Sameera. 'I'm tired.'

'We've been sitting around all day,' remarked Ayesha. 'Why are you tired?'

'I need to take a shower. I'll see you later.' Lisa spoke directly to Sameera, ignoring Ayesha completely. Then she turned on her heel and walked away.

As soon as she got to her room, Lisa yanked off her tank top and wrap-around skirt and headed to the bathroom for a shower. She slammed the door behind her and stripped off her wet swim-suit, angrily squeezing the excess water out before she threw it on the bathroom floor. How dare Ayesha speak to her like that! Who did she think she was? Bloody hell, she hadn't been able to hold on to a single relationship for more than two seconds, and here she was, passing snide remarks about her and her personal life. Well, if that was how she wanted it, then Lisa wouldn't spare her feelings either. Next time she said something, she would tell her a few home truths too. It wasn't as though they hadn't ever had a fight before, but Lisa couldn't believe how insensitive and thoughtless her friend had been today. And she hadn't even apologized! Despite a great start, it hadn't been a nice day at all! And then to add to everything, there had been that stupid phone call from Milind too. He'd been hysterical as usual, screaming about some presentation that he had to make to the Board, and that trip to Paris for that fashion show, and how the travel agent hadn't been able to get him a seat in first class at such short notice. Well, that wasn't her responsibility and she couldn't help it if Milind's assistant was such a moron, could she? But she'd had to listen to him while he ranted on and on for ten minutes and then abruptly hung up because his ex-wife suddenly called. Half the time he treated her like a punching bag and Lisa was getting fed up of it all. In fact, she was so livid, she was actually muttering to herself as she stepped into the shower cubicle and turned on the water. It was hot and usually she found it comforting, but today, she just couldn't relax. She had half a mind to just pack her stuff and take a flight back home, but that would have been taking things a little too far and she knew it. Well, to hell with Ayesha and her mother-in-law, and even Milind! They could all go to hell as far as she was concerned! Turning the hot water faucet all the way out, Lisa sighed and closed her eyes as she tried her best to calm down.

When she met Sameera for cocktails at the Sunset Bar an hour later, she was feeling a bit calmer. Ayesha had already left to have dinner with Vinny, which was good because Lisa knew she wouldn't be able to keep her temper in check if she so much as exchanged a single word with her. Deciding not to think about it right now, she managed to smile at Sameera and looked around. The Sunset Bar, which was one of the hotel's resident-only bars and right on the beach, was teeming with people at this time since there was a popular jazz band playing and everyone was enjoying the music. The atmosphere was festive, and most people seemed to be drinking cocktails since there was a celebrity bartender there tonight. The girls decided to try the Daiquiris and ordered a portion of Teriyaki Chicken Bites to keep them going until dinner.

'These Daiquiris are potent,' remarked Lisa as she took a sip tentatively. 'I'm going to be terribly hung over in the morning.'

'Well, at least tomorrow I won't have to deal with my nosy Brahmin landlady, who, every time I go home in an inebriated state, as she calls it, does a shuddhi with agarbatti and dhoop the next morning to drive away the devil,' grinned Sameera. 'Thank God for small mercies!'

They both laughed and Lisa leaned back in her cane chair, looking around at the people milling about, talking, laughing – just having fun. She felt completely at ease with Sameera, and for once, it was nice to be alone with her. Sameera always had a calming effect on her.

'So, where did Ayesha go for dinner?' she asked casually, reaching for the honey peanuts on the table. 'Must be some place fabulous since she's going with Vinny.'

'I'm not sure where she's gone but she's certain that he's going to propose to her tonight.' Sameera smiled at Lisa's stunned expression and shook her head. 'I know what you're thinking. She's lost her marbles. Even I don't understand why she's rushing into things like this. I mean, marriage for God's sake! After two weeks!'

'I thought it was just a holiday affair. But what makes her think he's going to propose?' asked Lisa.

'She said that he mentioned something about a surprise he'd planned for her tonight. She was sure it's going to happen.'

'Don't you think she's being a little presumptuous?'

Lisa hesitated for a minute and then told her friend what Ronit had told her about Vinny. Sameera shook her head in consternation and sighed.

'She even told me to wait up for the big announcement.'

'Well! I'll be damned! Maybe I should have been brutally honest with her and told her exactly what Ronit had said. I just didn't know how she would react. Besides, I didn't realize she was this serious. Do you think it'll happen?' Lisa looked seriously worried.

'Stranger things have happened,' said Sameera, trying to keep a neutral tone. 'But honestly, sometimes I feel that behind that veneer of bravado, Ayesha's just a scared girl desperate to find true love. By the way, what do you think of Vinny? Do you like him?'

'What is there to like? Or dislike? I hardly know him. I agree he's good-looking and rich and charming. But that's not always enough. And I told you what Ronit said about him.'

'Well, I just hope she uses her good judgement and takes the right decision,' said Sameera as the waiter came over with their appetizers. 'I don't know, but something about him just doesn't ring true. Really Lisa, sometimes I worry about that girl.'

Karan walked into the DLF Golf and Country Club at exactly eight-thirty, and took the elevator to the bar on the first floor. The party was already going strong and Karan was a little surprised to see the number of people gathered there. Most people seemed to have turned up with their spouses or girlfriends or boyfriends; even Sameer had brought his latest girlfriend along. For no particular reason, Karan suddenly felt a little lost, almost as though he wanted to turn back and go home. Just then, Vivek spotted him and waved him over to where he was standing with the Director of Human Resources and her husband.

'Hey Karan! This is Mallika's husband, Pranav. Pranav, this is Karan, one of my best boys. Couldn't do without him. Problem is, he knows it.' Vivek laughed uproariously at his own joke, and Karan smiled politely as Ria Khanna joined them and smacked Vivek playfully on the arm.

'You have to learn to laugh less loudly. You're much too noisy darling,' she admonished her husband jokingly and then turned to smile at Karan.

Ria Khanna was a tall, slim woman in her late forties with a warm face and a very pleasant, lilting voice. It was rumoured that she'd aspired to be a singer once. She certainly had a lovely voice though, and Vivek and her made a very striking couple as they stood there, arm in arm.

'How are you, Mrs. Khanna?' Karan asked politely with a smile. 'And the children?'

'Fine, fine, Karan. My younger one is learning to play the violin these days. How have you been? I hear you're working much too hard. Don't let Vivek slave drive you too much.' They all laughed politely and she paused to accept a glass of champagne from a passing waiter. She sipped it delicately, careful not to smudge her lipstick. 'So, how's Lisa? I haven't met her in ages.'

'She's fine,' answered Karan, 'has gone to Goa with her two best friends.'

'Well, well, I guess that's what you young, modern couples do,' laughed Ria Khanna. 'I would never dream of going on a vacation without Vivek. I guess I'm needlessly dependent on him to take care of me.' Vivek smiled and slipped an arm around her as she leaned forward to straighten his tie for him. Karan felt a pang inside as he watched them, and couldn't help thinking about how unfailingly Lisa always remembered to do it for him.

'Nor would I,' agreed Mallika with a smile. 'Pranav and I have gone through phases when we've barely spent two days together at a time, but I don't think we've ever planned a vacation without each other. But like you said, these young, modern couples are different.'

A couple of hours later, Karan decided that he'd had enough of the party. 'I think I'll call it a night.' He downed the bourbon he was drinking in one gulp. He knew he drank much too fast when Lisa wasn't around, but he couldn't seem to help it. He picked up his jacket and swung it over his shoulder.

'You're leaving? Already!' exclaimed Mayank looking surprised. 'But it's still early. Dinner hasn't even been served yet.'

'Yeah, but I think I'll probably eat at home. This really isn't my scene.' Karan waved at the party that was now in full swing and Mayank looked baffled.

'Why not? It's quite a rocking party.'

'Yes, but it's mostly what I would call a couples party,' explained Karan. 'Look around buddy! Most people have come with their spouses or their girlfriends or boyfriends. Frankly, I'm feeling a little out of place.'

'Well, you have me,' pointed out Mayank, looking hurt.

'Well, I shouldn't,' said Karan with a dry smile just as the band started playing "Everything I do" by Bryan Adams and some of the couples scrambled for a place on the dance floor. 'I should be here with Lisa by my side. But of course, she isn't here. That's our song they're playing by the way.'

Mayank could hear an unmistakable tremor in Karan's voice, and for a minute he thought his friend was going to cry. But he was much too dignified for that. Nevertheless, Mayank was convinced that he'd had a bit too much to drink.

'Maybe you should get a cab, Karan. Let me order you one.'

'What? You think I can't drive? You think I'm drunk? You think I'm pining for Lisa?' His eyes were glazed, his words slurred. 'Damn right you are, Mayank! I'm pining for her! I want so much to be with her right now! I want so much to hold her in my arms. She would have been the most beautiful woman here and …..' His eyes were closing and he could barely stay steady.

'I'm calling you a cab,' said Mayank firmly as he helped his friend towards the elevator. No one paid any attention to them. Quite a lot of people had had too much to drink by then but Mayank was worried. He'd never seen Karan like this. He wondered if everything was all right between the two of them. He'd sensed a bit of tension recently, but Karan wasn't the type to wash his dirty laundry in public. He'd never discussed his private life with his friends. Mayank just hoped things would work out for both of them. It would be a real pity if they didn't. After all, they loved each other desperately, any fool could see that.

□

Nixed liaisons

Lisa was the first one to wake up the next morning. She yawned and opened her eyes, but when she tried to sit up, she realized that her head was pounding. It didn't take her long to gather that she had the worst ever hangover. Slowly and cautiously, she sat up in bed and then immediately winced at the bright sunlight that was streaming into their room. They'd forgotten to draw the curtains at night and Lisa groaned as she hauled herself out of bed to do it. Sameera was still sleeping soundly in her bed, face buried deep inside the covers of the double duvet. Her peaceful breathing was occasionally punctuated by gentle snores, and she looked blissfully serene in her slumber. Wait till she gets up, thought Lisa wryly as she held her pounding head in her hands and thought about the previous evening. Was it the cocktails or the wine? Both probably!

Surprisingly, there was no sign of Ayesha anywhere. Lisa had forgotten all about the argument they'd had the previous day as she checked to see if her friend was in the bathroom or the balcony. She wasn't in either. Probably got up early for the first time in her life and went off to the gym to work off the celebratory champagne she'd obviously drunk in honour of her engagement. If, as she'd claimed, she'd really found true love this time, then Lisa was truly happy for her.

Her head was throbbing even more painfully by the time she staggered to the bathroom, but she managed to splash cold water on her face and brushed her teeth. The toothpaste tasted acrid and she rinsed out her mouth and stumbled back to the bedroom. The room suddenly spun around her and she had to sit down on the bed to steady herself. Why, oh why had they ordered that bottle of wine after those daiquiris? Everyone knew that wine and rum were such a lethal combination. Even the thought of having consumed the two in quick succession made her queasy now. Glancing at the clock, she suddenly realized that it was already ten o'clock! Breakfast was served till ten-thirty and they would start clearing up the buffet like maniacs at exactly ten-thirty-five. Lisa wanted – no needed – a strong cup of coffee, and she knew she should probably eat something even if it was only a piece of dry toast so that she could take a couple of aspirins. So, she mustered up all her energy and pulled herself out of bed. It was going to be a challenge to get Sameera moving too.

'I don't want any breakfast. I want to sleep,' mumbled Sameera, as they rode down in the elevator together. Getting her out of bed had been a herculean task! She pressed a hand to her head now and groaned loudly. 'God, my head hurts! Was it the wine? Or the cocktails?'

'Probably both,' grinned Lisa who was feeling slightly better. 'I haven't had so much to drink in ages. I always drink too much when I'm with Ayesha and you.'

'Speaking of Ayesha, where is she? Has she gone to the gym?'

'I guess,' answered Lisa who had tried to call her on the mobile. 'Her phone's off and she wasn't here when I got up. What time did she get in last night?'

'Dunno. I fell asleep right after you did,' said Sameera. 'I didn't hear her when she came in. Actually, to tell you the truth, I was out like a light.'

'Same here. I guess she came in pretty late and was considerate enough not to wake us. I'm assuming Vinny must have proposed. I'm actually surprised she didn't shake us awake the moment she came in to tell us everything about her date. Very unlike her. Anyway, I'm sure we'll meet her at breakfast, so we'll hear all about it then.'

The two girls staggered down to the hotel's open-air restaurant and Lisa grimaced at the thought of sitting out in the sun. The indoor area was closed for minor repairs. 'We should have ordered room service,' remarked Sameera as they made their way to a table under the shaded canopy of a banyan tree. At least it wasn't nearly as humid as usual, which made it bearable. They ordered fresh orange juice, whole-wheat toast, muffins and strong coffee, and sat back in the comfortable cane chairs. They'd thought they would be the last people there, but surprisingly, most of the tables were still occupied as people lingered over a last cup of tea or coffee. Lisa checked her phone for messages but there were none. She was a bit disappointed that Karan hadn't called or messaged her since the previous night. She knew he had a meeting that morning in Cyber City, but how long did it take to send a quick SMS? She sent him one instead and then sipped her black coffee thoughtfully. Maybe he had had an early start and was already in the meeting but even so...

'Hey, there's Ayesha!' Sameera's voice interrupted her thoughts. 'She doesn't look too good.'

Lisa turned around to see her friend slowly making her way to their table. She was still wearing the clothes she'd worn to go out last night, her hair was dishevelled and her eyes were red. It was clear even from a distance that she'd been crying. Sameera and Lisa scrambled to their feet and rushed to their friend.

'Where were you? What's wrong?'

'Have you been crying? What happened, Aysh?'

'I've been so stupid,' she murmured at last, turning away so that her friends wouldn't see her tear-streaked face. 'So incredibly stupid!'

'Come on,' said Sameera, slipping an arm around her friend, 'let's get you a cup of strong coffee.'

'I want to be on my own for a bit,' muttered Ayesha, shaking her head as Lisa took her hand and squeezed it.

'You're crazy if you think we'll leave you alone like this. Tell us what happened. Here, this should help.' She handed her friend a cup of strong, black coffee and a Snickers bar.

Ayesha was quiet for a few minutes as she sipped the coffee. Lisa and Sameera were very concerned about her but they waited patiently for her to finish her coffee. She took a final sip before setting the cup down and then sighed.

'I guess you might as well hear the sorry saga,' she sniffed, looking utterly miserable. 'So, to cut a long story short, he didn't propose or anything. Actually, the surprise that he'd planned was a suite he'd booked for us to spend the night together.' She unwrapped the Snickers bar and took a bite. It was gooey and sweet and comforting, and she felt instantly better. 'In fact, he told me that since he was returning to Delhi and it was going to be his last night in Goa, I should make it extra special for him. You should have seen the look of surprise on his face when I refused his offer of a one-night stand.'

She sighed and looked away, obviously embarrassed. 'I know you guys think I've been behaving like a complete moron. I know it was too much to expect after two weeks. But you don't understand. I really thought what we had was special.' She spread out her hands and looked helplessly at her friends.

Lisa sighed, remembering Ronit's warnings. How right he had been. But she didn't say it to Ayesha. Lisa knew that this was no time to be rattling off things like, We told you so, or You should have known better and you deserve it for being so stupid. No, this was the time to be good, sensitive friends, who listened, understood and sympathized.

'He even had the audacity to look surprised when I asked him why he'd gone out with me if he didn't have anything serious in mind,' said Ayesha, looking hurt and baffled.

'So what did he say?' asked Sameera curiously.

Ayesha shook her head ruefully. 'He said that we'd just been having a good time and we could still be friends and meet up for the odd coffee or drink once I got back to Delhi.' She rubbed her nose with her handkerchief and angrily wiped away the tears that were threatening to fall any minute. 'Why do I always make a mistake with guys? Why does it always happen to me? Why?'

'Everyone does,' explained Lisa gently but Ayesha shook her head, looking suddenly like a little child.

'You and Sameera don't,' she said. 'You're always so bloody sensible!'

'Oh, believe it or not, we've made our fair share of mistakes too.' Sameera squeezed her friend's hand and smiled. 'Remember that banker I went out with? He was cheating on me and I never knew! You live and you learn. Forget about the cad. He's just not worth it.'

'I guess you're right,' said Ayesha miserably. She crushed the empty chocolate wrapper in her hand and Lisa handed her another Snickers bar with a smile.

'So anyway, what happened after all that?' questioned Sameera after Ayesha had calmed down a bit. 'What time did you finally get back to the room?'

She looked at Ayesha expectantly, who sighed and looked the other way. 'Wait a minute! Don't tell me you never came back last night!'

'Please don't ask me. It's so embarrassing.' Ayesha looked at them imploringly, but Sameera shook her head firmly.

'No, we have a right to know. I hope you didn't go and do anything stupid. I hope you had the good sense to...'

'Sam, please!' Ayesha put a hand up to stop her and then nodded her head. 'Okay, I'll tell you what happened, but only if you promise not to start lecturing me again. I'm feeling stupid enough as it is. Go on, promise.'

Sameera looked doubtful but Lisa nodded immediately. 'Okay, Scout's Honour. We promise. We won't preach to you. Just tell us what happened.'

'Well,' began Ayesha, still looking very embarrassed. She paused and took a bite out of the Snickers bar. 'So, after our conversation, I didn't wait for dinner or anything. I just said goodbye to him with as much dignity as I could muster, left the restaurant, and walked down the beach. I kept walking for a while because I really didn't feel like coming back to the hotel. I couldn't face you guys after the way I had bragged.' She looked so downcast that both her friends felt sorry for her.

'Afterwards, I found this quiet spot and went and sat down,' she continued. 'I wanted to do some thinking. I figured I had some serious self-introspection to do. After a while, this guy came over to talk to me. He must have seen me sitting around all by myself and so he just came over to chat a bit. What was his name now? I don't know, I've forgotten. He had a bottle of whiskey with him and we had a few drinks. Then...'

'Had a few drinks?! With some random guy?' interrupted Sameera, astounded at Ayesha's recklessness.

'I know it was stupid of me, but I didn't know what I was doing. I was feeling so down,' said Ayesha, looking at her friends helplessly, 'and I know you're going to kill me for what I'm going to tell you next.'

Lisa and Sameera exchanged worried looks as Ayesha sighed and continued. 'We finished the bottle, and by then it was already one o'clock in the morning, so he asked me where I wanted to go. I told him I didn't want to go back to my hotel, so he took me to his house. It was about five minutes away from the beach.'

'Oh God, Ayesha!' exclaimed Lisa. She couldn't help it. This was too much, even for her. 'How could you go and do something so stupid?

What if something had happened to you? You didn't even know the guy! He could have been a psycho, rapist, murderer! I can't believe you could have been so foolish!'

'I know,' agreed Ayesha mournfully. 'Right now, neither can I believe that I did something so crazy. Anyway, to put your minds at rest, nothing happened. He put me up in his guest bedroom and even gave me breakfast this morning. He was quite nice actually. Afterwards, I thanked him profusely and took a taxi and came back. That's it.'

'That's it? Do you realize how reckless you were?' Lisa scolded her friend. 'God, Ayesha you should have come straight back to us. We're supposed to be your friends. We wouldn't have laughed at you or anything. We would have understood.'

'I know. I'm sorry.' Ayesha squeezed Lisa's hand and sighed. 'And while we're at it, I want to apologize to you for all the horrible things I said to you yesterday. I don't know what happened to me. I don't understand how I could have been so insensitive.' She looked genuinely contrite and Lisa put an arm around her friend.

'It's okay. Don't worry about it. All forgotten.'

'Well, I'm just glad that you're safe and sound,' said Sameera, looking grim. 'Do you realize what a dangerous situation you could have put yourself in? In fact, I'd say that you were very, very lucky that you didn't get into trouble. Didn't we tell you not to rush into things? Didn't we warn you about something like this? Didn't I say...'

'Look, you guys promised that you wouldn't preach,' interrupted Ayesha. 'I know I was stupid and I'm sorry. At least, I didn't sleep with him.'

'That's probably the only smart thing you did,' scolded Sameera, shaking her head.

'Do you think she's going to be all right?' whispered Lisa to Sameera as Ayesha drifted off to sleep. The two girls were standing on the patio drinking hot cups of mint tea as they chatted about the events of the day. It was well past midnight and expectedly, Ayesha had been feeling depressed all day. She'd refused to go anywhere and hadn't even joined them for a swim in the pool. It was just as well that Vinny and his group had gone back to Delhi. It just wouldn't have been a good idea to have had them in the same hotel, and would have only led to even more awkwardness. After quite a bit of coaxing and several vain attempts to draw her out, Sameera and Lisa had let her be for a while. Perhaps she needed to be on her own. So, they'd stayed by the pool and read while she went for a long walk on the beach that evening. Later, even though she joined her friends at dinner, she went up to the room before anyone else, which was certainly rare for Ayesha. But it hadn't been an easy day for her. It seemed she wanted to burst into tears almost every few minutes, and once she had returned to her room and slipped into bed, she realized that she just couldn't go to sleep. This was surprising considering that she'd hardly slept the previous night. She tried to keep the unpleasant thoughts away but her mind felt like an overactive, tangled mess. She did eventually drift off, more out of exhaustion than anything else. Her friends were glad to see her sleeping peacefully finally, and they sighed in relief.

'Of course, she is,' said Sameera in answer to Lisa's question. 'She's heartbroken right now. These things always seem like the end of the world when they happen. It won't look quite as bad when she looks at it in perspective. Give her a few days. She'll be right as rain.'

'But I still don't understand why she went and rushed into things like that,' said Lisa, looking mystified. 'Imagine believing that it was something special after only two weeks! Talk about being unrealistic!'

'But that's how vacations are,' smiled Sameera. 'There's something so utterly, perfectly romantic and idyllic about them.'

'Like my first holiday with Karan,' agreed Lisa. She had a dreamy look in her eyes as she spoke and Sameera smiled. 'We'd gone to Thailand and...'

Just then her mobile rang and she jumped in surprise as it vibrated in the left pocket of her jeans. Who could be calling her at one o'clock in the morning?

'I wonder who that is?' she said, whipping out her phone and glancing quickly at the caller ID. 'Oh, it's Preeti. I wonder what she wants. I hope Milind's not throwing another tantrum. Why does he always do these things at ungodly hours when everything is twice as difficult?'

Sameera giggled as Lisa made a face and flipped open her phone. 'Hi, what's up? Everything okay? What?' Lisa's face creased with concern as she listened to her friend. 'Stop crying, Preeti. Preeti, are you there? Sweetie

I can't understand what you're saying.' She made a helpless gesture and pointed at the phone. 'She's incoherent,' she whispered to Sameera, turning her attention back to the phone. 'Preeti – listen, get a hold of yourself. I know, I know, but please stop crying. How did this happen?' Sameera watched in concern as Lisa listened for a minute and nodded her head gravely. 'Okay, yeah. Yeah, I know it's crazy. No, it doesn't make any sense. Okay, I'll call you back in the morning. Sure, but try and take it easy till then. Where are you? At home? Good. Now stop crying and try to get some sleep.'

'Gosh! What happened?' asked Sameera as soon as Lisa had hung up. Lisa turned to her, looking dazed as she shook her head slowly. 'They've split up,' she said in a shocked voice and Sameera narrowed her eyes as she stared at her friend. 'Who? Who are you talking about? Who've split up?'

'Preeti and Aman,' whispered Lisa. She was barely able to speak. It was absolutely unbelievable. A long silence followed, and Sameera stared at Lisa incredulously, obviously as shocked as her.

'You can't be serious!' she managed at last. 'Are you joking?'

'No, I'm not,' answered Lisa. 'I would never joke about something like this. I can't believe it.'

'But I thought they were the perfect couple. They were so wonderful together,' said Sameera. 'I thought…'

'I know,' answered Lisa, still looking very baffled. 'That's what we all thought.'

'But what happened?'

'I don't know all the details. But basically, to cut a long story short, he said he's gay. Go figure.'

Another shocked silence followed, and Sameera stared at Lisa, open mouthed: 'What? I mean… what the hell!'

'Yeah! Crazy, isn't it?'

'But he's been with Preeti for years!' exclaimed Sameera. 'I mean, how could she not have known? Why didn't he tell her?'

'He says he's always been bisexual, but he's finally realized that he prefers men and he doesn't want to be unfair to Preeti. He said he wanted her to know the truth before she made a huge mistake. Apparently, he's in love with someone in his office. Another guy, I mean. They've been together for a little over a couple of months.'

'Well, at least it's not another girl,' said Sameera. 'That's some consolation at least.'

'Hardly,' said Lisa dryly. 'Preeti's totally shattered!'

'How exactly did he break the news to her?' asked Sameera curiously. 'Not that it makes a difference, but still.'

'He took her out for a drink to a pub and told her,' answered Lisa, looking disgusted.

'In a public place!' exclaimed Sameera. 'What cheek!'

'I still can't believe it,' said Lisa, shaking her head in distress. 'Preeti and Aman. They were so perfect. I thought their story was something out of a fairy tale. You know – happily ever after and all that. Who could have imagined?'

'Well, like I told you before, no relationship is perfect. There's always more to it than meets the eye.' Sameera tried to catch Lisa's eye as she spoke, but Lisa looked away and stared out at the pool instead. She didn't want to discuss this anymore. There was no point. Aman was in love with someone else and had no qualms about admitting it, while poor Preeti, and everyone else who'd ever known them, wondered what in heaven's name had gone wrong in their perfect relationship. The thought was just too dismal and Lisa didn't want to talk about it anymore. She was exhausted. Between trying to get Ayesha to get over her misery all day and now this, she was too spent to even think straight any more. Two heart-broken friends! She could hardly believe it. What a day!

After Sameera had gone to bed, Lisa decided to go down for a walk. Sleep had become elusive these days anyway, and there was no point lying in bed and tossing and turning for hours. She quickly took off her dressing gown and changed into a pair of shorts and a tee shirt. Slipping her feet into a pair of comfortable slippers, she picked up her mobile and padded out of the room. She glanced at her sleeping friends before she shut the door behind her. A wave of guilt, unexpectedly, swept over her. She realized as she took the elevator to the lobby, that for the past few months she'd been so obsessed with her own issues and wallowing in self-pity, that most of the time she hadn't even bothered to get to know what was happening in her friends' lives. But things were probably not easy for any of them. Sameera, for instance, lived alone. Her family was in Lucknow and she lived in Delhi all by herself. It couldn't be easy for her – a single woman living alone in one of the most notoriously dangerous cities in the world. Sameera was strong and mature – but still. Lisa knew how lonely and lost her friend felt sometimes without anyone to take care of her. She had no one to come home to in the evenings, no one to spend the holidays with, no one to care for her when she wasn't well. It couldn't be easy. Lisa suddenly remembered how sorry she had felt for herself the day she hadn't been well in Goa and there had been no one to take care of her. She didn't even want to imagine how Sameera did it all the time. Then there was Preeti. Dumped at the altar! Practically everyone had thought that Preeti and Aman were the perfect couple – the way they smiled at each other, the way they understood each other's thoughts without exchanging a single word, the way they cared about each other. Lisa still couldn't believe that they'd actually split up. All she could hope and pray for now was that somehow Preeti would get through this and be okay.

Sinking down into one of the deck chairs by the pool, Lisa's thoughts shifted to Ayesha. It was very quiet and tranquil at that late hour, and she breathed in the calmness as she listened to the chirping of the crickets and the rustle of the leaves. She could hear the distant sounds of the sea from the beach. The sky above was alight with millions of stars, and on the beautiful full moon night, everything around was bathed in silver moonlight – almost like something out of a fairy tale. Usually Lisa, who was a very romantic person, loved full moons, but with two heartbroken friends to deal with, she wasn't feeling particularly romantic tonight. She shook her head as her thoughts went back to her third friend. Ayesha was so terribly desperate to find the right guy but had somehow, along the way, lost focus of what she really wanted. Most of Ayesha's friends were getting married or were engaged, and Lisa knew that Ayesha had started panicking. She didn't want to be the only one who attended social functions alone. She didn't want to be the one, despite her wealthy family background and good looks, to be the last one to get married. She didn't want to be left out. But that was no reason to plunge into a relationship or to get married. You'd think that these days with more and more women declaring themselves to be independent and liberated, young girls like Ayesha wouldn't feel pressured. What about all the stupid surveys that talked about how so many women were opting for late marriages, while others were delaying plans of motherhood and pursuing their careers, or just having fun instead? Why then, did girls like Ayesha have to feel pressurized about stability?

She felt thankful that she hadn't had to worry about things like that. She'd been in love. Their relationship had been just what it should have been. Romantic, passionate, spontaneous, perfect! She hadn't thought about how old she was or whether it was too early or too late to commit herself to Karan. She hadn't had to consider how many siblings he had, what kind of parents he had, or how much they had in common. She hadn't even been worried about her dragon of a mother-in-law. Because everything else had been insignificant! They'd been in love and that was all that had mattered. Love is strange, thought Lisa, as she twirled a strand of hair between the fingers of her right hand. Love has a way of making you forget about everything else as though nothing matters. Love is delusional, in that it makes you see everything through rose-tinted glasses to the point where you only see and believe what you want. And that's how much in love they had been. Everything had been so wonderfully perfect, particularly in the beginning, that their first fight had been like a rude shock. But it was only in the past year that they'd had serious issues. She couldn't deny that during the previous year, there had been times when she had even hated Karan; times when she'd gone to the point of thinking that marrying him had been a stupid, reckless thing she'd plunged thoughtlessly into. Sometimes, in moments of extreme despair, she'd even wondered whether he'd ever loved her at all. But now, as she closed her eyes and thought about her husband, she couldn't help thinking about what a good man he really was, and that she was indeed lucky to have him. Or maybe they were just lucky to have each other. Perhaps Sameera was right after all, and everyone wasn't as blessed to love someone and be loved in return. At that particular instant, as she looked up at the brilliant, glowing, full moon again, she suddenly felt very, very fortunate to have Karan in her life. There was nothing Lisa wanted more than to feel Karan's arms around her, holding her the way he always did. She certainly needed that. What a day it had been!

□

Basking in blessings

'We have two days left,' announced Sameera on Friday morning. The three girls were drinking their morning tea out on the patio. The sun was shining, the birds were chirping, and they could hear the sounds of the waves in the distance. 'Let's try and make the most of them.'

'Two? I thought we have three days left. Don't we leave on Sunday evening?' asked Ayesha, pouring herself another cup of tea from the teapot. She was still not her usual self, but was feeling better. She had decided earlier that morning that Vinny hadn't been the love of her life after all, and didn't deserve more than a couple of days of pining. Lisa and Sameera were just glad that she was looking better.

'Sunday doesn't count,' pointed out Sameera in answer to Ayesha's question. 'We'll have to spend part of the day packing and the airport is an hour from here.'

'Thanks for pointing it out,' said Ayesha, making a face. 'Really, Sameera! You can be such a killjoy sometimes.'

'What time's our flight on Sunday?' asked Lisa as she bit into a cookie. She didn't want to say it to her friends, but she couldn't wait to get back.

'I'm not sure. Let me check.' Sameera reached for her bag and pulled out their return tickets. 'Seven o'clock in the evening,' she announced as Ayesha groaned.

'We'll barely get home by eleven. I won't even get time to eat dinner or unpack. My dad wants me in the office on time on Monday,' she said sulkily, looking like a petulant child. 'You'd think he'd let me take a day to unpack and settle down, and start with a fresh mind on Tuesday.'

'We'll never have a fresh mind as far as work's concerned,' laughed Sameera. 'You can eat dinner on the flight. You're the one who wanted that flight. I'd suggested an afternoon one but you wanted the extra time here.'

'No, I didn't. It was only because you didn't want to fly that other airline and. . . .'

While Sameera and Ayesha argued about who had said what, Lisa considered her options. If she got home at eleven on Sunday, she'd barely get enough time to take a shower and sleep, let alone talk to Karan. Milind expected her to be in the office on time on Monday and she didn't want to invite his wrath. Not to mention how unprofessional it would be to be late on her first day after a holiday. But she wanted to, needed to spend time with Karan. She'd missed him so much! She had so much to say to him, so much to talk about. No, no, she needed to be back before that.

Lisa didn't tell her friends about her change of plans immediately. She didn't want to answer any questions or invite any comments. It was only Friday morning; there was plenty of time to tell them. She smiled and hugged her little secret to herself as they went about planning the day.

'So? What do the two of you want to do today?' asked Sameera. 'Should we go shopping? We haven't done much of that on this trip.'

'I'm glad someone else noticed,' remarked Ayesha. 'I thought I was the only one. What's a holiday without shopping? I can't believe I haven't bought anything worth speaking of in two weeks!'

'You were too busy,' remarked Sameera with a sly smile. 'You know what I mean.' She knew Ayesha was almost okay now. Well, okay enough for them to tease her a little bit.

'Stop that, Sameera Qureshi!' glared Ayesha. 'I do not want to be reminded of that cad ever again.'

'Well, that's certainly a good sign,' remarked her friend. 'Being angry is much healthier than pining for him. Coming back to shopping, should we check out the Mapusa market? I hear it's great for clothes, antiques, souvenirs, spices – you name it! And I still haven't bought any cashews. I promised my mum I'd get her the pepper ones.'

'Okay then,' said Lisa. 'It's already ten-thirty. Let's put a step on it girls. I'm going for a shower.'

Despite the late start, they managed to make good time and were at Mapusa by one o'clock. Amazed at the variety of stuff available there, they enjoyed themselves thoroughly, shopping for pickles, local spices, preserves, harem pants, cashews and curios. Lisa wanted to buy something special for Karan but couldn't find anything suitable. There were all kinds of shops selling gaily colored shirts and shorts, footwear, accessories, beach wear, but nothing that he would like. At last she stopped at a tiny gift shop with an interesting display of quirky knick-knacks in the window. She had a feeling she might find something there that her fussy husband would like. And sure enough, she chanced upon a sterling silver tasselled bookmark that she knew he would love. It came with its own blue velvet box and polishing cloth and they said they could get it engraved if she wished. It was expensive, but it had been so long since she'd given him something special that she didn't even think about the price. It was the perfect gift, and she was absolutely thrilled as she wrote down the message on a piece of paper. It was an ideal opportunity to say what she wanted to.

It was a very enjoyable morning but by mid-afternoon, the sun got considerably hotter and all of them were beginning to feel tired, hungry and longing to rest their legs a bit. Looking around for a place to have lunch in, they finally settled on a modest Goan restaurant. It wasn't more than a shack in size but it was pleasant and looked clean enough. The girls were just relieved to be out of the sun, and they flopped down into their seats and called to the waiter to bring them some chilled water.

'How can it be so hot?' exclaimed Lisa as the waiter poured out iced water into glasses and handed them the menus. 'I'm completely fried!'

'And we're completely starved,' said Ayesha, opening the menu. 'Let's order before one of us faints.'

'Well, I'm having Prawns in Coconut Curry with Steamed Rice,' announced Sameera, decisively closing her menu. 'Oh yeah, and a beer.'

'You've been drinking beer every day. You'll get a beer belly before you know it,' teased Ayesha, but Sameera looked at her smugly. 'No chance of that happening.' She patted her flat stomach. 'Overactive metabolism, you know.'

'I hate that term,' muttered Ayesha. 'A gift that I clearly haven't been blessed with.' They placed their orders and sat back in the cane chairs.

'Our consumption of alcohol has certainly increased on this holiday,' commented Lisa. 'I wonder how much weight we've put on.'

'Come on, Lisa!' said Sameera. She took a swig from the bottle of beer that the waiter had placed in front of her. It was a local beer but it was good and very refreshing on a hot day like this. 'Fancy counting calories on a holiday! From Monday it's back to cornflakes for breakfast and daal-roti-sabzi for lunch and dinner. Isn't that a dismal thought?'

Just then, a group of girls chattering loudly in Russian strolled in and sat down at the table next to theirs. They were all wearing tiny bikinis with wrap around skirts tied loosely around their trim waists, and huge sunglasses.

'Look at them,' whispered Ayesha enviously. 'I love the ease with which they can carry off those bikinis. They're not at all self-conscious. I wish I could be like that.'

'Oh, we're just self-conscious because Delhi's such a notoriously dangerous city,' pointed out Sameera. 'Hey, did you see that number that Swati was wearing on her engagement? The choli was no better than a bikini top so I wonder what the fuss is all about!'

'I thought her future mother-in-law was going to have a coronary,' remarked Ayesha, 'and frankly I think it looked positively vulgar on Swati.'

Sameera laughed at her friend and leaned back in her chair, enjoying the feeling of the sun on her bare shoulders. 'You're just jealous of her because she's getting married to this loaded businessman and is going to live in LA after the wedding.'

'Sounds glamorous,' agreed Lisa who was quite enjoying their girly banter. She sat back and sipped her iced tea. It was so relaxing to just sit around and chat with her friends about nothing in particular – the sound of the waves, the sun on their heads, good food, great company. This is what she loved about being with Sameera and Ayesha. They always managed to have so much fun together and there was always a lot to talk about. True, they had their fair share of arguments and all that, at least Ayesha and her did since Sameera was mostly always too busy playing the role of peacemaker and reconciler to do much arguing herself, but it was always fun to be with her best friends. The most important thing was that she could really be herself with them. And it certainly had been a great vacation. In fact, it had been just what she'd needed. It had given her the mental and emotional break she'd needed so desperately, and restored her peace of mind and ability to think and act coherently after all the stress she'd gone through. It had given her the opportunity to gather and put the pieces of her life back together. Even though they hadn't spoken about it, Lisa had sensed that this vacation had done not just her, but also her relationship with Karan a world of good. It had given them the time and space away from each other to look at things in perspective, and to think rationally. Absence had made the heart grow fonder after all, and Lisa was glad that she'd taken the decision to get away for a while. Now she just had to wait and see if Karan felt the same way.

As he drove home from work that evening, Karan was glad that he'd been able to wrap up his meeting on time. It had been a follow-up after a final report had been sent, and thankfully, it had gone very well. The report had been very well received and the client had even accepted quite candidly that of all the research companies they'd worked with in the past, Karan and his team had given them the highest degree of accuracy and detail in information. In fact, he'd gone on and on about what a difference this report would make to their strategies for the following year, and how he could now go to his headquarters in Germany and present the report to the CFO and his team. He'd been so pleased that he'd even told Karan that they now wanted to hire them on a retainer for three years, which was wonderful news to say the least. Karan couldn't wait to tell Vivek about it.

His thoughts turned to the office party as he drove home. How many drinks had he had? He must have had too many if Mayank had felt the need to call a cab for him. He knew that Mayank wasn't a fool, he must have figured out that something was wrong. Karan sighed as he remembered how close to tears he had been. It hadn't been easy to sit there and watch all the other couples dancing, sharing intimate conversations, wrapped up in each other while he yearned for Lisa, all the time wondering what the future had in store for them. Over the last few months there had been several instances when he'd felt that he couldn't live with her anymore. The day they'd had that big fight, he'd actually believed that his marriage was on the rocks. But since the day she'd left for Goa, he'd missed her like crazy. He hadn't thought he would; he had actually heaved a sigh of relief when she had called him from the airport and informed him that her flight to Goa was on time. He'd been so fed up of their daily fights and constant squabbling. But now he couldn't wait to see her, to put his arms around her, and just hold her. Yes, he had missed her very much. He was tired of having his morning coffee amidst the sounds of his mother's continuous grumbling about the maid, Mrs. Luthra's new S-class Mercedes, and his father's irritated grunts and mumbles as he tried to read the newspaper. He'd had enough of his friends too. Sure, he'd enjoyed going out with them occasionally, but he missed Lisa's very presence around him. Waking up next to her in the morning, watching and wanting her as she emerged dripping wet from the shower; seeing her face cloud over with concern when he told her he'd had a bad day in the office – yes, he had missed her very much. He hadn't expected it; in fact, it had been the last thing he'd thought would ever happen to him, but it had happened, there was no denying it. Admittedly, he regretted all the bitterness of the past few months, all the unpleasant things they'd said to each other, all the times they'd intentionally or even unintentionally hurt each other. He still didn't know whether things would ever go back to the way they had once been between them. There was still so much that was unsaid and unresolved, but he had to confess that he'd finally realized that he still loved her as much as ever. He was still hurt about some things and he knew she must be too. He wondered if she had missed him and thought about him as much as he had. Had she suddenly discovered too, that contrary to what they'd recently believed, they might actually indeed be lucky to have each other? Or had she just enjoyed the time she'd been able to spend without him around? Relieved to have got a reprieve from all the unpleasantness that had been a part of their life recently. Karan didn't have the answers but he was willing to do whatever it took to patch things up. He now knew for certain that despite everything, there was a deep love that existed between them, a bond that is unique to two people who love each other so completely that nothing else matters. Thinking about it almost took his breath away, so powerful was the feeling. He'd actually come to the point of yearning to hold her, touch her. Her absence had not felt like a few days; it had felt like years!

Well, just two more days to go. And with this project nicely wrapped up and the other one mostly done too, he would have more time to spend with her. Just thinking about it made him smile. Things were looking up. Even the usually jammed roads were relatively clear, and he thought that he might even have time to go to the gym and squeeze in a workout. He hadn't had time to go in four days and he felt he was getting softer by the minute. All in all, Karan was feeling better about things, and he was actually humming merrily to himself as he parked his car outside his parents' house and hopped out. He hoped his parents were there. He was due to go back home soon, and he thought it would be a good idea to spend some quality time with them that night.

□

The true taste of love

Saturday dawned sunny and bright, and even though it was going to be their last night in Goa, the three girls were in an upbeat mood. The holiday seemed to have done them all good. It was difficult to believe that it was almost over and it was time to go home. Two weeks had seemed like a really long time when they'd planned it but now it all seemed to have passed by in a flash.

'I just wish we had a couple of days more,' said Ayesha, looking longingly out of the window of their suite at the azure sky and palm trees swaying gently in the breeze. Why were vacations always so idyllic? It made it all the more difficult to leave!

'But that's the thing about holidays,' smiled Sameera. 'They go by in a flash and you always wish you had a couple of days more. And before you know it, you're getting ready to go back.'

'Go back to what?' demanded Ayesha with a disgusted expression. 'Work pressure, deadlines, and oh yeah, don't forget, no boyfriend! I don't even have Hemant anymore. Total gloom!' Her friends laughed and she glared at them and then sighed, 'Oh, for one day more!'

'Well, we still have one night left,' said Sameera, trying to cheer her up. She poured herself another cup of tea and sat back in her chair. They'd finished most of their packing the previous day since they didn't want to leave things to the last minute. 'Let's make the most of it,' she continued. 'I was thinking, why don't we head towards Baga Beach tonight? I hear there are some pretty good clubs there.'

'Way to go!' agreed Ayesha, who was always ready for a night out. 'Let's have a really rocking time before we head back. What do you say, Lisa?'

'Well,' said Lisa, glancing at her friends. She placed her cup of coffee on the table and smiled. It was time to tell them. 'I'm not really staying back till tomorrow.'

'What do you mean?' Ayesha looked at her in surprise. 'We've paid up till tonight. Haven't we?'

'Well, yes. It's just that I've preponed my return by a day. I'm leaving tonight.'

'Why?' demanded Ayesha. 'Is there a work-related problem? Did Milind call?'

'No,' said Lisa, looking mildly embarrassed. 'Milind did not call. Actually, I wanted to get back a day earlier because...'

'You wanted to spend some time with Karan,' finished Sameera, smiling at her friend. 'Am I right?'

Lisa nodded and smiled back sheepishly. 'Yeah, I figured that I won't get a minute to talk to him if I get back tomorrow night. Milind wants me in the office at 9.00 am sharp on Monday morning.' She couldn't help thinking about Karan's reaction on seeing her there that night. Would he be delighted? Would he be just surprised? She knew he was returning that evening to stock up on groceries and get the house cleaned, so at least she was sure that he would be there. She smiled to herself as she realized that whatever his reaction, she couldn't wait to see him tonight.

'You know what, Lisa?' Sameera squeezed her friend's hand then and nodded. 'You did the right thing. It's what I would have done in your place.'

'I completely agree,' beamed Ayesha. 'You need to get back tonight.'

Since Lisa was leaving that evening, the girls had a quick breakfast and then took a hotel car to Candolim Beach. They reached the beach in good time, and though it was as hot as ever, the beach was swarming as always. Not feeling particularly adventurous that morning, the girls decided against any of the water sports and rented out some fishing gear instead. They found a peaceful spot away from the crowd and sat down in a line with their gear all hooked up. It was lovely to just sit there in companionable silence and listen to the birds; and even though they didn't catch anything, they enjoyed the tranquility and peace of listening to the sound of the water and feeling the sun on their shoulders. It was all very idyllic and Sameera suddenly burst out laughing.

'What's so funny?' demanded Ayesha looking at her in surprise.

'Nothing,' said Sameera with a grin. 'I was just thinking about how calm and restful everything is and how terribly frenetic and crazy it's all going to be when we get back.'

'I don't even want to think about it,' groaned her friend. 'I know it's going to be awful!'

'Well, as they say, "Rejoice in the Present,"' laughed Lisa, glancing at her watch. 'I say, it's almost lunch time!' she announced. 'Twenty minutes more and we should look for a restaurant.'

They sat around for a little while before conferring about where to go for lunch. They finally decided on a cozy little Italian restaurant that Sameera had discovered. It was just off the beach and though it was a small place, the food was superb. As was the wine they ordered on the recommendation of the manager. It was an Indian Red, and even though none of them had heard of it before, it was delicious and went well with the thin crust pizzas they ordered. After lunch, they poured what remained of the wine into the three glasses and sat back in the wicker chairs. It was still scorching outside but the beach was bustling with people, sitting around languidly, sipping cocktails, reading or just soaking in the sun. They seemed to have all the time in the world, and the three girls stared at them enviously. They still couldn't believe that their holiday was over.

'I wish we didn't have to go home,' sighed Ayesha for the hundredth time that day. 'Why can't we stay here forever?'

'It's okay, Ayesha,' laughed Sameera. 'There'll be more vacations.' She smiled and squeezed her friend's arm, but all of them felt a little sad as they looked out at the blue waters and sandy beaches that had been their home for more than two weeks.

'Absolute bliss!' declared Ayesha. 'In fact, this is where I'd like to come for my honeymoon. What could be better?'

'Well, now all you need is a guy,' teased Sameera. 'You can start working on it as soon as we get back.'

'On second thoughts,' said Ayesha, suddenly looking serious. She turned to face her friends and they were surprised at the look of maturity they saw on her face. 'What's the hurry? After all, I'm only twenty-nine. I have plenty of time. So what if Swati and Sumita and whoever else, is getting married? I'm not going to compete with other people and make a mistake. This time, whatever decision I take, whenever I take it, I want it to be the right one.'

'Hear, hear!' Lisa gave her friend a thumbs up: 'Good for you, Ayesha! Take your time. I'm glad you're being sensible about this. Seems like this vacation's been good for you. It's taught you something. We need to thank Vinny for this.'

'We absolutely do not need to thank that creep for anything!' Ayesha pretended to look outraged. 'I was too good for him anyway.' She grinned cheekily then, and Lisa came forward to give her a quick hug while Sameera raised her glass for a toast.

'This one's for you, Ayesha! To waiting for the right guy! And to making him stick!'

'Cheers to that!' said Lisa and they clinked their glasses together and laughed.

'So, Karan, what time is Lisa's flight tomorrow?' Prakash Chopra poured himself a cup of tea and delved into the biscuit tin for his favourite Marie biscuits.

'Seven o'clock in the evening,' answered Karan as he sipped his coffee. For a change, things had been quiet in the office that day and he'd managed to get home early. 'She'll be home around eleven.'

'That's quite late,' remarked his father. 'She'll be exhausted by the time she gets home.' He rummaged around in the biscuit tin but couldn't find a single Marie biscuit in there. 'No Marie biscuits as usual!' he remarked, looking irritated. 'How can I drink my tea without Marie biscuits?'

'Oh ho, you!' exclaimed Anju Chopra, shaking her head. 'Inflexibility toh dekho! The world will not come to an end if one day you have your tea without Marie biscuits. There are so many other biscuits in there. Orange cream, chocolate cream, Good Day.'

'No thanks,' said Prakash Chopra declining the offer. 'I don't like any of them. So, when are you going home, Karan?' he asked, turning back to his son.

'This evening,' answered Karan, accepting an orange cream biscuit from his mother. 'In a little while, in fact.'

'Today! But why?' Anju Chopra stared at Karan in surprise. 'Lisa is coming back tomorrow, na? Then why do you want to go home today?'

'Mom, the maid is coming back this evening,' explained Karan patiently. 'I need to get the house in order before Lisa arrives. She'll be exhausted when she gets in.'

'Tsk, tsk, what is the world coming to? You boys these days have absolutely no brains,' said his mother, looking more disapproving than ever. 'Why should you get the house cleaned? That's her job! Anyway, she's been on a holiday while you've been working like a dog.' She looked shocked, outraged almost, and Karan had to resist the urge to laugh aloud. It was amazing how convinced she was about how she felt and had no qualms about admitting it. He actually couldn't help being a little touched at how blindly partial she was to him all the time.

'I cannot understand why some of you women insist on making things difficult for other women! Where's your loyalty to your own gender?' Prakash Chopra ignored his wife's glares and continued to sip his tea.

'Bolo, aur bolo! You never support me anyway.'

'Mom, Lisa will be exhausted when she comes in,' repeated Karan, 'besides, it'll be too late to get any cleaning done.'

'She should have taken an earlier flight,' argued Anju Chopra. 'Why does she expect you to get the cleaning done? I tell you, she takes you for granted, Puttar. You are a very beeba bachha. Even when you were in school…'

'Mom!' exclaimed Karan, clearly exasperated now. 'Stop it, will you? What's the big deal if I get the house cleaned? It's my house too. Why are you always picking on Lisa?'

'What? How can you even say that?' His mother drank the last of her tea and set the cup down noisily on the saucer. 'Do you know she hasn't called me even once since she left?'

'You could have called her, Mom,' retorted Karan.

'I did! She did not answer her phone; she did not even call me back. That girl is beyond disrespectful but you are too blind to her faults. Anyway, since you have already decided to go home today, there is no more to be said. I know you young people need to get on with your lives, not hang around doddery old women like me.' She sounded hurt and annoyed.

'Mom, let's drop it please.' Karan ran a hand through his hair and sighed wearily. 'I didn't mean to upset you or anything. I'm sorry if it sounded that way.' He'd never spoken to her like that before but this time he had felt the need to make his stand clear. Rising from his chair, he straightened himself to his full height. 'Why don't the two of you drop in for dinner sometime next week? After all, you haven't met Lisa in a while. I know she'd like to see you. And I'm sure you've missed her.' He looked pointedly at his mother and she ignored him completely, turning her face away.

'Sure, Karan,' answered his father at once, looking pleased. 'We'd love to come. Check with Lisa and let us know when.'

'Will do! Bye Dad, Mom. See you next week.'

Though his mother still looked mutinous, Karan smiled as he bent down to kiss her cheek. 'Take care, Mom. I'll call you later.' She nodded as he went to get his suitcase and swung his laptop around his shoulder.

'Well, now that you are going back, be sure to get that Rama girl to make you dinner, and don't forget your milk and...'

'It's okay, Anju,' Karan's father put his arm around his wife's shoulder as Karan waved to them and walked out of the house. 'Karan isn't a child anymore. I'm sure he can take care of himself.'

'He will always be a child for me.' Anju Chopra wiped away the tears from her eyes. 'I am, after all, his mother.' Her face had taken on a rather petulant expression and Karan's father was suddenly reminded of the twenty-three-year-old girl he'd married. She'd looked at him the same way when he'd refused to finance a trip to the US every year just because her sister lived there. It was amazing how some things never change!

'Of course, you are,' agreed Prakash Chopra, patting his wife's hand soothingly. 'You will always be his mother. No one is refuting that. Now come on, call up the grocery store and get me my Marie biscuits so that I can have a decent cup of tea.'

When Karan walked into the house in DLF, the sun was streaming joyfully in at the windows. He strode in purposefully, placed his suitcase and laptop carefully in a corner, and looked around. Even though they'd both been out for more than two weeks, the house looked reasonably clean since Lisa had made arrangements with Kriti to let the part-time maid in every three days for the basic cleaning and dusting to be done.

Karan walked into the kitchen and opened the fridge. Except for a bottle of jam, a bar of chocolate, and a jar of olives, there was nothing in there. Karan knew that Lisa would be thrilled if the fridge was well stocked when she came back the next day. He whipped out his cell phone from his jacket pocket and speed dialed the local grocery store. He rapidly ordered bread, butter, eggs, juice, milk, some fresh fruit and vegetables, and some chicken and fish. That done, he hauled his suitcase up and carried it into his bedroom. The house seemed a little silent without Lisa there, but Karan tried to ignore it as he went about unpacking his suitcase. He then headed to the bathroom for a shower. She would be back soon, and that was all that mattered.

By eight-thirty the house was spic and span. Every corner was gleaming, and Rama, who had dutifully returned at the promised hour, had carefully put all the groceries away and tidied up the kitchen. Karan had cleaned the bedroom himself and put fresh flowers in a vase which he carefully placed on their bedroom window sill. He looked around the house, happy and satisfied with all the effort they'd made to get it in order for Lisa when she returned the next day. Smiling to himself, he called out to Rama to make him a mushroom omelet for dinner. Then he settled down in the couch in the bedroom and ate it while watching an old war movie. Everything was peaceful and quiet, and when the movie came to an end, Karan leaned back into the couch and shut his eyes. He hadn't felt this relaxed in ages. It was good to be home. It was certainly good to be home.

When the doorbell rang at eleven-twenty, Karan was fast asleep in the bedroom. He sat up with a jolt and listened. Rama, who had retired to bed long ago and was a heavy sleeper, did not even stir. For a minute Karan thought he'd imagined the sound, who would ring their doorbell in the middle of the night? But then it rang again, even more persistently this time. The sound reverberated around the house and Karan quickly sprang out of bed. 'Jesus! Who in hell could it be at this hour?' he muttered to himself. Rubbing his eyes, he fumbled into his dressing gown and then glanced at the clock as he tied the girdle around firmly. Grabbing his keys, he padded out of the bedroom and down the corridor, snapping on the lights as he went. The bell rang for the third time just as he was unlocking the door. Karan swore to himself and turned both the locks, extremely irritated at being woken up. It had taken him a while to fall asleep in the bed he shared with Lisa, and he had tossed and turned for a full hour before he had finally fallen into a deep slumber. Needless to say, he was not amused. This had better be someone in serious trouble or he wouldn't be very understanding about being disturbed at this ungodly hour. When he swung open the door, the last thing he expected to see was Lisa standing there in front of him, looking tired but very happy to be home. For a minute he looked confused and stared at her as though he was seeing a vision. It was a full minute before he realized that it really was Lisa and his face broke into a delighted smile.

'What?' he asked, shaking his head in bewilderment. 'But… you're supposed to be back tomorrow and… I mean… I thought…'

'Can I perhaps come in?' asked his wife with a slow smile.

'Huh? Oh yeah, of course.' He took the suitcase from her hand and ushered her in. She smiled to herself as she thought about how courteous he was even at a time like this. She stepped in and closed the door behind them.

'Lisa? Is everything okay?' asked her husband, looking concerned as he set the suitcase down and turned to look at her. 'Are you okay?'

She smiled at him then and lifted her hand to trace a single finger down the entire length of his face. 'I missed you,' she said simply, looking up to meet his eyes as he sighed and pulled her into his arms.

When they finally parted after what seemed to be an eternity, both of them were crying. Their lovemaking that night was as special as it had always been, but this time there was also an intensity and fervour about it that took them both by surprise. Later, they lay in each other's arms, talking until the wee hours of the morning. There were no explanations, no apologies, and no mention of the past few months. There was no need. They both knew exactly how the other one was feeling and that was enough. Never had they been surer of their feelings and their relationship. Lisa remembered what Sameera had said to her on the flight to Goa and smiled to herself. How right she had been! It was as though being away from each other for a few days had been a blessing in disguise.

Later, since neither of them was feeling sleepy, they decided to have a drink together. As they settled down in the living room, Karan went to the bar and selected one of his best bottles of sparkling wine.

'I don't have any champagne so this will have to do,' he said as he opened the bottle.

'Are we celebrating something?' Lisa teased him.

'You're back and that's enough reason to celebrate as far as I'm concerned,' he said and handed the glass to her.

They smiled at each other and Karan leaned back in his chair, looking completely relaxed. 'So, tell me more about Goa. All that you told me earlier was about the gorgeous beaches, the water sports, how much alcohol the three of you downed among yourselves, and that creepy guy Ayesha was dating.'

'Well, I think I covered most of it,' smiled his wife.

'What about sightseeing? And oh yeah, shopping? I can't believe the three of you didn't do any shopping.'

'Oh, no!' exclaimed Lisa, 'I almost forgot.' She hurriedly pushed back her chair and got up. Karan looked after her in surprise as she disappeared into their bedroom. She appeared a minute later holding a small box. 'Actually, I brought you something.' She handed the box over to him and he opened it at once. The moment he saw the beautiful silver bookmark nestled there in cotton wool; his eyes widened.

'It's beautiful,' he said softly, looking at his wife, 'really it is.'

'It's engraved.' Lisa gestured to him to turn it over. Her heart was beating harder as she waited for him to read the 3 words inscribed at the back of the bookmark in a flowing italic font.

'Love conquers all,' he read aloud and then smiled widely. 'You know what?' He pulled her close and kissed her lightly on the lips. 'It's exactly what I wanted to say to you too.'

'Too mushy?' she teased him then.

'Mushy, but true. We're a living example, aren't we?' Karan turned the bookmark around in his fingers and smiled again. 'Thank you, sweetheart. It's beautiful.' He put the bookmark back into its box and placed it gently on the mantelpiece, before turning back to his wife, 'and now, I have some news I want to share with you.'

'Oh, my God! Karan! But this is fabulous news!' Lisa whooped with joy and jumped excitedly up and down like a little girl. 'Executive Vice President! I'm so, so, so proud of you.' She flung her arms around him and hugged him tightly. 'But why didn't you tell me before? We spoke twice on the phone yesterday!' She made a face at him and he laughed, happy to see her so excited.

'I know. But I didn't want to tell you over the phone and I wanted to see your reaction. Anyhow, I only got the news myself last evening. Vivek hasn't even made the formal announcement yet. As a matter of fact, you're the first person to know.'

'This is wonderful,' sighed Lisa happily. 'But we must celebrate this properly. Let's go out somewhere special tomorrow and open a bottle of champagne. You really deserve it.'

'We both do,' he said as she rested her head on his shoulder and said a silent thank you to God.

They listened to some old English tunes that they both loved as they drove to the restaurant the next evening. Karan had booked a table at Olive Bar and Kitchen since it was where they'd celebrated their first anniversary, among several other important occasions. They had some very special memories there, and it was inarguably, one of the most romantic places in Delhi. Lisa loved it anyway: it was one of her favourite restaurants and even though Karan had teased her often enough about how it was the hundredth time they were going there again and didn't she ever want to try anything new, she knew that secretly he loved it just as much as she did. Now, as they drove down MG road, Karan talked animatedly about the promotion and Lisa listened to her husband, thrilled at how excited and happy he sounded.

'I just hope it doesn't mean even more work than before,' she commented blithely and he grinned.

'Well, it certainly means more responsibility, but it also means extra perks.'

'Like what?' asked Lisa, pushing her seat back to a more comfortable position. 'Our own company-sponsored villa with a heated pool and state-of-the-art gymnasium? And a butler and housekeeper for me?' she teased, clapping her hands as Karan laughed.

'No, I don't think so. But yes, it means that I'll finally have my own secretary and assistant. They'll be doing a lot of the legwork like fixing my teleconferences, typing out my sales call reports, checking and answering my emails, and so on. So that's going to be a major relief. It also means that I can call the team home sometimes instead of spending weekends in the office when we have a deadline. You know, that kind of stuff.'

'Sounds good to me,' said Lisa. She nodded approvingly and then leaned forward to sniff his cologne. 'Dunhill?' she asked, and he raised his eyebrows and laughed.

'Yes, my darling, you're very perceptive.' The truth was that they'd both made an extra effort that night, and they both looked good. This was no ordinary evening after all; it had been a long time since they'd gone out to dinner together like this. Lisa suddenly felt very, very happy and she leaned towards her husband and kissed him passionately on the lips as he stared at her in astonishment.

'My, my, someone's in a good mood,' he remarked with a laugh, pulling into the quaint looking, little, One Style Mile complex that housed Olive Bar and Kitchen as well as a number of famous designer boutiques. 'I have a feeling tonight's going to be fun.'

'By the way, I wanted to mention one thing. I think we should invite Vivek and his wife over for dinner one of these days,' said Karan, handing the car keys to the valet. 'I've wanted to do it for a long time but we haven't been able to. He is my boss after all.'

'Sure,' said Lisa easily, smoothening down her dress as Karan gave his name to the maître d', 'whenever you want.' She slipped her hand through Karan's arm and smiled up at him. The restaurant was as lovely as they both remembered it. Beautiful people everywhere, twinkling fairy lights, open skies. The maître d' greeted them both politely and escorted them up the gravel path that led to the restaurant. The path was a little uneven and Lisa found it challenging to walk properly in her four-inch stilettoes. She wobbled a little as she tried to balance herself and Karan put an arm around her shoulders to steady her and helped her to the table. She smiled to herself and snuggled closer to him, trembling slightly as his fingers touched her bare skin. It felt nice to know that he still had that effect on her.

'Those heels are precariously unsteady,' he warned her as she smiled at how unaware he was about the effect his touch had on her. 'So anyway, I think you'll get along well with Vivek's wife considering that she's a creative person too.'

'Really? What does she do?' asked Lisa, smiling at the maître d' as he settled them at their table. It was one of their best tables under the banyan tree, and the weather was perfect for sitting out. The restaurant looked as pretty as a picture with its minimalistic white décor, spectacular flower arrangements, and breathtaking foliage. It was famed for that understated and classy look that all the Food and Nightlife magazines couldn't stop raving about. There were pretty white candles here and there, and the sweet, scented air was crisp and clean, giving the place an air of tranquility, and offering a short respite from all the noise and stress that came with living in a city like Delhi.

'She's a jewellery designer. Works with Ritu Bhalla,' said Karan in answer to Lisa's question. 'I understand she's doing very well.'

'That's impressive,' nodded Lisa. 'But I didn't think you'd even know who Ritu Bhalla was considering that you're not… um, shall we say… much of a patron of the arts!' Lisa looked at her husband in surprise and accepted the menu from the waiter.

'Well, that's certainly a nice and polite way to put it.' Karan looked a little sheepish. 'But I don't mind admitting that I wasn't exactly open-minded about some things.' He laughed as Lisa raised her eyebrows questioningly at his words. 'Anyway, going back to Vivek's wife, I think you'll get along with her. She's very bright, creative and enormously talented. Almost as talented as you,' he added softly, taking Lisa's hand. 'I'm sorry I behaved like an ass at times. I know I've been insensitive. I didn't appreciate your work or understand its demands simply because it was so different from mine. But that's no excuse for the way I've behaved with you at times.' He looked into her eyes as he spoke, and she could see that he meant every word.

'It's okay,' she sighed softly. It was the first time in months that they'd spoken that honestly with each other. 'I've been difficult too,' she admitted, 'very difficult in fact. I know I haven't been the easiest person to live with these past few months.'

'Let's leave it all behind,' smiled her husband as the waiter brought the champagne they'd ordered and poured the bubbling golden liquid into crystal flutes. 'Instead, let's look ahead to a wonderful life together and promise to love each other to the point of distraction. Just like before.' He smiled at his wife and she squeezed his hand.

'That sounds like a good idea,' she said. 'It sounds like a very good idea indeed.'

'Great!' Karan ran a hand through his hair. 'I'm glad we've been so honest with each other. So, now that all that's behind us…'

'Actually, I do have one little thing to tell you.' Lisa hesitated as she contemplated whether this was a good idea or not. Where was the need to tell him? What was the big deal anyway? It wasn't as though she had done anything, was it? But she felt guilty about the lie every time she thought about it, and she wanted to get it off her conscience.

'What is it?' he asked, looking happy and relaxed as he crossed his arms in front of his chest and waited for her to speak. Lisa licked her lips nervously and tried to smile as she spoke, but she couldn't be sure about how Karan would react to something like this.

'It's not a big deal I guess, but it's just something that's been bothering me,' she began tentatively. 'When I was in Goa...'

'You didn't go and have a holiday affair, did you?' he joked, leaning back in his chair. She was quick to shake her head. 'No, of course not,' she said firmly. 'But... I did go out to dinner once with a guy.'

Almost at once, Karan sat up straighter, his relaxed mood gone in an instant, and stared at her as she continued: 'He was a part of the group that Ayesha and Sameera were friendly with. A travel photographer.'

'Mr. Creative himself, huh?' remarked Karan wryly, narrowing his eyes. 'That must have been interesting.'

Lisa smiled sheepishly. 'Anyway, he invited me out to dinner.'

'And?' asked Karan. He was as poker-faced as ever, and she couldn't help thinking that at a time like this, she found it impossible to penetrate her husband's mind. He could be as unreadable as he wished.

'And nothing really,' she continued, feeling a little nervous. 'I mean, we went out for dinner and all, but it wasn't really a date. In fact, I accepted his invitation because I was just fed up of sitting around alone while Sameera and Ayesha went out with the other guys. All we did was talk, and I have to admit that he was interesting in his own right. We chatted about places we'd been to, food, and life.'

'Very philosophical,' commented Karan, 'go on, I'm listening.'

'Well, that's it really. He was a thorough gentleman actually, and even though he did invite me out a second time, I think he did it more out of courtesy than anything else. Anyway, I turned him down the second time.'

'Did you tell him you were married?' Karan quizzed, still as deadpan as ever.

'Of course,' replied Lisa at once, 'right in the beginning, in fact. But like I said, it wasn't a date. It was just dinner.'

Her husband looked at her for a minute and then raised his eyebrows. 'So, why has it been bothering you so much if it was just a casual dinner?'

'Because I should have told you about it earlier.' She looked deep into his eyes as she spoke, and he couldn't help thinking how lovely she looked tonight. 'We've always had such an open and transparent relationship. Yes, we've had fights and the last few months have been difficult – almost hellish actually – but we've never had secrets or concealed things from each other. And I felt terrible about it. I'd never concealed anything from you before and it was not a nice feeling.' She looked at her husband earnestly, and his face broke into a big smile. She felt relief wash over her.

'I'm glad you told me about it,' he said, placing his hand over hers. 'You didn't have to but you did. That obviously means a lot to me.'

'You're not upset then?'

'No, I'm not. Despite what you may think, I'm not as traditional as the pin-striped suits I wear that you hate so much.'

'Don't hate them,' muttered Lisa, looking appropriately embarrassed.

'Don't you?' he teased her and then looked serious again. 'I can't say I'm thrilled that you went out to dinner with another man, but your honesty means the world to me. And I do realize that it's not entirely your fault, sweetheart. We've both been going through a trying time lately, haven't we? I know I haven't been the most understanding husband. But I promise to change. Anyway, let's forget about all this. It's not important any more. The important thing is that I love you and that is enough reason to celebrate. So let's get to it.' He lifted his glass of champagne and raised it.

'Thanks for understanding, Karan,' said Lisa softly. 'I appreciate it. And by the way, I love you too.' He laughed and they clinked their glasses together. The cool night air gently caressed Lisa's bare shoulders and she shivered slightly as she sipped her drink. The champagne was cool and luxuriously delicious, and she suddenly felt incredibly happy as Karan rose from his seat and came around to wrap her shawl loosely around her shoulders, bending down to kiss her as he did so. It was such a simple gesture but there was a tenderness about it that brought tears to Lisa's eyes. She closed them briefly as she silently thanked God for bringing them together again. She knew there would still be times when they would not agree, there would of course be the occasional row, they would still go through difficult phases, but she also knew for certain that come what may, they would never again give up on each other.

□

Epilogue

'Can you even believe it?' Lisa looked at Karan incredulously as she threw another wrap-around skirt into her suitcase. 'Ayesha's agreed to meet this guy after all.' It was the end of March and summer was just around the corner.

'Well, what's so unbelievable about that?' asked Karan, pulling out his drawers and flinging things on the bed. 'Jesus, where the hell are all my vests?'

'Come on, Karan! This is Ayesha you're talking about! Ayesha, who swore that she would rather die than settle for an arranged marriage.'

'Who is the guy?' asked Karan with interest as he pounced on a pile of vests and underwear stuffed into a corner of the drawer and started sorting through them.

'He's her mother's friend's sister-in-law's son.' Lisa shook her head incredulously. 'The very route she swore she would never consider. I don't know what happened to her.'

'Probably realized that it's the person that counts, not the route through which he comes,' said Karan sensibly as his wife laughed. 'You sound like Sameera. Anyway, I'm really happy for Sameera and Mayank.'

'Yeah, I can't believe they're going steady,' remarked Karan, neatly placing the vests and underwear into one side of his suitcase. 'We should have introduced them earlier.'

'Oh, God! Where are those dresses that I sent to the dry cleaners?' Lisa clapped a hand to her mouth and panicked: 'Don't tell me he didn't bring them back! Oh God, Karan, all my evening wear, all my...'

The bell rang and a few seconds later, Rama peeked her head in at the door. 'Didi, that was the drycleaner. He brought your clothes back.' She held out the wrapped bundle and Lisa squealed and jumped for joy.

'Oh, thank God! Bless you, Rama!' She placed the bundle carefully on the bed and turned to her husband. 'Karan, this is such an amazing feeling!' She suddenly threw her arms around him and hugged him hard. 'I'm so happy! We're finally off to Bali!'

'Well, someone as talented as you, deserves the best,' said Karan, glancing at his wife with a smile. 'Milind certainly gives you all the credit for the phenomenal success of the anniversary issue. And the launch of the supplement. Did you read his interview in Delhi Times the other day? He said you are one of the most talented people he's ever worked with.'

'Oh, Milind just gets emotional,' she said with a dismissive wave, looking a little embarrassed at Karan's lavish praise.

'He's no fool,' pointed out Karan. 'He knows how committed you are. That's why he agreed to give you a second vacation so soon. He knows how hard you've worked. Particularly after Preeti left. How is Preeti, by the way?'

'Good! Having fun in Mumbai. It's only been five months but she seems to have adjusted pretty well to the fast-paced life there. She's coming home for a visit next month.'

Karan's mobile suddenly vibrated, and Lisa unplugged it from the charger and handed it to him.

'I think it's Vivek,' she said, going back to her packing.

'Thanks,' he murmured, flipping it open. 'Hi Sir, how are you?' Karan shifted the pile of clothes on the bed to one side and sat down to speak to his boss. 'Aha. I see. Well… no, no, I understand Sir. It's pretty last minute, isn't it?'

Lisa looked up from her packing and glanced at her husband. He was frowning and nodding as he listened to his boss. 'Yes Sir, of course. I know how it is these days. Yes, of course I understand. Yes, I'll tell Lisa, yes. No, no, please don't worry about all that.'

Lisa felt her heart skip a beat as she sat down on the bed and closed her eyes. Karan was still talking to Vivek but she wasn't listening any more. It didn't matter. She wouldn't fight with him. She wouldn't complain. She wouldn't say a word. It wasn't his fault. He was Executive Vice President after all, and he had to do his job. She wouldn't stand in the way of his career. She would be a supportive wife. They'd have to call the airline and the hotel. The airline would charge them full for this flight, but they could still cancel the return. And most probably the hotel would charge them one night's charges. She would talk to Milind and tell him that she didn't need the vacation after all and…

'Lisa? Where are you lost? I'm trying to talk to you.' Karan shook her gently by the shoulder and she blinked at him as he smiled down at her. 'Everything okay, sweetheart? You look like you've seen a ghost.' He sat down next to her and took her hand, 'I have something to tell you.'

'I know,' she said, trying to put on a brave face, 'It's okay. I don't mind. Don't worry, I'm not going to fight with you. I'm just concerned about the money we'll lose and…'

'What are you talking about, Lisa?' asked Karan in surprise. 'I'm trying to tell you that Vivek had our tickets upgraded to first class. It was a little last minute and the flight to Bali was full, but he managed. He's a gold card holder with the airline. He said it's the least he can do for the Executive Vice President of his company. We're travelling first class!'

Lisa blinked again as her mind tried to fathom what Karan was saying. She looked blank for a second, then her face suddenly broke into a delighted smile. 'Oh Karan… but I thought… well, never mind then!' She threw her arms around him again and he laughed as he kissed the top of her head. 'Well, hurry up then and finish your packing. We have to leave for the airport in less than an hour.'

□

Manufactured by Amazon.ca
Bolton, ON

23491152R00127